SHIFTING LOYALTIES

DANIEL CANO

Arte Público Press
Houston, Texas
1995

This volume is made possible through grants from the National Endowment for the Arts (a federal agency) and the Andrew W. Mellon Foundation.

Recovering the past, creating the future

Arte Público Press
University of Houston
Houston, Texas 77204-2090

Cover illustration and design by James F. Brisson

Cano, Daniel
    Shifting loyalties / by Daniel Cano.
        p.   cm.
    ISBN 1-55885-144-5
    1. Vietnamese Conflict, 1961–1975—Participation, Mexican American—Fiction. 2. Vietnamese Conflict, 1961–1975—Veterans—Fiction. 3. Mexican American families—United States—Fiction. I. Title.
PS3553.A535S55   1995
813'.54—dc20   95-13564
                                                  CIP

My sincerest thanks to Ernesto Padilla and Yolanda Luera for their continual encouragement, to Steve Steinberg, Gary Soto, Gloria De Necochea, for early readings of the manuscript, to Nicolás Kanellos and the staff at Arte Público Press for finding merit in this work, and a special thanks to Linda Feyder, whose keen eye helped bring about a sense of order.

For my parents, Ray and Esther Cano,
and my children, Diane, Danny, and Reina.

CONTENTS

SHIFTING LOYALTIES

ONE
TWENTY YEARS TOO LATE

August 27, 1985

Dear Mr. and Mrs. Podleski,

It's difficult digging up the past, reliving what one had hoped to forget. But one doesn't forget. Ghosts don't leave us because somehow we won't allow them to. We force them to stay with us, to walk by our sides, to both protect and terrify us. If my writing comes out fragmented, some points not completely explained, some characters out of place, some incidents explained too much, forgive me, for that's how Vietnam lives in my mind. Twenty years disfigures the faces, muffles the words, blurs the scenes, yet the stories remain honest, the memories sincere.

I was nervous the day I called you on the telephone. For years I've racked my brain at the idea of talking to you. As an excuse, I'd tell myself there must be fifteen or twenty Podleski families in Clairton, and chances are I'd never find the right one. I was stunned—that's the only way I can put it—when the operator told me there was only one family with your name. It was a pleasure and a relief talking to you, but now I've decided to write, to tell you all the things I couldn't remember, or was hesitant to reveal over the phone.

Your son Wayne and I were in the same unit, A battery, 320th Artillery, 101st Airborne Division, assigned to the same section, the Ammo Section. We took care of the battery's ammunition needs, directing helicopters, unloading, stacking and counting the ammunition that was delivered to us. When we weren't "humping ammo," as we called it, we "pulled out-post," which meant guarding the battery's perimeter.

For nine months, Wayne and I slept side by side. We ate together, talked, joked, shared stories, letters, pepperoni that you sent him and canned *tamales* my mom sent me.

The years have wiped away so much. I'm now thirty-eight. In Vietnam, I was nineteen. I don't remember Wayne's birthday, but I remember him being a few months younger. I treated him like a little brother. In Vietnam the only time that really mattered were days of the year, 365, and we marked off each 24 hours as they passed, one day shorter, one day closer to home.

I arrived in Vietnam three months before Wayne. Maybe that's why he seemed younger. He was still fresh. Two months in a combat zone and I began to see myself as a veteran, not necessarily an old timer, but experienced enough to know when to keep my head down, and I taught Wayne what little I'd learned. Seniority, rank, ethnic background, or class meant nothing to Wayne. The only thing he cared about was whether he liked you or not, or whether he could talk to you or not. He hated pretense and games. Either you were real or fake.

Wayne loved to talk and laugh. He had the kind of laugh that grew on you, that made you want to laugh right along with him. He laughed like a little kid being tickled, a high-pitched giggle that turned his face to wrinkles, his blue eyes disappearing in his long brown eyelashes. But I guess you know that even better than I. Because we were paratroopers, we shared a special bond beyond our friendship. Somehow education failed us (or we failed it), so to us, the 101st Air-borne Division, Screaming Eagles, was our alma mater—our Harvard, or Columbia. This was our "rite of passage." Here is where we got our chance to leave home and live in the dorms. Here is where we had our own versions of hazing. We had mascots and insignias, uniforms and battle cries, fight songs and...history, a long history of heroes who had come before us, and we felt as much pride as Notre Dame football players walking across the gridiron in South Bend, Indiana. We shared secrets and feelings that only we understood.

Proud? Yes. Patriotic? Maybe. Loyal? Who knows? Our loyalties were never stagnant; they shifted, always shifting. We never talked politics. We didn't even care whether the war was right or wrong, whether we won or lost. We were teenagers in Vietnam because that's just where we happened to be. It wasn't complicated or confusing.

I wish that I could remember our most personal conversations. There were so many. Each day I feel a deepening love for Wayne, but the things we did and the talks we had aren't really important anymore. They are like the bricks, cement, and wood that make a house. After a while only the house is important, not the materials used to construct it.

Wayne often talked about Clairton, about you, his girlfriend, friends, the town, the river, the steel mills, the mountains. I can only imagine what the town is like.

I was shocked a few years back when I saw a movie called *The Deer Hunter.* The first hour of the movie was set in Clairton. I saw the steel mills Wayne had described. There was the factory noise, trucks thundering up and down the highway, crazy kids in their cars. I remember thinking: so this is why Wayne could never sit still. He always had to be doing something, talking to someone, planning something. Clairton seemed to be a place where a kid could get into a great deal of mischief.

Wayne was an explorer, an adventurer...and curious about the world. He was ready to try anything. He possessed such a strong presence. When I saw the Allegheny Mountains in the movie, I wondered if Wayne had ever gone up to those

15

mountains, maybe with high school friends or relatives. In those mountains I saw a spiritual tranquility, the same peaceful feeling that was inside Wayne, for although he was rambunctious and alive, he was at peace with himself. He was completely satisfied with his place in life. There was a confidence in him that told everyone he loved life. Wayne trusted people, and if anyone shattered that trust, he'd be deeply disappointed.

I remember a time when we were positioned on a mountaintop outside of...who knows where? We had a breathtaking view of the valley and rice paddies below, and the Vietnamese villages scattered throughout the green, watery countryside. Wayne and I were sitting on a sandbag wall. We heard shooting coming from the valley. A firefight erupted. We watched as soldiers, both Vietnamese and American, chased one another across the rice paddies. Excited, Wayne leaped from the wall and pointed. "That's what I wanna do," he said. "Get down there with those guys, where the action is." I told him he was nuts and not to talk stupid. He said, "I wanna be down there feeling what those guys are feeling, seeing what they're seeing." Then he told me he was going to transfer to the infantry. I reminded him about Jesse Peña, a friend who had transferred and later realized he'd made a terrible mistake. Wayne must have listened to me because he never spoke about it again.

We'd go to Mass and Communion together, along with some other friends, Danny Ríos, a guy we called Little Rod, Doc Langley, and another friend, Alex Martínez, who wasn't Catholic, but it didn't matter. Whenever a chaplain came out to the jungle, we all went to services anyway, usually on a Thursday. We seldom knew one day of the week from another. It was just, "Oh, here comes the chaplain...must be a Thursday."

When the Catholic priest came, he'd find a nice spot, usually a clearing in the jungle—one time right next to a stream—and he'd set up his portable altar. We didn't even need confession. He'd just make the sign of the cross over the whole bunch of us and give us all general absolution. The Mass never lasted more than thirty minutes. The priest's sermons were short but important to us. He had a way of making us feel that what we were doing was good and right. Strange, though, Wayne and I never talked much about religion or God, not that I can remember, anyway. We simply accepted that part of our lives as fact. I remember Wayne always wore a medal around his neck, a St. Christopher. I wore the Virgin of Guadalupe, a gift from my mom. In her letter, my mom said she had made a *"manda,"* kind of like a promise, a deal with God. She promised to visit the basilica in a town named San Juan de Los Lagos, Jalisco (where my family originates) if I came home safe. God kept his part of the deal; I'm not sure about my mom.

During operations, Wayne and I joined a group of friends, a sort of secret society. We'd hold meetings that we called sessions. Other than Wayne and me, there was Noah, a tough but gentle kid from Harlem. There was Fox, the most educated of the group. Sgt. Dabon wanted to join, but because he was an NCO and we were all privates, he had a hard time sneaking over. Of our group, Noah and Dabon were black, Wayne and Fox were white, and I was Mexican. But I had them calling me Chicano in no time. We didn't care about skin color. What was so great about the group, though, was that we came together because of interests and intellectual stimulation, each of us bringing our own individuality and uniqueness to the others. Dabon was the oldest, married and with one child. He, too, died the morning Wayne died.

17

But cultural ties are difficult to break, so once we were out of the jungle and back in the "rear area," we associated with other guys, Wayne, usually with guys from Pennsylvania or someplace back east, and I with guys from the Southwest, mostly Californians and Texans, guys who were from the same part of the country and of the same ethnic background as I.

Once we started a new operation, and all our friends went back to their various units, Wayne and I would be back together again, working, eating and sleeping side by side. When I look back on those days, I realize now that we really were happy, considering the circumstances. I think our friendship was the most important thing back then, the war secondary, although we never forgot where we were, not for a minute. The war hung over us, stalked us like a boogeyman, giving no warning, just waiting to jump out of the bushes and take us away. Sometimes when we'd get homesick, usually when we were camped in the jungle and it was late at night, Wayne would be talking, then he'd stop. "You know, I'm really hungry," he'd say. "Aren't you?"

I'd answer, "Man, am I ever. I feel like a hamburger and a chocolate shake."

Wayne would reach into his pocket as if he were pulling out money. "Look here," he'd say. "I'll buy if you fly."

I'd look at him and smile. "You got a deal."

He would start that high-pitched giggle. "Go on down to the drugstore and bring back some stuff, an' get plenty of french fries an' ketchup, an' hurry up."

We'd sit quietly for a moment and imagine the jungle turning into a city street and me running down the sidewalk looking for some kind of drugstore. Then we'd turn to each other, stare, and start laughing.

The last time I saw Wayne was around October 15, 1967. We were camped in the jungle outside of Chu Lai. I'd just arrived back from R&R. I spent two days in the field, and my tour was about to end. I was ready to go home. Wayne, Alex, and a couple of other friends wanted to throw a small party. My rucksack was packed and I told them, "Thanks but no thanks." They argued, but it didn't help. Wayne said he'd see me back in North Carolina, where we'd continue our sessions.

The next morning, back at base camp, I heard the battery had been overrun, Wayne and Dabon killed, Alex wounded, and a lot of other guys killed or wounded. I didn't want to know the truth or find out what happened, so I left, and five days later I was home in Los Angeles.

To surprise my parents, I didn't call or let them know I was on my way. A taxi dropped me off at home. It was about 10:00 P.M. Nobody was there. The house was dark. I walked straight to the den, sat down and cried, very hard.

After my thirty-day leave, when I first arrived at Fort Bragg in North Carolina, some guys who'd recently returned from Vietnam saw me and were shocked. They thought I'd been killed. That's what the word was. I asked about Wayne, but they said he didn't make it. I figured if they'd made a mistake about me, maybe they made a mistake about Wayne. I waited, but neither Wayne, Alex, or Dabon showed up.

A few weeks later, I ran into a friend, Ritchie Oyas. He'd survived the attack. He told me what he remembered. He said that everything had been normal. The outposts were set, sentries posted, and the battery settled in for the night. Then the mortars dropped, direct hits ripping the length of the battery area, immediately taking out three howitzers. Everyone was half asleep, but when the mortars hit, guys panicked and rushed from their hootches, in direct line of falling mortars.

19

Wayne was in the ammo section, a short distance down the mountain. When the ground attack came, an enemy soldier ran past Wayne's hootch where five guys were sleeping (I would have been right next to Wayne) and lobbed in a grenade, immediately killing two guys. Wayne must have grabbed his M-16 and made his way out of the hootch into the dark. The battery area was filled with Vietcong. Wayne, I'm guessing, felt that it was safer up by the howitzers, so he took off, running up the hill. He was hit in the chest, some say by a rifle, others say it was a grenade. They later found him on a hillside, not far from gun section three. They choppered him to the field hospital, and he was still breathing. I'm not sure if that's where he died.

It was something he and I had talked about: what we would do if we ever got attacked. The best thing to do was stay put. We'd gone through the entire year without having to face any full enemy assaults. We'd been probed a lot, mortars, snipers, grenades, but nothing like what happened that night.

Last November, my job sent me to Washington D.C. It was my first time there. Reluctantly, I walked to the Vietnam Veterans Memorial. The closer I got, the slower I walked. I didn't know whether I was shivering from cold or fear. I stepped to a directory and turned the pages, looking for Wayne's name, believe it or not, still hoping I wouldn't find it in the huge list. But reality set in. There was Wayne's name, date killed, and his hometown. Then I found Dabon and Noah's names, Sgt. Morris's name, Mac's name, and the names of other friends, close friends who'd been killed during other battles.

I moved to the black-marble wall. All of the names were there. I must have stood in front of them for an hour, just staring. As the sky darkened, the air got colder. I saw my name up there, right next to Wayne's, and it was no longer me looking at the wall. I became a part of the wall, and I was looking down at the people standing there. I saw my mom and dad standing where I had stood, and I felt the pain they would have felt. The names on the wall became eyes, fifty-five thousand pairs of eyes staring down at the faces staring at us. We watched the people lay down flowers, photographs, letters, and the hundreds of candles that flickered for us, lighting up the base of the black-marble wall.

Mr. and Mrs. Podleski, I'm not sure if this is the type of letter you expected. I'm not sure if I have said too much, and if I am causing you more pain.

Mrs. Podleski, you said something over the phone that's stayed with me. You said you missed Wayne more as each day passed. I thought that maybe the pain would lessen with time. It doesn't, and I wish every congressmen and senator in Washington could understand that, because usually it's not their sons and daughters who fight wars, but the sons and daughters of the working class, those of us who struggle every day to scrape out a living.

I feel Wayne's presence stronger now than I ever have. He was special. At eighteen, he had experienced life's joys as if he'd lived forty years. He was a good and dear friend. He'll always be remembered.

Sincerely,

David Almas
Santa Monica, California

TWO
PLANTING THE SEEDS
(DAVID ALMAS)

David Almas played Little League in the rich part of town, where kids got full uniforms and played on a regulation-sized baseball diamond, freshly cut grass shimmering in the infield. There was an outfield fence, dugouts, an announcer's booth, and a P.A. system that called the names of players, teams... and lost kids. It was like the big leagues.

His neighborhood friends weren't there, though many were good players. Some didn't have the registration money. Others wanted to stay close to home, play at the neighborhood park, where everybody knew each other, was sure to make a team, and played more for fun than anything else. Instead of uniforms, they wore colored t-shirts and caps printed with cheap letters that peeled off after a few months.

David's dad could barely afford the registration fee, but he always said Little League was worth it, just like private school was worth it. "It's all a part of the training, being a man, doing your duty, like being drafted in the Army when there's a war. One day you'll see. I'm planting seeds."

It all started one Saturday morning when David stood in the outfield at the Little League park near Westwood Village and UCLA. He felt butterflies and a knot in his stomach as he waited with a hundred other kids who were trying out for a team. Around him were mostly light-skinned, blond-haired kids who had new mitts and baseball shoes, not scratched and soft like his. He knew that not everybody would make a team.

He hit the ball hard and scooped up everything that came at him. Driving home, his dad told him what he did right and what he could have done better. "Hustle," he'd said, "all the time. Run...get your glove down in the dirt. Attack the ball...don't let it attack you. Keep your cap on and don't stand around jabbering for Christ's sake. Show 'em you mean business, that you're there to do a job."

Two nights passed, and no one called. He worried. Three nights later, the phone rang. It was the coach of the Tigers.

"David...David Almas?"

"Yes, sir."

"Congratulations, son. You're a Tiger. See you at Thursday's practice."

"I made it! I made it!"

"Sure," said his Dad.

"Good, *m'ijo.*" His mom hugged him.

Four years later, as a twelve-year old and senior player of the Tigers, he knew every bump in the field, could play any position, studied the opposing pitchers, and as a pitcher himself, knew the strongest and weakest hitters in the league.

It was the championship game, 1959, a standoff between the two top teams, the Tigers and Cubs. The year before, the Cubs had won and David's team finished second. This year, he was determined to win.

On game day, before he went to work, David's dad woke him and said, "Don't go to the beach. You'll get tired and won't be strong enough to pitch a good game, hear?" Then David heard his dad tell his mom as he left the house, "Eva, you make sure he rests."

David stayed home, lay in bed most of the afternoon, his hands behind his head. He listened to Ritchie Valens's album over and over. His little sister, Christina, teased, saying the needle would wear a hole through the record, and he chased her into the living room.

His mom made lunch at 2:00 P.M., *nopales*, mixed vegetables, and fresh beans. By 3:30, she spread his gray wool uniform, socks, and undershirt on his bed.

"Thanks, Mom," he said.

He closed the door, turned the music off, and blocked out the noise from the other room. His knees weakened. In his stomach, the butterflies stirred inside the cocoons and a knot formed. He stepped out of his jeans. Like a warrior preparing for battle, he moved slowly and carefully. His dad taught him that everything must be done right, orderly, nothing forgotten.

Stripped to his shorts, he slid the thin, white stockings to his knees, running his hands up his ankles and calves, taking out all the wrinkles from the soft cotton. Just below his knees, he attached rubber garters to keep the stockings from slipping down. Next, he took his green baseball socks and slid them over the white stockings, stretching them tightly. He stood in front of the mirror and turned. A lot of people would be watching. Since wool made him itch, he put on his cotton pajama bottoms, then slipped into the wool pants that his aunt had said looked like knickers.

His mom bought him a long-sleeved green undershirt that matched the color of his socks and hat. It fit perfectly. Over it, he put on the wool baseball jersey, the same gray as his pants, with a black number eleven on the back. He made sure the buttons on his shirt were lined with the seam of the fly, so it looked like one straight line, broken only by his black leather belt—Army style.

Arriving home early from work, his father called, "Time to go!"

The cocoons in David's stomach cracked and the butterflies fluttered.

He heard nothing as they drove to the field. His parents said a few words to him, but they knew not to talk too much.

David thought about a hike that he and some friends had taken to Camp Josepho, just above Sunset Boulevard in the Santa Monica Mountains. They had walked alongside a shallow creek, into a steep canyon where they spotted a trout swimming in a clear pool. It was trapped, caught between two boulders. The four boys had leaped in. The fish tried to get away, flapping its tail, dropping into the deepest part of the pool at the base of the rock, but the water was only knee deep. After a few minutes of yelling and splashing, one of the boys had brought it out in his hands, a big smile on his face, his thick glasses spotted with water.

David's dad turned their clunky '53 Chevrolet onto a dirt road, dried weeds on both sides, dandelions swaying. Once, when cleaning the yard, his father had shown David a long-stemmed dandelion. "See this plant?"

"A weed," David had said.

"It ain't a weed."

"What do you mean?" he'd asked.

"I mean it's a plane, a B-14 carrying a thousand guys, paratroopers, Screaming Eagles, who're about to land behind German lines." He hummed, making the sound of an engine. Then he raised the dandelion, moving it, like a plane flying. David watched.

"They jumped at night, hundreds and hundreds of guys. Your uncle Ted jumped. Got his legs blown to hell. They were scared, but one thing stayed in their minds. They were there to do a job, do their duty, to do the things men do. And if you're the best trained, you stand the best chance to come out alive."

Then he had put the dandelion to his lips and blown. The fuzzy ball exploded, sending the white motes in every direction, thousands of paratroopers filling the sky, rising and descending, slowly, until they covered the ground. David had

25

watched as the last bits of fuzz hit the grass. His dad had said, "I went to jump school at Fort Benning, then was stationed at Fort Campbell...Kentucky. Good men...paratroopers."

He moved the steering wheel back and forth, dodging potholes. Their car bounced up and down, squeaking. Hundreds of shiny cars were parked on both sides of the dirt road. David's dad found a vacant spot and pulled in between a Jaguar and a Lincoln Continental. On his team, David was the only Mexican. Most of his teammates lived in Mandeville Canyon, Westwood and Bel-Air. He thought, chuckling, that he was like the family car: both were out of place.

As he walked past the Senior League field and snack bar, David said hello to the guys and their parents who said hi to him. Mr. Woods, manager of the Dodgers, a Senior League team, called, "Hey, Davy, Davy Almas. Next year, you'll be with us, huh?"

David smiled, shyly. Mr. Woods was a successful screenwriter, and Mr. Lancaster, a famous movie star, was one of his coaches.

In the dugout, David removed his tennis shoes and slipped into his rubber-spiked baseball shoes, tightening the yellow laces and folding the long leather tongue over the double knot. His stomach tightened. The butterflies crashed into each other. David's manager called, "Okay, you'se guys! Show 'em what it's all about. Look like a team out there. Look like champs."

David walked onto the grass, just outside the third-base line and stepped to the practice pitcher's mound where he began to warm up. A few men yelled encouragement, and he smiled. People crowded into the bleachers and others started to line the outfield fence. He threw to the second-string catcher, who was good with the mitt, lousy with the bat. With each pitch, his arm warmed and got stronger. After about ten minutes, the coach, who was six feet, five inches tall and the biggest man David had ever seen, said, "Okay, Dave, enough. Get yer jacket on and come in and sit down."

The bleachers were filled and the sideline fences crowded with people standing shoulder to shoulder. David stepped from the dugout.

He saw a group of men wishing his dad luck, as if he was the one pitching. David realized that in a sense, through him, his dad would be pitching. These men were rich, and they enjoyed being around his father. They had visited the Almas home, and David's mom had cooked their favorite foods. Secretly, though, he had always been embarrassed when they came over because the men's living rooms were larger than David's house. None of this seemed to bother his dad who was a carpenter and a hard worker. For some reason, these men were relaxed with Mr. Almas. They could be themselves, speak slang, share what they had in common and leave what they didn't locked inside their cars.

David's team straddled the third-base line, the Cubs the first-base line. The players removed their caps and held them over their hearts. An afternoon breeze blew in from the ocean. Except for a few honking horns and the traffic buzzing on the boulevard, there was silence all around. All David heard was a couple of hundred different toned voices saying, "...with liberty and justice for all." And together, like one voice, the fans cheered.

He walked towards the pitcher's mound. The guys on his team threw the ball around and called to each other. The Cubs yelled at the first batter, encouraging him to hit it out of the park. Their coach kept saying, "Just a hit, Barry. Just a hit."

David's name flew out of the bleachers, the fans' voices getting louder, wilder. "Throw it past 'em, Davy, boy! No hitter, babe!" Mrs. Silverstein winked at him, her hair blowing in the breeze. Often, she'd been a fantasy in his dreams.

The umpire tossed him a new ball. He picked up a handful of dirt and rubbed it into the soft leather. He stepped to the mound, placing his toe on the rubber, kicking the dirt, spreading it over the mound for traction.

He threw the ball to the catcher, easy at first, then harder with each pitch. He felt strong as he let the ball go, and it shot out of his fingers quickly, dropping in a straight line. It popped as it hit the catcher's glove. "Play ball!" the umpire hollered.

The first batter stepped to the plate, digging his right foot into the dirt, clenching his bat, then holding it out over the plate, measuring his distance. He took a practice swing, pulled the bat up high over his shoulder and waited.

David's eyes found the catcher's mitt and never lost it, not even for a second. He wound up, and his body moved, his arm a slingshot flinging the white hardball towards home plate. The batter swung, his thick piece of wood cutting the air, missing the ball.

✪ ✪ ✪

Driving through the gate and down the street, his dad talked mostly about the guys who made errors or didn't come through with hits when they needed them. He didn't say much about David's pitching, only that he needed to get faster if he was going to pitch next year in the Senior League. "More practice," he said. "We've got to practice more."

David had been practicing since he was five-years old. Every afternoon of every baseball season his dad would hit him grounders, the ball speeding across their front lawn, slapping his mitt. He loved the crack of the bat, the perspiration and smell of leather.

"No, it was a good game. You couldn't have pitched any better," his mom said. "Sometimes you win, sometimes you don't. The important thing is that you're having fun."

"The important thing is that you learn to be a man," his father cut in.

"*Ay*, Abran," his mom said, shaking her head.

They talked about the end-of-the-year party at the Schwartz's, who lived in Brentwood Canyon. "What do you think I should cook for the party, Abe?" she asked.

"*Arroz con pollo*," was all he said.

Once they arrived home, David changed clothes, ate dinner, got on his bike and rode to see his friends who were waiting to hear what happened. He told them they lost, seven to five.

"You should'a played here with us. Those guys over there are sissies. We got the best players," one boy said, walking around barefoot, tossing a baseball into the air and catching it in his bare hand.

"What ya' mean?" David said. "Nobody else here even knows how to play."

They argued.

David thought about Dickie Laughlin. He could have scored a run, but he'd gotten tagged out as he ran to third base. He'd been daydreaming. The coach yelled at him, but it didn't make any difference. Dickie went into the dugout smiling the same silly smile as when he'd driven away from the field in the back seat of his dad's Mercedes.

"I'll strike out any'a those guys. I ain't afraid of a bunch a rich dudes," said a boy who could throw a baseball harder than anybody in David's league. The boy's coach usually pulled him out of the game by the fourth inning because he'd start hitting guys on purpose then laugh at them.

"Wait 'til we get to Unihi," another friend said. "Those guys you play with won't even make the team."

David didn't answer. He knew that the guys in his league wouldn't be going to the public high school. They all attended private schools.

"Hey, how come you gotta be different? You go to Catholic school when there's a public school right down the street. You go way out there to play baseball with rich dudes and there's teams right here, near your house."

"That's what my dad wants."

"Why don't you just go to school with us?"

"Me and my old man already fought about it, a lot. He says for me not to ask no more. I'd rather go to public school. But it's better to play baseball at the Little League, because it's like playing in the majors. You've seen my uniform and the field where we play. It's way better than the stuff the park gives you guys."

"Yeah. They say some day we'll get uniforms," someone said.

"How come the rich kids get all the breaks?"

"We don't need no uniforms," said the boy who was a wild pitcher, as he sprinted into the parking lot, turned, and came back. "We don't need nothing we ain't already got."

They all laughed.

"Let's go play. All this talkin' is getting on my nerves," said another.

They jumped onto their bikes and raced across the asphalt lot, heading to the high school. David slowed and watched his friends pull ahead of him.

As he pumped the pedals, he rode past a clump of weeds and saw dandelions growing in the center. He remembered his father's stories, about war, paratroopers, airplanes, and about men doing what they must do. He heard the hum of a low flying airplane and imagined the dandelions, feathery balls filling the sky, like paratroopers careening in all directions. David felt the parachute's risers tugging at his shoulders, the harness tightening around his legs and arms, the wind whipping past his ears. On the ground, far below, he saw men hitting the earth, scooping up their chutes, and rushing into a treelined jungle, enemy rifle fire barking across the drop zone.

It was what he dreamed about, what he saw in his visions. Maybe that's why when he asked his dad if he could do what all the other guys in his neighborhood did, just hang out, go to the neighborhood school, play at the neighborhood park, his dad always said, firmly, as if preparing him for something bigger, more important, "Don't ask." He never explained it, as if David was supposed to figure it out for himself. His dad just said, "Don't ask. One day you'll see."

THREE
FIRE MISSION
(DANNY RÍOS)

Danny Ríos wore his fatigues so that little skin was exposed, even buttoning his shirt at the neck. His uncle Monte, a construction worker in the Berkeley Hills, had once told him, "Don't be like the crazy *gabachos* who let their skin burn. Protect yourself, *hijo*. When you sweat, your shirt'll get damp, then, when a breeze blows, it'll cool you down."

Danny once wrote to his mom and dad, "Tell *Tío* Monte there aren't too many breezes over here."

His mother had written back, "Your *tío* says to wait. They'll come. Have patience."

Danny's ears rang from the incessant roar of the howitzers. The smell of sulfur filled his nose. He wiped his face and watched Lt. Elario Villarreal walk across the smoke-filled battery area, down an incline, and into the ammunition dump. Villarreal pushed aside boxes of grenades and flares. A corporal had already told Lt.Villarreal that no high explosive rounds remained.

"We damn near used up a thousand H.E. rounds, sir. Ain't nothing left," the corporal said.

The lieutenant peered into the boy's jittery eyes, "Did I ask you, numbnuts?"

Unable to locate a single H.E. round, Lt. Villarreal kicked a crate of smoke grenades from a stack of boxes. The crate hit the ground, clanked, tumbled and came to rest against a box of trip flares. Scowling, Lt. Villarreal strutted back to the officers' hootch.

From the mountaintop, the artillerymen listened to the embattled "grunts" fighting in the valley below. The cracking rifles, exploding grenades and mortars sounded too much like a Fourth of July celebration.

PFC Richie Oyas pushed his way through the Fire Direction Center's canvas flaps, a circular tent at the corner of the battery area. His job was to figure coordinates, calculate enemy positions, and direct outgoing fire. He lit a Lucky Strike and walked to where Danny sat on a sandbag wall.

Danny looked into Oyas' dazed eyes. "Choppers bringin' in anymore H.E.?"

"Where you been, Ríos? We put a ton a' shit on that mountain and ain't even scratched the bastards. Infantry's gettin' the shit kicked out of them down there...we called in the B-52's."

"Hey, hey, brother Ree-cardo, what's going on? Our brothers catchin' some nasty shit down there," said Wayne Podleski, swaggering forward, shirtless, his dog tags hanging from his neck, gleaming against his tanned skin.

"Haven't you guys been hip to what's going on? Ya been on them guns all damn day."

"Say, cool it, brother Richie," said Wayne, thickening his adopted black drawl. "All's we do is the fire mission, man. Ya'll in FDC got the brains. Ain't that right, Danny Boy?"

Danny shrugged.

"I'm just cooked, man. B company, 1st 327 walked into an ambush. NVA...dug into a mountainside, got cement bunkers, machine guns and mortars...heavy shit, man. Got B company pinned down. B-52's gonna have to drop their shit right on 'em."

"Ain't that a bitch. An' all we kin do is sit up here an' listen," said Wayne, taking a wrinkled pack of Camels from his trouser pocket.

"There it is," said Oyas, placing his foot on top of a sandbag wall and pulling at his cigarette.

Someone pointed. Danny looked up, straining to see through the hazy sky. There they were, like silver termites crawling along a blue ceiling. Danny's stomach tightened. Everyone looked up.

"...Whoo-ee, best not miss," said another soldier. "From up there, all this shit looks the same."

The ground rumbled. Danny grabbed the sandbags to steady himself. Like kettle drums pounding in an empty auditorium, the B-52's rocked the valley. Then, as if they'd never been there, the bombers disappeared and the wilderness fell silent. The firing in the valley stopped.

❂ ❂ ❂

The sun had begun its descent as the first chopper rose from the valley floor. Danny, who had been cleaning his M-16, took the weapon by the handle, and with some other artillerymen, walked to the mountain's edge and watched as the chopper, flying low, came towards them. It landed on a grassy knoll 75 meters downhill. A range of jungle-covered mountains filled the horizon.

As the helicopter landed, blasts of wind rustled the grass. The two door gunners jumped from behind their M-60's and grabbed the body of an American infantryman. Stepping carefully from the chopper and walking hunched over to avoid the powerful blades, they placed the body on the grass and returned to the chopper, where they lifted another body, carried it, and placed it beside the first. After the helicopter lifted and dipped back down into the valley, the bodies of six dead Americans lay neatly, side by side on the grassy knoll.

The next chopper was a minute behind the first. As it landed on the knoll, the door gunners rushed, unloading one body at a time, laying each alongside the other. After the

34

chopper's skids rose above the earth, twelve bodies lay together in the grass.

Danny watched and remained silent. Some other artillerymen walked away. Danny couldn't move, his rifle an anchor.

The sky darkened and a stream of choppers rose from the valley, one following the other, all depositing their loads. Danny didn't know how many helicopters were involved in the grisly delivery. After a while, they all looked the same.

The door gunners moved fast, fighting the darkness. They no longer stacked the bodies side by side. Instead, as the helicopters hovered, the door gunners, balancing in the doorway, shoved the bodies onto the growing pile.

Danny could barely see as the last chopper dropped its cargo. He listened as the plopping sound of the chopper faded and died. The mound of flesh looked like a messy pyramid, the sides so steep a couple of bodies rolled from top to bottom, coming to rest against other bodies. Darkness was nearly complete, and most of the artillerymen had returned to their gun sections.

The mountains lay silent and stars shone overhead. Danny turned to a soldier who stood next to him, opened his mouth to speak, but said nothing. Both strained to see the corpses, but night had swallowed them. The soldier walked away. Danny stood alone, wondering about his mother and father and how they were. He hadn't written them in a long time and felt guilty.

He turned to the battery area, stared into the night, and walked towards the whispering voices of faces he couldn't see. Every now and then, an orange glow of a cigarette lighted a man's lips and nose. Danny walked into his hootch, where three of his friends were talking. The blast of a mortar echoed somewhere far away, and then came the crack of a rifle, one single shot, and the jungle fell silent.

It was Danny's turn on the outpost, so he grabbed his helmet and rifle. He put on his webbed harness, made sure the grenades and ammunition were in place and walked a short way down the mountain to the outpost—a small bunker surrounded by sandbags. One of the soldiers teased, "Sure took ya' sweet time getting here, Ríos baby."

They played Rock, Scissors, Paper to see who would get the first watch. Danny won, his paper to Wayne's rock. Wayne and the other man slid farther into the bunker, talked low, and prepared to sleep.

Danny sat on a sandbag, the open sky above him. He looked at the night and listened. He heard a shrill chirp echo across the mountains, and he heard the soft call of a wolf or tiger...a lion, maybe a jaguar. He didn't know the difference. He remembered an eighteen-foot boa constrictor he'd seen at the brigade zoo in Phan Rhang. The zoo was filled with animals captured during the various operations. When he was a kid, all of these animals scared him, their eyes, teeth, pointed snouts. Even his mother's "*llorona*" stories had frightened him. Tonight they all seemed harmless. He peered into the dark. The VC were out there somewhere, and he watched carefully.

FOUR

OUTPOST
(CHARLEY YAÑEZ & MANNY CARDOZA)

The three artillerymen built their outpost six feet above the banks of a slow moving river. As the water flowed past, it whirled and splashed against protruding boulders. The howitzer gun crews were positioned twenty-five yards to the rear of the outpost, behind a veil of bamboo and weeds. On the opposite side of the river, the foliage spread, clinging to trunks and branches high above the jungle floor where the infantry moved, penetrating, searching.

Sergeant Timmons ordered Charley Yañez to help carry ammunition to the ammo dump.

"Hey Sarge! I'm pulling outpost," Charley said.

"I don't wanna hear it, Yañez."

"Outposts never have ta 'hump' ammo," Charley responded.

"Can it!"

Charley turned to his friend, Albert Alvarez, as Timmons walked away. "That sorry son-of-a-bitch."

"Tell him," said Albert.

"It wouldn't do any good."

"Fuck that, *ese*. I told you before. The lame *puto's* jealous. Always pushin' shit on us." Albert glared at Timmons's broad back, then strutted towards him. "I'll go tell his ass."

"No," said Charley, grabbing Albert's arm. "You're already on his shit list. Next time he'll give you an Article 15. You don't need that. You'll be home in three weeks."

"The shit ain't right, that's all," said Albert, moving towards Charley.

By the time the thermometer reached 117, Charley had helped move five-hundred rounds of ammo, lifting the heavy projectiles onto his shoulders, a human pack mule, walking back and forth, carrying, dropping, picking up and walking again.

Exhausted and sore, Charley walked back to the outpost and joined Albert and Manny Cardoza. They all complained, laughed, talked, bickered over small things and laughed at absurdities: some truths, some lies.

Albert started it. He stripped down to his olive boxer shorts, neatly folding his fatigue trousers and shirt, felt his way into the tepid water, spread his thin, pale body onto his air mattress and floated into the current.

It wasn't a large river, maybe a hundred-feet wide and chest high at the deepest point. Like a moat, the water flowed around the artillery battery, and Albert never had to leave his air mattress to return to the outpost. He put his arms into the water and paddled slowly.

During the last operation, Albert had spent thirty-two days on the outpost, waking every two hours throughout the night and early morning. This operation he was supposed to stay in the ammo section, where it was safer and he could sleep five, six hours straight. But Sgt. Timmons assigned him to the outpost again. Albert had stood up to the stodgy NCO, accusing him of favoring the kiss-asses, calling him a *pendejo*, but it hadn't helped. As he moved down river, Albert breathed deeply.

Reggie LaBeet, who manned the next outpost, hollered, his voice an echo among the trees, "Ay...Beh-toe! Ay... Beh-toe! You'se a crazy spic...*es—say*. There's snipers out there."

"Them's Puerto Ricans. I ain't no spic. I'm Mexican. Chicano! *¡Pura raza!*" Albert yelled, cocking his head to one side.

Manny walked into the water next, dove towards the middle, and disappeared. A moment passed, and his head broke

38

the surface, water splashing from his hair, a smile on his face. "Come on in," he called to Charley.

"Wait 'til the '*cholo*' comes out," Charley said, his voice echoing down river. He wiped down his M-16, checking for dust in the chamber.

Minutes later, rubber air mattresses filled the river. Wearing green boxers or rolled-up fatigue trousers, the other artillerymen, lanky arms and legs, wrestled in the water and jumped from the bluff, bodies tucked into tight balls. The water exploded into giant ripples, scattering the air mattreses, the men laughing and hollering.

Albert stepped to the muddy bank. His shorts dripped. "I heard that '*cholo*' shit, you hick. Go on, get yer Bakersfield Okie ass in the water so I can watch you drown," he said, drying off and sitting on a sandbag.

"Modesto."

"What?"

"Modesto, not Bakersfield."

"What the fuck's the difference. You're all Okies."

Charley didn't speak.

"Say something, *ese*."

"What?"

"You always get that dopey look on your face, like your brain's speeding, like you're way inside yourself. It's kind of scary. Why don't you tell me to go fuck myself...anything, man? Put yourself on the cross, stretch yourself, your horizons."

"Horizons are stretched inside the head, not outside."

"Man, I'm about to lose all respect for you."

Charley laughed and walked to the water's edge.

Albert slipped on his fatigue trousers, running his thumb and forefinger down the front, like he was putting creases in the material. He put on his shirt, buttoning up, careful to avoid unnecessary wrinkles in the sleeves. He spread pomade on his hair, lightly, so the VC could not smell it, and he combed until each strand was perfectly in place. He smiled at himself in the mirror, ran his fingers over his smooth cheeks and chin. He eased on his sunglasses, took his post behind the M-60, aiming the cold steel barrel at the jungle.

Charley plopped down on the air mattress and the water washed over his body. He floated around the island, his arms and hands submerged in the water. Rocks glittered along the bottom and fish darted into the shadows. He looked at the jungle canopy overhead, the tree branches so clumped that only glimmers of light penetrated. It reminded him of a spot along the Tuolumne River back home in the canning town of Riverbank, where on hot summer days, the air reeking of rotten tomato, he and his friends would swim, cold beer waiting for them in the grassy park that lined the shore.

He closed his eyes and nearly fell asleep.

✪ ✪ ✪

Darkness came early. They dressed, ate canned meals, loaded their weapons, checked the machine gun, grenades, and drew straws to see who would get the first watch. Charley picked the short twig and drew the midnight to 3:00 A.M. shift. "Hell with it," was all he said.

He and Albert crawled into the hootch to get some sleep when Manny whispered, "You hear about the blip?"

"The what?" Charley said, his voice low.

"It's a joke, man. Called the blip," Manny hissed, rubbing at a medallion, a peace sign hanging around his neck.

It wasn't really a joke, more a story about a guy traveling around the world looking for the right place to build this thing called the "blip." After ten minutes, listening to Manny add suspense by throwing up his hands, making weird faces and smothered sounds, Albert and Charley protested and threatened to stop listening.

Manny said, his voice hushed, "No, man. Check it out. The guy finds the perfect spot in Polynesia. Dig it?" He raised his voice, then dropped it to a whisper. "Someplace off the coast of Morocco, the guy starts his hammers hammering, saws sawing, glue gluing, wrenches wrenching, and he comes out of a warehouse holdin' a square box in his palm. This is it! The blip. The guy opens the box, takes out a pebble and drops the pebble off a pier, and when the pebble hits the water it goes, 'blip.'"

Albert and Charley sat quietly. Manny chuckled, struggling to keep his voice quiet.

"You made me stay up to listen to that shit?" Albert whispered.

"That's it?" Charley murmured. "Just blip?"

Manny nodded, smiling triumphantly.

Albert said to Manny, "Just 'cause you get first watch, Cardoza, you tell that long-ass story to keep us awake, to keep you company?"

"Man," whispered Manny. "I don't need no company. I can take care of my damn self."

"Shit, tomorrow night I get first watch. No drawing straws and no blips. And neither of you fuckers better fall asleep on yer watch. Eighteen days and a wake-up. That's all I got left," said Albert, crawling into the camouflaged hootch. "Goddamn hillbilly and Hollywood punk, that's what they give me for partners, shit."

"Hollywood's the place of dreams, bro'," said Manny. "I got women left and right."

"Hollywood's a dump, *tapado*," said Albert. "Nothing but dizzy broads and winos."

41

"Man, Beto, the more you talk, the more you show how low your I.Q. really is. Go doze off into your *'cholo'* Nirvana."

"Can't everyone be a *cholo, pinche,* Manny."

"A bunch of dead-beat drug addicts."

"Don't knock it if you never tried it."

"I wouldn't touch that shit in a million years."

"Never say never, *pendejo*. You can't tell the future."

"Never! Dig it! Never would I stick a fucking needle in my arm," said Manny.

Charley slid onto his air mattress and pulled the poncho liner over him. Albert did the same. They whispered something, chuckled, and minutes later, they slept.

○ ○ ○

Charley's body shook. He rose to his elbows, eyes closed. "What?" he asked, wiping his eyes and face.

"Shh...come on. It's your watch," said Manny.

"Bullshit. I just got to sleep."

"Damn sure seems that way, don't it? But it's midnight, both hands straight up, cowboy."

Charley stretched his arms. He pushed his poncho liner to one side. He didn't remember what it was like to sleep an entire night, none of them did. Dizzily, he slid from the hootch to the bunker, yawned, rolled down his shirt sleeves, and buttoned his cuffs and collar. On the outpost, they never removed their boots. Charley reached down and tied his laces, then he took a canteen and poured water on his face, into his mouth, rinsed and spat out.

"Hey, Charley, your ass awake?" Manny whispered. "It's trickier 'n hell out here."

"Shit," he said, still yawning, sitting dazed.

"Timmons is a sorry son-of-a-bitch for makin' you 'hump' ammo while you're on outpost," said Manny.

"Oh, man, I'm beat."

"Keep alert, brother."

"Yeah, I got it."

"See you in the mornin'."

"Manny...you hear anything?"

"Damn straight, 'lotta night and 'lotta sound. Ya' gotta keep a good ear."

Charley stared blindly into the blackness. The river splashed, like feet sloshing in the water. He grabbed the machine gun. The noise had a rhythm, a pattern. He released his grip on the heavy weapon and picked up the lighter, quicker M-16.

"Hey..."

Charley spun.

"What time's it?" Albert asked.

"Goddamn, Beto, you scared the shit out've me."

Albert chuckled. "Take it easy, damn hillbilly," he said, moving around in the hootch.

"It's 12:15, stupid. You still got a couple'a hours sleep."

"All right..." said Albert, mumbling.

Charley heard rustling from behind, but his concentration was on the jungle.

His vision adjusted, and the trees and foliage took on gnarled, freakish forms. He watched the shadows and listened to the river. He knew that the VC crawled on bellies and thighs for two, three days, making no sound, moving a few yards a day, unheard, unseen. He remembered when he first arrived in country, and David Almas, before he rotated home, had told him about "B" battery getting wiped out at Dak To. David swore that the VC had popped out of the earth, attacked and disappeared, no warning, nothing.

Charley's heart thumped. He shook his head. Millions of multicolored spots merged into various shapes and patterns before his eyes. He heard a splash and spun to his left, concentrating on either side of the noise, never directly towards it. Nothing. He stared at his watch... 12:17. He coddled his rifle and clicked the safety to the ON position, breathed deeply and wiped his eyes.

Again he heard the noise, jerked his M-16, aware it could be a frog or fish. He gripped the rifle's plastic stock and fingered the trigger. The river fell back into its natural rhythm.

His stomach tightened. He searched the area to his front, surveying the shadows.

A week ago, an outpost from C battery had been killed. He hadn't heard or seen his assassin, not a shot fired. His buddies, sleeping, quickly jumped when they heard the muffled scream. They looked and saw nobody, only the body of their friend slumped over the sandbags, his throat cut.

Charley searched the water and sand, checked every shadow, tree trunk, and shrub. He listened to every sound, taking nothing for granted. The blood raced through his veins. He shook his head, grasped his rifle, watched and waited.

To his left, a footstep crashed on dry leaves. He whirled, and instinctively pulled the trigger. The bullet ripped through Albert's forehead and slammed him into a tree. He slumped to the ground, a wheezing sound slipping through his nostrils.

From an outpost down river, a machine gun opened up. Grenades exploded. Red tracers lined the jungle. Manny scrambled around inside the hootch, grabbed his rifle, crawled outside, blind, feeling his way towards Charley, who sat still, staring at the tree trunk where Albert sat, his body twitching, his head cocked to one side.

Manny got on the field telephone and yelled for a medic. The howitzers sent flares into the sky, illuminating the jungle. A medic, sergeant, and lieutenant reached the outpost. The medic worked on Albert, the others surrounded Charley, questioning him. He tried to answer but kept repeating, "I don't know. I don't know," as he knelt in the dirt next to Albert. Someone pulled Charley to his feet, took his arms and walked him to the infirmary. He mumbled but made no sense.

"Careless shit, man," said a soldier.

The medic stuck a needle into Charley's arm and the darkness took him.

✪ ✪ ✪

The next morning when he emerged from his sleep, Charley rubbed his sore arm, just below the crook of his elbow. Rising from the cot, he straightened his wrinkled fatigues and stepped into the morning glare. He saw his ruck-sack leaning against a sandbag wall. The medic approached and said, "Yañez, you're going back to base camp for a few days. You need a break, man."

The words reverberated and didn't mean much. There was a throbbing pain at the nape of Charley's neck. He looked up and saw the colonel's two-seat observation helicopter hover overhead and descend, setting down in the middle of the bat-tery area. Charley's eyes followed the tall officer as he stepped down from the chopper. His fatigues were starched and his jump boots gleamed. The man lowered his head, held his hel-met, and ran beneath the twirling blades.

Charley knew that the senior officer came to the field only when there was an investigation of some sort. The colonel double-timed to Captain Edwards, the battery commander. The two officers talked. The colonel nodded and shrugged his shoulders. The captain pointed, and the colonel turned and walked to where Albert's body lay stretched on the ground, covered with a plastic poncho, only the soles of his muddy jun-gle boots visible.

When Charley saw the body, he fell backwards against a low sandbag wall. His heart pushed against his chest and his throat constricted. His vision became hazy and a sickness gripped his stomach. He couldn't believe what he was seeing. Everything had been like a dream, yet there was Albert's body, stretched out on the dirt. Charley looked at his rucksack then slowly looked back at the colonel, who had removed his helmet, his white hair cut close at the temples. Standing at attention next to the body, the officer saluted, turned, and jogged to his chopper. The aircraft lifted and disappeared.

"That's what an American's life is worth, man, a fucking salute," said Manny, his voice shaky as he approached Charley.

Charley stepped from the sandbag wall and moved towards Albert. Manny reached out and grabbed his arm, awkwardly pulling him back. "No, man," Manny said. "You don't wanna see. It ain't him anymore. Beto's gone. Just let it be."

Charley looked into Manny's eyes and stepped back to the sandbag wall. There were other words, which Charley didn't hear. He felt Manny's arm on his shoulder. Charley lowered his eyes and grabbed the sides of his head. Manny turned and hugged him, holding him tightly. Neither cared that others watched. Charley bit the skin inside his cheek, drawing blood.

A Medivac landed and Manny, the medic, and three other paratroopers helped load Albert's body onto the chopper. Charley didn't know what to do, what to say.

Soon another chopper arrived, and some men unloaded canisters of hot spaghetti, punch, and a bag of mail. Manny and the medic took Charley's arm and helped him board for the trip back to Phan Rhang, their base camp. Manny hollered above the din of the engines, "Get a grip, man. They'll have your ass on the outpost in a few days, and you ain't got time to crack up. Hold on, brother, just hold the fuck on."

Charley sat stiffly in the helicopter's web seat. He wanted to lie down and rest, get some sleep, and maybe when he awoke he'd feel better. He thought about Albert and wondered how long it would take for Albert's parents to find out. Charley felt tired. He stretched out on the seat, looked out the open door, and saw the blue of the ocean and the blue of the sky, a deep blue that surrounded the aircraft as it raced across the shoreline of the South China Sea.

He wrapped his arms around his M-16, the barrel pointing towards his chin. He reached down, and with an index finger felt the trigger. Closing his eyes, he envisioned himself placing his mouth over the barrel and pulling the trigger.

FIVE

ESPRIT DE CORPS
(DAVID ALMAS)

David Almas was tired of sitting in Raymond's bedroom. It was Friday night, almost 11:00 P.M. David hadn't wanted to steal the hubcaps, had said it was stupid. The other two thought it was stupid, too, but they were bored. They wanted to do something.

"Anyways," Kenny had argued earlier that evening, "ain't that what people say Chicanos do, steal hubcaps?"

"Shit, that went out in the 50's," Raymond said.

"Well, then let's do it just to see what it's like."

"Dumb, man," David said. "Nobody even uses hubcaps anymore. Everybody's got chrome rims."

"Fuck it. I'm doing it. I saw some spinners on a chopped Oldsmobile over at that used car lot on Pico and Steward," said Kenny.

"Man, the guys from Santa Monica catch us and they'll 'jack us up,'" Raymond said, cracking his knuckles then pushing himself from the wall.

"It'll take us five minutes. In and out, quick, clean. We'll be back here in no time," Kenny said.

"What do you think?" Raymond said, turning to David.

"Stupid, but what the hell. You guys go, then I'm game."

The whole thing took about a half hour. A ten-minute ride to the car lot, sneaking around in the dark, each guy pulling off a hubcap. They jumped back into the car and were back at Raymond's mom's apartment, where they sat around flirting with Raymond's older sisters until the girls' boyfriends picked them up.

"So...this is it, our Friday night?" said David, taking the hubcap from Kenny, flipping it over twice, and tossing it into a corner where it banged against the other hubcaps. "Let's go to Carole's party. We can get Julian to buy us a six-pack. There's probably all kinds of people gonna be there."

"No way!" Raymond answered, looking at the four hubcaps then scanning his narrow, windowless room where the single bed and a three-drawer dresser barely fit.

"Raymond's afraid Carmen's gonna be there," said Kenny, as if Raymond wasn't in the room.

"So let her be there, man," David said. "Show her you're glad to be free of her. Put on your Jimmy Cagney face."

"I can't, man. I never felt like this before, you know," said Raymond.

Carmen was an Italian who ran with Chicanas. She looked like a model, thin and shapely, light-brown hair, hazel eyes.

Raymond and David argued.

Kenny picked up the front page of the *Los Angeles Herald Examiner*. He read the captions under the photographs. His lips moved slowly.

"Well, if you want her back," said David, "you can't let her know how much it hurts. You gotta go in there and make her jealous; let her see you dancing with the other girls. Shit, forget Carmen. Barbara's crazy about your ass, has been for years. So is Helen...and Alice."

"I'd rather stay here."

"Man, when you get in your moods, Raymond, you're like an...an old man. This is bunk," David said. "We can't stay cooped up here all night."

"You're my friends! Aren't you?" said Raymond. "You're supposed to be here with me. We do everything together."

Kenny held the newspaper where they could see it.

"Check out this shit, man," Kenny said.

The newspaper's hazy black and white photograph showed a line of Marines lying in a prone position, hands holding onto their helmets, as if a strong wind was blowing. Smoke clouds hung over their heads. Thick brush surrounded them. Their rifles lay at their sides.

"Man..." David said.

"That ain't shit. We can go over there and kick some ass. I swear to God. You won't catch me hiding my head like that," said Raymond.

David read the article out loud. The Marines were operating around Da Nang. They'd run into an ambush and were pinned down. The reporter wrote that each year the Viet Cong were gaining strength and becoming more confident, hitting American troops in daylight.

"Yeah, let us in and we'll clean up that shit in no time," Kenny said.

They hadn't talked about the war before or about the military. They'd never discussed politics or much else, other than girls, parties, alcohol, and cars.

"The Marines are tough bastards, tougher than all them other units," Kenny said.

"They ain't nothing compared to the Airborne," said David. "My old man was a paratrooper. Nobody's badder than them."

"Ain't no way," said Raymond. "The Marines, man, bad dudes."

They argued for an hour. David knew some facts, like the 82nd and 101st jumping behind German lines on D-Day, the first Americans to make contact. He told them about the standoff at Bastogne, the New Year's Day jump in Belgium, and how many Chicanos from Los Angeles were in the Screaming Eagles, gave their lives for the country. Kenny and

Raymond argued more from emotion than from anything concrete or factual. They talked about war movies, *The Sands of Iwo Jima* and *Guadalcanal Diary*.

The three decided to join. Just like that. Why not? They were all eighteen. David had graduated from high school and was enrolled in community college. Raymond and Kenny had quit school in the eleventh grade. One was driving a delivery truck and the other was moving furniture. For each, it was their third or fourth job since leaving high school.

"All right, let's do it," Raymond said, his chin jutting out.

"Yeah...Monday we go down to the recruiting office together, just to check it out. Me and Raymond'll go talk to the Marines and you do your paratrooper thing. We'll go to Vietnam and clean that shit up in no time."

The next week, they talked again. David had read all the Army literature. He found out everything about going Airborne. The photographs in the colorful brochures showed guys leaping from planes, filling the skies with parachutes. The recruiter explained how David would go to basic training, probably to Texas, then travel to AIT, either in Louisiana, maybe Kansas or Oklahoma and then to Jump School at Fort Benning, Georgia. None of them had ever been more than 200 miles from home. It all sounded romantic, like it was a dream.

The three settled on a date. They wouldn't tell anybody about it, not even their parents, and surprise everybody.

"Man, wait'll Carmen sees me in my dress blues," Raymond said, running his hand through his dark, wavy hair. "She'll come begging me to take her back."

"Shit yes," said Kenny. "And when I walk down the street with my uniform, man, the broads'll be fighting over me."

"I don't care about all that. I just got to get away, see what it's all about," said David.

He had already signed all the papers. His mom and dad were sitting on the couch, watching television. His sisters were in the den and his little brother was in bed.

"Hi, *m'ijo*. Where were you?" his mother asked.

"At Raymond's."

"How's Bertha?" she said, referring to Raymond's mother.

"Fine...I need to tell you something."

His dad looked up from the television.

His mom's words came out slowly. "What is it?"

He looked at the two of them, opened his mouth, hesitated, turned away and said, almost whispering, "I joined the Army." He looked back at them.

No one spoke.

"What?" his dad asked.

"I went to the Army recruiter and joined. I'm going Airborne."

David's dad rose from the couch. He put his newspaper down and stepped around the glass-top coffee table. He moved towards David and stopped a few feet away.

His mother's face dropped, as if all the muscles had lost their power. She looked up at David, confused and dazed.

"Why?" his dad asked.

"I want to go Airborne, like you. It's time for me to do something on my own. You joined when you were seventeen. You told me all those stories about the paratroopers at Bastogne and Normandy, about the Screaming Eagles and the All-Americans, you know, the 82nd."

David's father wasn't sure what to say.

His mother sat still. She looked away from her son to the television. The actors flickered around like caricatures, their movements silly, uncertain. The light from the screen flashed against the wall, changing from dark to bright, like a strobe light. From the den, David's youngest sister yelled, "Mama!

Sally's teasing me again and she won't stop." His mother stood, walked to the television and turned it off.

"Why didn't you ask us?" she said.

"I wanted to make my own decision."

"There's a war going on. Those boys, every day more of them are dying. We have a right to know if you're thinking about doing something like that," she said.

"I'm sorry, Ma. It's something I had to do."

"You've never even mentioned the Army. What about college?" his dad said.

"When I get out, I can get the G.I. Bill. They'll pay for all my college."

His parents looked at each other. Then his mother turned to David. "I wish you would have talked to us. I wish you would have said something first."

She chewed the inside of her lip and moved back to the couch. His father returned to the couch and sat next to her. David stood there, hands at his sides.

"I just thought, you know...I want to be on my own. It's something I've always wanted."

"You could be killed," said his dad.

"I'll be all right. I know it."

"You don't know nothing."

"*M'ijo*, I wish you would have said something, at least talked to us," said his mom.

"It's something I want to do, something I need to do."

"You don't know what you need," said his father.

"*You* joined!"

"Times were different. We had nothing. You got everything."

"I want to be like you."

They didn't answer. His dad got up, walked to the television and turned it on again. He stared at the screen.

"Are you hungry? There's some food in the refrigerator. You can warm it up."

"No, thanks, Ma. I stopped at the Nu-way and had a chili dog."

"When do you go?" his dad asked.

"A couple of months, after the fall semester."

His father nodded, his eyes on the television.

David waited for them to speak. Nobody said a word.

He walked past the television, said excuse me, and went to his room. He threw his coat over a chair and turned on his radio. Some guy was singing, "How does it feel...to be all alone, with no direction home, like a rolling stone?"

David lay back in his bed and listened, wondering if maybe he had made a mistake. His decision had been so natural. The Army...just another step in growing up. His dad and uncles had done it. They'd fought in the big war. At family parties they laughed about it, joked about guys they'd served with. Now it was his turn. The voice on the radio sang, "You used to laugh about, everybody that was hanging 'round... now you don't laugh so loud, now you don't seem so proud, about having to be scrounging your next meal."

✪ ✪ ✪

On the morning of April 25th, David's mother drove him to the recruitment station on Spring Street in downtown Los Angeles. His dad had to work and couldn't get off. He woke David at before leaving for work, shook his hand, and wished him luck.

The tall buildings cast dark shadows over the streets. Horns honked as David's mother stopped to let him off.

"I'll park in that lot over there and meet you in the building," she said, and pointed to a brick structure where a crowd of men stood on the sidewalk.

"No, Mom. Go home. I'll be here all day taking a physical and getting my papers. They'll take us to the airport from here."

"But *m'ijo*."

"You can't, Mom."

"I…"

The horns honked behind her. One car sped past, tires screeching.

"I'll be okay. I'll call you later."

"But, where are they taking you?"

"I don't know. I'll get my orders here."

"David." Her eyes filled with tears. She reached out and he took her hand.

"Bye, Mama. I love you."

He closed the door and walked quickly down the side-walk. She watched him. He stood at the fringes of the crowd. She turned away for a moment. When she looked again, he'd blended in with the other boys. She stepped lightly on the accelerator and turned on Hill Street, got onto Olympic, and went home the slow way, rather than taking the new freeway back to Santa Monica.

David found Raymond, who was leaning against the building, hands in his pockets. He was wearing pressed khakis, a white t-shirt and a Pendleton, unbuttoned. Although there were a lot of guys standing on the sidewalk, few of them talked.

"Shit, man. I thought you changed your mind," Raymond said.

"I told you I was gonna do it," said David. "Where's Kenny?"

"I don't know. I called him all last night and his mom said he was out."

"Out? Shit."

"Maybe he went over to Lucy's house."

"He should've been here by now."

They stood next to the locked glass doors. They heard the lock jingling. The doors flew open and a Marine, stripes all over his sleeves, crewcut hair, looked at Raymond and bellowed, "Tuck that shirttail into your trousers, mister."

Raymond looked at him.

The Marine bellowed, "Now! Now, not tomorrow!"

Raymond quickly buttoned his shirt and tucked it into his waist.

"And the rest of you...do as I say."

They followed him inside the building, and for six hours they walked through various rooms, signing papers, removing their clothes, walking through lines of doctors, signing more papers. But mostly they waited in long lines, waited for the word to enter, to exit, to move, to walk, to stop, to stand straight and not slouch, and the bellowing echoed through the cold halls, strong, hoarse voices, commanding, and cursing.

They broke for lunch and were marched to a diner where they all ate in different shifts. After lunch they marched back to the induction center and stood in front of the building as dark green buses pulled to the curb.

"How many of you suckers joined?" hollered a Marine sergeant, talking to all of the new recruits.

David, Raymond, and about one-third of the crowd raised their hands.

"All right then, ya' all move to one side, next to those buses."

They did as they were told.

The sergeant called for all who had joined the Marines to get onto the first three buses. Those who joined the Army were ordered to board the last three buses. David shook Raymond's sweaty hand.

"I think we fucked up, *ese*," Raymond said, looking around nervously.

David wouldn't admit to anything. "We're in now, too late. Eight weeks and I'll see you back home. We get a leave after Basic."

"Yeah, okay. Be cool."

"You, too."

As he moved towards his bus, Raymond turned to David one last time. "Fucking Kenny, man. He didn't show. Fucker."

"Get yer ass on that bus and stop using that profane language around civilians. You hearing me!" a sergeant yelled, rushing up and putting his nose to Raymond.

"Yeah, I hear."

"Bullshit! Nobody says 'yeah' to me. 'Yes, sergeant!' that's all I wanna hear come out of your filthy mouth. 'Yes, sergeant!' nothing else."

Raymond lowered his eyes.

"Are you understanding me, spic?"

"Yes, sergeant," Raymond said, his voice monotone.

"What did you say? I can't hear you."

"Yes, sergeant!" Raymond yelled loudly, his voice cracking.

David boarded the last bus. His heart pounded. None of the recruits said a word.

"Open up them windows, pussies. It's like a furnace in here," said an Army sergeant.

David opened his window and the smoggy, downtown air, mixed with gas fumes, entered. He looked at the hundred or so men still standing on the sidewalk. In front of them was a Marine sergeant who said, "So, you didn't have the guts to join my Corps. That right?"

The draftees looked around at one another not knowing what to say.

"Sergeant Wilson," the Marine said to an Army NCO, "did these men join your Army?"

"No, sergeant! They waited for us to come and get their sorry asses. They're scum, maggots, got no guts."

"Line it up, ladies. Gimme one straight row, right here in front of me."

They scooted around until they stood in one long line stretching down the sidewalk.

"Draftees, are you?" said the sergeant.

None of them spoke.

"Think you're gonna get some cushy Army job, do you? Well, I got news for you gentlemen. When Uncle Sam drafts you, your ass is his and he puts you where he damn well pleases. So NOW! From my left, starting with the number 1...sound off!"

Silence.

The sergeant swiped the cap from his head, crunched it in his hand, and ran down the sidewalk to the first man in line.

He spoke softly, as if choking, the veins pulsating in his neck, his eyes bulging. "Did you hear me, young man?"

"Uh, yes, sergeant."

"Well!" came the burst from the sergeant's lungs. "Call out! Damn it. Say ONE. Scream it out like a man."

Down the row came the numbers, 1,2,3,4,5,6,7,8....

When they finished, the sergeant smiled. "Good. Very good. Now, all even numbers take one step forward."

Half of the men, about fifty or so, moved to the front.

"Sons, welcome to the United States Marine Corps."

A sound, something like a stunted sigh, came from the men who stepped forward. They turned and looked at one another.

"Board that bus right there," said the sergeant as a bus came up the street and pulled to the curb.

"The rest of you ladies jump onto the last three buses with the other Army dogfaces and say a prayer to your god that you didn't pick an even number."

The men rushed towards the bus and scrambled up the steps. David rubbed his palms over his thighs. He breathed deeply and fell back into the seat. He looked at the man next to him. The guy was staring straight towards the front, like a mannequin, no movement, not even a blink of an eye.

The sidewalk was clear. The glass doors of the induction center closed. A few men in military uniform, both Marine and Army, stood inside the lobby. The buses pulled away from the curb, smoke from the exhausts billowing into the air, the engines whining. David whispered the Act of Contrition as the bus sped toward the L.A. Airport.

SIX
SEMPER FIDELIS
(JOEY SERRANO)

The black 1951 Ford backed into the street, moved past rows of apartment buildings to the local park, and pulled alongside the curb. Joey's stomach tightened. "Oh, man," he whispered, kicking the dirt.

He heard the honk.

"I gotta go," he called to his friends.

"Come back later," said an older boy. "Maybe Frank'll let us play under the lights."

"Yeah, I'll try," he said, walking from the field, tucking his mitt under his arm.

As he neared the car he muttered to himself, "Not this time, dang it. Nobody's pushin' me around. I ain't takin' it no more."

He opened the car door, pulled hard, and jumped into the front seat.

"Did you do okay?" his mother asked, her eyes hidden behind her black cat-eye sunglasses.

"What?"

"Did you hit the ball?"

His eyes narrowed. He noticed that she'd quickly brushed her hair and put on lipstick.

"Into diamond number three," he said, placing his cap on the seat, wiping his forehead.

"That's pretty far?" She forced a smile.

"I'll prob'ly hit two or three homers this year."

"I wish we had the money so you could play at the Little League, you know... over on Sepulveda."

"It doesn't matter. Nobody I know plays there."

Ruth Serrano knew her son occasionally rode his bike out to the field to watch the Little League teams play. He'd once mentioned how much he liked the official baseball uniforms, the colors, lettering, and insignias. She wanted him to play there.

Ruth had argued with her husband about registering Joey for Little League. Herman Serrano had said, "The park league's good enough. Why the hell ya want him going way over there for, anyway? Let him go out there and pretty soon he'll be wantin' what those rich kids got."

Joey pulled the baseball shoes from his feet and slipped on his sneakers. His dad had slapped him once on the head for wearing his rubber cleats on the concrete, saying the hard surface would wear them down, and he couldn't be buying him any more shoes. "What...you think we're made out of money?" he'd said.

"Who was at the playground?"

"Park, mom...park, not playground."

"¡Ay tú!" she smiled. "All right then, ten and already a man. The park then, who was there?"

"Teeth, Marco, Magal..."

"Miguel?"

"No, mom! We call him Ma-gal."

"Ayyiii! Picky, picky. Who else?"

"Tito, Brian, Takashi...same guys as always."

"Those boys're all so big, older than you. They hit the ball hard."

He rolled his eyes.

"Yes, m'ijo, you're so tough."

"I can take care of myself."

He looked out the window, his eyes barely clearing the padded door frame.

"Well, you be careful, that's all. I don't need you breaking an arm. Remember, last summer, Tsumo...."

"Ma! You said it a hundred times already."

She blinked, her lashes moving behind the glasses.

"Frank said no more metal cleats," he said.

She downshifted and turned onto a boulevard. She didn't look at Joey. "Frank's the best playground director, so far. I'm glad they finally got a Mexican."

"Park, Mom. Park director, and what's Mexican got to do with it? Geez."

"He understands you guys, that's all."

"Ohhh, man, Ma. He got a crystal ball or something?"

"Don't be smart, Joseph. You know what I mean."

They drove along the boulevard, cars passing on both sides. Joey remembered muscleman Jerry Morales—elbows flying, knees rising, legs pumping—stealing second base and Tsumo Nakanishi, skinny, fearless, running from shortstop to snag the catcher's throw. Tsumo dropped to one knee to make the tag. Jerry, showing off, slid hard, the dust mushroomed, floated off, and Tsumo rolled on his back, holding his knee, gritting, his glove tossed to one side, the ball rolling.

Frank came running. He tore Tsumo's Levis.

"Goddamn it! No cleats. If I told you once I told you a thousand times...."

The boys froze.

Jerry's metal spikes had slashed the creamy part of Tsumo's leg, just above the knee, as if an ice pick had dug and twisted.

When the ambulance had disappeared, Joey walked to third base and stood there, the only kid on the field. After a few minutes, his friends had picked up their mitts and taken their positions.

"You know your dad...."

"I know, Mom," he sighed. "I done it enough times."

"Sorry you've got to do this, Joe."

She pulled to the curb and parked.

He lifted the chrome handle and pushed his knee into the vinyl panel. The door opened, and he stepped to the sidewalk.

"*M'ijo.*"

He turned.

"Joey, *m'ijo...*"

He smiled at her. "Yeah, Mom?"

She removed her sunglasses. She looked young, but tired. "Don't stay long, okay?"

"I'll come back fast, Mama...don't worry."

He started up the sidewalk, stopped, kneeled, reached down and folded his Levi's cuffs to his ankles. He tucked the bottom of his white t-shirt neatly into his belt and turned to see his reflection in a large window. He saw a round face, a flattop haircut. Sticking his tongue out at himself, he continued walking. People passed, but he paid no attention.

He nearly tripped over the outstretched legs of a man sitting on the sidewalk, back propped against a brick wall. Unshaven and dirty, the man looked up. Next to the man was another man, wearing a Marine cap. He was slumped in a wheelchair, no legs, just two stumps. The man coughed. He spat. A wad of phlegm flew through the air, sticking to the sidewalk near the curb. WWII and Korean War veterans, Joey's dad had once told him: war heroes who lived at the Soldiers' Home two blocks up the street.

He crossed an alley and came to the entrance of a square, brick building. Inside, the air reeked of alcohol, sweat, and spicy food. The jukebox blared. Two men staggered to the sidewalk.

Joey looked towards his mom's car, paused, and slid inside the building, moving sideways, his back brushing the red-velvet wallpaper.

Taking short breaths to keep away the stench, he pushed himself from the wall, straightened, and forced his way between legs and arms, deeper into the noisy cavern. The crack of billiard balls echoed. He turned. The colored balls scattered over the stained, green surface. Someone called his name.

"Joey! Joey! What'chu doing? Looking for you' daddy."

"Paja...I mean, Mr. García?"

Pájaro, a stumpy, dark man with a large head that tilted slightly to one side, put his hand on the boy's thin shoulder. "C'mon. You' daddy over here."

Most of the men knew Joey. He'd been going in since he was five.

"Looky, there's you' papa over there," said Pájaro, pointing to the farthest corner of the bar.

"Hey, *Papá!*" Pájaro called. "Look who's here to see you."

When he saw his dad, Joey clenched his fingers.

He approached cautiously. His father's face had already swelled. Long strands of hair parted in the middle and fell to the forehead, hanging over the ears. His shirt and pants were dirty, splotched with bits of roofer's tar.

"Sh-s-on!" The sound resembled a word. "Wha-a-at're the hell you do...doing here?" His dad's eyes tried to focus.

The gutty garbles came directly from the stomach, bypassing the vocal chords and throat—a radio with bad batteries. Joey wanted to turn and run.

The other men at the bar looked into Joey's face. He saw the distorted, smirking faces and smelled the sour breath. He attempted a stiff grin. In one swoop, someone lifted him from the floor and sat him on the bar, where he spilled a bottle of beer, the cold liquid soaking his Levi's and running down his leg. Others turned to look. Some came closer, rubbing against him, slapping his back, patting his head, their cigarette smoke stinging his eyes.

"My mom's outside," Joey hissed.

"Wait a minute," his father blurted. "What're yo-u talkin' abo-out. Tell 'em, *m'ijo*, wha-at you go-nna be when you…'re a man?"

"Please, Daddy. Just gimme the money."

"Tell 'em, damn it, Joey. Don' be…ash…shamed. Sh-s-peak up. Wha…t're you going to be?"

Joey's legs dangled over the edge of the bar, his toes curled inside his Keds.

"C'mon, Joey. Te-ell 'em! Tell 'em! Siempre Fidelis, huh."

"A Marine," he answered, rubbing his knees with his knuckles. "An' it's semper not siempre."

"Why-y-y-y? Wh-y-y a Marine?"

Joey looked to a sign that read, Rest Room, Men Only.

"'Cause nobody's meaner or tougher than a Marine, Iwo Jima, Guada'canal, Guam…" Joey uttered.

"Hey… Yey-y. Now, *m'ijo*, tell them, damn it! Tell 'em what the Ma-rrines did at Iww-wo Jima."

Joey flushed. His throat hardened. He choked, as if he couldn't answer. He opened his mouth, swallowed.

"Tell 'em, son! Te-ll-l 'em."

Joey saw the strange eyes staring. His father's voice rose above the jukebox music. More men inched forward.

Joey spoke slowly as he told of the beach landing and the Marines hitting the sand, the move inland, the planting of the flag, and whenever he hesitated, his father asked more questions, orders, and like a parrot, Joey spat out more answers, dates and times, and as he did, he felt stronger, in control.

"Lou-ow-der, son. Louder. Who was the admiral in charge of all Marines?"

The boy sat silent.

"Huh, son? Tell 'em."

Joey looked directly into his father's eyes. "No! Dad, that's all. I ain't sayin' nothing else."

A few men applauded. His dad insisted, question after question, but Joey sat mute.

"What co-l-l—ege you going to, sh—on? Annapolis, in Maryland. Tell 'em where you go...oing to graduate from? Who's the com...manding gener...eral 'a the Marines? Tell 'em about Corr—rigador? The Marrr-rianas? You kn-n-ow it, sh—on." He turned to the others and said, "The Reds is lucky my kid was too youn...nng fer Korea. He...eed, a showed 'em."

Joey looked at the dark floor.

"Tell, son, so's they kin hear you. Siempre Fidelis, damn it. The Navy's a bun-unch a wat—tter lilies. Army's al-l-lll dogfaces. You join the Mar-rrrines. Die fer yer coo-uuuntry. Be proud. Siempre Fidelis."

Still, Joey didn't talk. He looked into his dad's dull eyes.

One man walked away, followed by another. Some applauded, and one patted Joey's back. The bartender gave him a Coke and said, "Only one, then ya gotta get him outside, Herman."

"I came for our money," Joey said. "Mom's waitin' in the car. Gimme the money."

"Wait, Jo-oo-ey...wait a second," his father said. "Fir-r-r-st, who co-oommanded the American troops in the Pa-aaacific?"

Joey turned away.

"Co-o-me on, son. You know. Te-e-ll 'em." His dad said, weakly, "Siempre Fidel—ish. Who was com—mmander, *m'ijo?*"

He barked, defiantly, "No Dad! No more. My mom's outside an' she wants our money 'fore ya spend it all. I ain't ans-wrin no more."

"Jo-o—eyy! Tell em how we ansss-wer the gunny in boot camp. What...what're we say? *M'ijo*, you know."

"You're a phoney!" Joey hollered, leaning forward, his arms stiff. His voice was sharp-edged. "You didn't even go to the war. They wouldn't even draft you," he yelled, his body tense, fists tight. "You didn't pass the physical. They didn't want you. Flat feet...right? Right? You couldn't even be a Marine. Even the Navy didn't want you. Nobody wants you... nobody. My mom don't want you. I don't want you...stay away! Leave us alone."

His dad's face sagged and wrinkled like an old cushion. He looked confused.

Joey leaned back, his legs quivering.

A man who stood a foot taller than the rest, dark skin, straight black hair and piercing eyes, limped forward, pushing through the crowd. The others stepped aside. Joey looked up at his uncle. Maimonides Serrano moved to his nephew, pulled him from the bar, and sat him on a stool. He turned to his brother. "What the hell you doin', Herman?"

"No, no-o-thing, Mo,...jez...jez talking to my boy."

"In front of these *pendejos*...like my nephew is a circus freak or somethin'. I tol' you 'bout this before. It ain't right. He's just a kid. It ain't right!"

Maimonides took the Coke from Joey's hand. "C'mon, José, you gettin' outta here."

The boy could smell the alcohol on his uncle's breath.

"I came for the money. My mom's outside waitin'," said Joey.

"Goddamn it, Herminio. Give him what you got."

Clumsily, Joey's dad dug into his pocket and pulled out a handful of crumpled bills. He didn't look at his son.

"That all?"

He reached into his other pocket, unfolded a ten and handed the money to his brother.

"Tha...'s al—ll I got."

"You sure?" said Maimonides.

"Christ is my witness."

"C'mon, José. This is no place for a boy."

Joey slid from the stool, started to walk away but turned to look at his father.

When his eyes found Joey, Herman said, "Go-ooo with your uncle."

Joey wanted to speak, to say something. His eyes remained on his father.

Maimonides saw a shot glass on the bar, poured the liquor down his throat and walked to the door, dragging his right leg across the sticky asphalt floor.

"I'll be home soon, Joey," Herman called, raising a glass of beer, a silly smile on his face.

Once Herman Serrano started drinking, he wouldn't come home until two or three in the morning. He'd continue drinking for days, sometimes weeks, lose his job, and disappear. He'd stumble through the streets, sleep in parks and borrow money, trying to get enough for a bottle of wine, a can of beer. He'd become ill, so ill that he couldn't eat. He'd finally find his way home. Joey and his mom would bathe and shave him, sit—at scheduled intervals—like guards, keeping him home, watching his body convulse. Then came words, sobs, confessions, apologies, promises, moans, and pleas. As the days, hours and minutes passed and the swelling subsided, the tanned, handsome face would return. There'd be room to breathe, to smile. There'd be another job, a paycheck, food on the table, laughter, play, rides to the beach, but then, they'd all wait, for the silence, the irritability, the vacuum of time, and the cycle would begin all over again.

As they stepped outside, Maimonides placed his hand on his nephew's shoulder and they walked towards the car.

"I hate him," Joey said.

"No! *Hijo*."

"He hurts us."

"He's your daddy. He works hard."

"So what? He spends all the money in there."

Maimonides stopped walking and put his hand on his nephew's shoulder.

"You got on'y one daddy. He makes mistakes, but he loves you...because he's your daddy."

"Why does he have'ta drink?"

Maimonides looked into the boy's eyes, smiled, and continued walking.

They neared the car. Joey waited for his uncle's reply.

Maimonides didn't answer.

"He didn't even go to the war. Wasn't even a Marine."

"That don't matter. I went, and your uncle Ned...and a lotta guys. See we was all a part of it, even your daddy. He lost good friends. He wanted to go but was too young. Tried hard, but they wouldn't let him. He went to three different cities and tried to join up. Even lied about his name and how old he was."

Joey was silent, then said, "I'll never be a Marine. I hate the Marines."

"There's no more wars, *hijo*. That's why we fought, so you don't have to join nothing."

"I'm going to be a paratrooper, like you," said Joey, ignoring his uncle. "I'll show him. I'll never be like him, never be what he wants me to be."

"Yeah, and you wannu spend your life with a bum leg like this," he said, slapping his thigh. "People give me work because they feel sorry for me, not because I'm a good worker. How can I? Sometimes it hurts so much I can't get up in the morning. You want that?"

"But you're a hero, Uncle Mo. Everybody respects you. My dad told me all about it, how you jumped at Bastogne, killed Germans, helped free the Jewish prisoners. Dad said you were one of the first soldiers at the camp."

"I'm a wino. I drink 'cuz I can't do nothing else. Being a hero don't put food on the table. It don't feed your family."

Joey didn't understand.

When they reached the Ford, Maimonides opened the door and Joey stepped inside, reached into his pocket, and handed the rumpled bills to his mother.

"Thank you, *m'ijo*. He would have spent it all, if it wasn't for you."

Maimonides interrupted, "No. He wouldn't have spent it all, Ruthie."

"We've gotta go, Mo. Take care of yourself."

"Okay. And I'll get Herminio home."

"Don't bother. We don't need him."

Maimonides shrugged and said to Joey, "You be a good boy, *hijo*, huh? And remember what I told you."

"Okay, Uncle Mo."

Joey's mom looked at the boulevard, waited, and pulled into the traffic. Joey hoped that she didn't mean what she had said.

"He would have spent all of the money," she said as they drove down the street.

"You don't know, not really you don't."

She looked over her shoulder, put out her arm and changed lanes. "Did he give the money to you right away?"

"He bought me a soda first and then we talked to his friends for a little while. Then Uncle Mo came by and we talked some more. My dad gave me the money right away. I think he was savin' it, like he knew that I was comin' to get it."

Ruth Serrano looked at her son.

"That's good. I'm glad," she said. "Thank you, Joey."

He looked out the window as they drove down the wide, crowded boulevard, past the library, police station and post office. One orange cloud hung low in the west. Some daylight remained.

His mom left him at the park. His friends were no longer playing baseball, but they sat talking, scattered about the bleachers. Joey grabbed the railing with one hand and pulled himself onto the wooden seats.

The lights above the baseball diamond flickered, and with a pop, brightened the infield's dark brown soil. They heard Frank's voice: "You guys got the diamond for forty-five minutes! Forty-five... no more."

The boys cheered, grabbed their gloves and bats. Joey batted first. He swung at the first pitch and missed. He remembered what his father had told him about not backing away, so he placed his lead foot closer to the plate and raised his bat high, right elbow even with his shoulders. He heard his father's voice: "Tha's the way to look like a hitter." The ball came chest high, fast and straight. "Go get it, Marine. Hang tough, never quit." Joey heard the buzz of the speeding ball and didn't back away. He swung hard, level, and drove the ball into left field, into the deepest corner of the outfield.

"Semper Fidelis," Joey whispered.

"Whadda ya say?" said the catcher.
"Just some words."

SEVEN

SOMEWHERE OUTSIDE DUC PHO
(DAVID ALMAS REMEMBERS)

I.

Inside the fifth-story condominium overlooking the Santa Monica coastline, David Almas sat back in the L-shaped gray sofa and sipped coffee from the "Best Dad in the World" cup his grown children had given him on Father's Day. His wife Luz wore a thin cotton robe. Her auburn hair flipped lazily about her head. She pressed a red pillow to her breast and curled her legs on the cushions. The sun had started its descent over the Pacific, and the evening shadows entered the sliding glass doors.

An hour before, during a wrenching argument, David had thrown open the front door and started to walk out. Luz lunged in front and pushed him back inside. She shouted, more apprehensive than angry, "Yeah, go on...take the easy way out."

He stood there, unable to move.

"Run...run like a kid, but don't expect me to come after you, not again," she said.

He stayed and fought, bringing up confused emotions, arguing until both were exhausted, until both had forgotten what started the initial argument.

Now on the couch, in the dim shadow and orange glow of the sun's last light, she reached out and touched his fingertips.

"David, you should go into counseling."

"Come on, Luz."

"Okay, okay, I know...you don't have any...*¿qué?* profound psychological problems," she said, raising her fingers as if making quotation marks, "but you've got to learn to feel."

"I can't stand the way our generation rushes to therapy for any little thing, like it's a cure-all, a 90's fad taking the place of the 60's love-in. And I am 'in touch', sometimes too much. Just because I don't hang my emotions on my face, doesn't mean I don't know exactly what I feel."

"You're in so much denial."

He looked at her, a smile forming at the corner of his mouth. "It's a skill," he said.

"Be serious. Counseling helped me when Sergio died," she said, referring to a close friend who had committed suicide in his early twenties.

"You don't think I've lost friends, close friends? I deal with my losses. Maybe in my own way, but I do deal with them," he said.

"Running? That's not dealing."

He winced but quickly recovered. "Life is like a story, each incident another chapter, each person another character. And I'm a part of that story, sometimes fiction, sometimes reality. Maybe that's why you've been in therapy for the past twenty years, because you stopped believing in stories. You're caught in facts."

"Stories are, are...unreliable."

"That's the point. Everything is unreliable. There is no truth, no reality."

"Your...stories. They won't get you through everything," she said, frustrated.

"Yes, they will. Especially when I feel myself weaken, and I have no answers. Jesse Peña...." he said, then paused.

"The guy who disappeared?"

David looked toward the double glass doors. "It's weird, stupid...hard to believe, but it'll be with me, forever...letting me escape, maybe that's why it happened."

He stopped talking. She rolled her eyes.

Most guys denied it ever happened," he said.

"But it happened?"

"Probably not like I remember."

"Tell me."

"How much you want to hear?"

"All of it. The whole thing."

He drank his coffee and put the cup on the glass table.

"My first year home from Vietnam," he said, "I was... what? Twenty-one years old. I stayed awake every night 'til one or two in the morning, sipped beer, smoked 'weed,' dropped acid occasionally, listened to rock and roll all the time, didn't give a shit about work or anything. All night, just thinking, remembering, seeing the faces of friends, hearing them laugh, argue, fight...."

He told her that he had tacked a map of Vietnam to his bedroom wall, and placed red checks in areas where he'd been, where an operation had taken place, a friend killed or wounded. He'd colored a round blue mark over Chu Lai, where his friend Wayne Podleski had died. David said that he relived the war over and over every night, every hour, pondering, reminiscing.

He told Luz that after one particular operation, while he and the guys, mostly Chicanos from California and Texas, had been back at base camp for a brief stand-down outside the city of Duc Pho, someone had reported their partner, Jesse Peña, missing, AWOL. They'd all been together the night before, drinking and partying, so they were confused by the news. At first, they bragged about Jesse's bravado, but then they became concerned and decided to search the bars downtown, before Jesse got into serious trouble.

As he spoke, David's eyes were on the bearded wizard in the mural-sized oil painting hanging on the opposite wall.

David remembered how the ill-fated search party had been ready to start its mission when orders came through, restricting them all to base camp. The next morning at 5:00, a long line of double-propped Chinook helicopters lifted them to a mountaintop in Kontum province, where sharp-peaked ridges stretched in every direction, the valleys and mountains buried in dense jungle.

David described how he and the other artillerymen rushed to unhook the howitzers from the choppers and push the big guns into position.

He said that throughout the day, the men had hacked away brush, unloaded tools, equipment, packs and ammunition, carrying hundreds of heavy canisters into the ammo dump...long lines of shirtless men, sweat pouring from their bodies, shoulders raw and burning, the sledgehammers clanging against metal stakes, the gun crews digging in the howitzers. They had filled thousands of sandbags and stacked them into long curving walls around tents and jeeps. The shouting voices, striking metal and popping smoke grenades echoed, but more powerful was the roar of the landing helicopters, kicking up dust, dropping their cargo and lifting, fast.

"At night it got cold and windy, like ice. Wayne and I were pulling outpost. We'd become tight, real close. He arrived in Vietnam a few months after I did," David said, his voice calm, monotone.

Moving close to him, pulling her robe over her exposed legs, Luz said, "Your friend from Pennsylvannia?"

"Yeah, a little town called Clairton, a good-looking kid, smart, cool, and wouldn't take shit from anybody, a damn good friend, almost like a brother."

Sitting back and taking hold of Luz's toes, rubbing, kneading, he remembered one night when the wind had whipped the jungle and a trip flare had ignited...a shrill, piercing sizzle, lighting up the thick foliage. A shadow had darted across the perimeter. Grenades pounded the jungle and machine guns chattered. The howitzers exploded, shooting bright flares into the sky. The firing stopped as the flares burned brilliant, descending, oscillating beneath white parachutes. Seconds later the darkness had returned and the world, again, rumbled.

An explosion had shaken the outpost. The ground vibrated, ears buzzed, and David's left arm had felt warm. He'd slid his fingers under his shirtsleeve, felt the wet skin, and touched the punctured flesh below the shoulder.

"Wayne, I'm hit, man," David had said, as Wayne reached for a hand grenade.

"You shittin' me?"

"Feel my sleeve."

It was soiled, slimy.

"It don't look too bad, Almas. I'll get Doc Langley out here."

"Hurry up, man."

"All right...goddamn it! Got yourself a Purple Heart," said Wayne, cranking the field telephone. "Shit. I oughtta get half. It's probably from the grenade I threw. I knew I threw it too close to us."

"You asshole."

Wayne laughed.

The next morning a chopper had flown David to the field hospital at Pleiku. Doc Langley, the battery medic, went along to take care of the paperwork and refill his supply of drugs.

The doctors had sewn David's arm, and a nurse rolled him to a crowded room where he slept the whole day, until Langley barged in, waking him. Langley spoke, excited... telling David that Jesse had been spotted.

"You believe that shit, man. The Tiger Force," Langley had said, smirking, "was on a listening post, keepin' an eye on a squad of dinks movin' along the trail, and there, right in the middle of the VC column, they see Jesse—or a chubby Mexican-looking-type guy in fatigues, black headband, rucksack, an M-16. Dig this, Almas. The dude ain't a prisoner. He's like a...a commie, man, walking right along with them gooks. A fuckin' stroll in the park, man."

"Maybe he was takin' his dog for a walk," David had suggested, chuckling.

"No shit. A gook German shepherd, man."

David told Luz how he had looked at Langley and Langley at him, and they laughed. Langley said, "Tiger Force dudes probably got hold 'a some good dope, man."

"Yeah, the shit was probably dipped in acid."

"Or fuckin' opium."

After they had joked a while, David told Langley that maybe Jesse hadn't gone AWOL, but had gotten himself captured or something.

"Shee-it, I guess it ain't impossible," Langley had said, "but I sure as shit wouldn't bet my paycheck on it."

"It ain't like Jesse to go AWOL."

"That it ain't, David," he'd said. "That it ain't."

Luz interrupted, "When was the last time you saw Jesse?"

"In the rear area, the night before he was reported missing." David explained how after each operation, when they'd get back to the rear area, in the evenings about five or six guys, mostly Chicanos, would find a secluded place in the brigade area, drink beer and talk all night. That last evening Jesse had acted like a stranger... hadn't said much. He'd smiled, nodded, eaten a couple of cans of peaches and just watched and listened. Danny Ríos, a religious, easygoing, baby-faced Chicano from Redwood City, California, had asked Jesse if he was cool. Jesse had just nodded.

It was early when Jesse stood and said that carrying the radio during the last operation had kicked his *pinche* ass, and that he had to go. Little Rod and Alex Martínez tried to talk him into staying longer, but Jesse said he had to keep his mind clear... something about being "short," only three months to go and needing to have things ready. He had touched his fingers to the tip of his cap and said, "*Me voy,*" and walked into the darkness of the brigade area. That was the last they had seen him.

David described Jesse's round, boyish face, his five-feet, seven-inch, rotund frame and his mischievous smile, like a Buddha statue. He was handsome, with wavy hair, creamy skin and dark eyes, childlike, innocent, pure, immediately likeable. Two deep dimples, one on each cheek, brought a glow to his face.

After each operation, the guys looked forward to their sessions and Jesse's stories. His humor wasn't slapstick or silly, but sharp—David used the word, poignant—and always with a point or moral. Sometimes, he'd reminisce about family and friends back home, like his cousin Bernie who was so much against the war that he had traveled down to Eagle's Pass, Texas, pretended to be a *bracero* and had been picked up by U.S. Immigration. According to Jesse, Bernie, who was American and fluent in English, spoke only Spanish to the INS agents. He was deported and went to live with relatives in

Piedras Negras. All this, Jesse had said, just to beat the draft. Bernie could say he hadn't dodged the draft; it was the U.S. that rejected him.

Jesse's stories had always led to questions, analyses and laughter. Everyone participated. He was never egotistical and always came across as sincere, gracious.

He'd switch from English to Spanish in mid-sentence, his voice rhythmical, a blend of talk-laugh, where even tragic stories became lighthearted. He didn't pass himself off as educated or intellectual. His speech had a sophistication that didn't come with schooling but with breeding. Someplace in his family's poverty, there was an honest appreciation of language.

David said that Jesse loved Texas as much as Puerto Ricans loved New York. To hear him talk, one would think that San Antonio was San Francisco or Paris. "San Anto," as he had called it, had culture, personality. No music matched Willie Nelson's or Little Joe's. Jesse played their music on his portable tape recorder, and the guys from California had laughed and called him a goddamn cowbody, a redneck Mexican out of step with the times, and they'd slip into arguing about their states and which was best, and how the city was better than the country...and on and on until they'd drained themselves.

✪ ✪ ✪

David told Luz that after his release from the hospital, the scab on his arm healed, the field operation finished, he and the guys had all gone back to the front-area base camp, still near Duc Pho, preparing to move someplace else, never knowing where, always outside somewhere or other.

"When I got back with the guys," David said, "I found out that Langley and I weren't the only ones who'd heard the rumor about Jesse being seen with the V.C. All the guys knew about it. Big Rod..."

"I thought you said his name was Little Rod?"

"There were two Rodriguezes, Big Rod, from San Antonio, tall, about six-foot, good-looking, tanned, always neat, at base camp wore starched fatigues and spit-shined boots—a real joker who laughed a lot. Then there was Little Rod from Brownsville...looked like a tree stump, short and dark, *puro Indio*, fatigues too big, always wrinkled; some guys called him *Changuito*, serious, superstitious as hell, hardly laughed, and couldn't control his left eye that looked at the sky whenever he got too emotional.

"Big Rod knew some guys from the Tiger Force who had told him that it was definitely an American they'd seen out there, and no question, big as shit, had to have been a Mexican, something about the eyes and hair.

"Alex...."

"You've mentioned him before," Luz interrupted.

"Yeah, he was a tough bastard, from Woodland Hills, always cussing, kind of disrespectful and *muy agabachado*. Anyway, he said it was all a bunch of bullshit and called the Tiger Force a bunch of fuckin' racists grunts...told Big Rod that he should have asked the Tiger Force if they also checked to see whether Jesse had a green card...stupid bastards.

"The whole thing put the fear of God into Little Rod. He forced us to move the location of the next session, said that the evil eye would follow us if we met in the same place where we'd last seen Jesse...wouldn't explain, just said to find a new place or count him out."

David laughed at the memory.

"Alex had said the only evil eye was Little Rod's left one, the one that kept checking out the clouds."

He went on to explain how Danny Ríos and Alex had found an isolated spot, an eerie-looking place near the camp's perimeter, separated from the rest of the brigade by a decaying sandbag wall about four-feet high. Empty wooden ammo boxes, broken and black with mildew, were scattered all over the place. To one side, no more than twenty-five yards away, the jungle grew thick—not like in the field, but still dense enough to hide someone or something. They waited until the night moved in and the trees and brush turned to shadows. The perimeter watch was some yards beyond—a gun tower manned by two paratroopers.

It hadn't taken long before the guys were all sitting around. Even Wayne and Doc Langley came. Langley said he had a surprise. He brought two Chicanos, engineers, one was from Culver City, Hector Medrano, a tall good-looking guy whose brother Rudy had stepped on a mine and been killed three months earlier.

Hector had told David that everything back in the Westside was still cool, a lot of hard-core *cholos* were leaving the gangs and joining the anti-war movement, wearing *sarapes* and *huaraches*, growing ponytails, beards, even enrolling in city college. "Ain't that some shit," Hector had said. "Take a war to make them *pendejos* stop killing each other."

"Hey, *ese* Medrano...your brother was a bad *vato*, man. *De aquellas*," said Little Rod.

"That's what I've heard," said Hector.

"All the guys knew who Rudy Medrano was...called him the Pointman," said Danny. "He stayed pretty much to himself. Always was wearing a black *sombrero*."

Hector smiled, a quick jerk at the corner of his mouth. "My old man bought it in Mexicali. Rudy had it pinned to the wall over his bed in our room back home."

There was small talk, the usual *"Orales"* and "What's happenings."

"Jesse's either been kidnapped or gone AWOL," David had told his friends, wasting no time.

Alex piped up, "Ain't nobody gonna get kidnapped from this here place, man."

He was right. The camp was a fortress: guards securing the perimeter in guntowers, M.P.'s patrolling in jeeps, units posting watches throughout the night.

"No way, *pura locura*," called Little Rod. "Who in hell wants to kidnap a *gordote* Chicano PFC radio operator? Only thing Peña gave a shit about was getting back to his ol' lady and kid."

"There it is! That's what I think, too," said David.

"I'm with Almas," said Alex. "Peña split, man, A-W, fuckin' O-L. I say he's shacked up with some ol' red-tooth bitch downtown. Tiger Force don't know shit from gold, man; prob'ly saw some fat gook dressed in fatigues and thought it was Gordo, man. Gordo'll bring his ass draggin' in. Give him a few more days."

"Okay, but, you know, he's been gone more than three weeks. That's a long time," said Danny, his olive-colored baseball cap high on his head, showing his young, beardless face. Danny read the Bible every day, and spoke in a soft spiritual voice, but he wasn't 'square' or a nerd.

Doc Langley had reminded them how Michael Oberson, a six-foot-five, two-hundred-and-thirty-pound cook had gone AWOL, changed his name, and shacked up with a Vietnamese waitress in Saigon for fourteen months. "Shit," Langley had said. "Oberson got himself a sweet honey, a job with an American insurance company, and a slick-ass apartment in downtown Sai...ass...gon. Stayed there 'til his woman got too serious. Ask me, I say he knocked-up the honey."

Wayne blurted out how Oberson had finally tired of being AWOL and turned himself in. That's how all the guys had met him. While Oberson waited for his court martial, the Army assigned him to the artillery.

Danny reasoned, "Jesse's got three months left and he's back in the *world*. Nobody goes AWOL with three months. Makes no sense, man."

"Damn! Maybe Gordo couldn't take no more...'punkass,' Danny. Maybe he just had to get the shit away, someplace where he wouldn't be gettin' his ass shot at."

"Three weeks...still a long time, Alex," said Danny. "And if he's AWOL, it's the Saigon stockade. Ain't a dude in his right mind wants more time in this shit hole."

Passing his hand through his neatly combed hair, Big Rod spoke, his English accented, slowly drawing out the words.

"I been thinking, you know. Not too long ago Peña tol' me son'thing was wrong...inside. I ask't him like if 't was his *vieja* or kid, but he say'd no, wasn' like that. Say'd it was more like a feeling, like son'thing what grabs your stomach and turn and twists and don' let go. Not a pain, *¿sabes?* you kno', more like a chunk a' metal glue' to your stomach, son'thing that jez' hang and pull 'til it feel like your insides're falling. Say'd it wouldn't go away. Woke up feeling like that...*todos los días*. I thought he was sick, you know."

David stopped talking. He stared at the mural across from him. He and Luz had bought the painting from a Vietnam veteran at a sidewalk art show in Westwood, across from the UCLA campus where David taught Latin American History.

Luz offered a glass of water. David drank, then continued the story, saying that Wayne, Doc Langley, and the engineers had gone back to the battery area. Those who had stayed continued talking.

"Hey, Hector, maybe I'll catch you later, talk more about home," David had said as Hector walked away.

"That'd be far out, man, but they're assigning me to some shit duty with the Marines, up around Da Nang. We'll be buildin' some bridges up there or something. ¿Quién sabe?"

"All right. Be cool."

"Later."

David had called, "And Wayne, you keep your ass out of trouble. We got a bunch of shit work to do tomorrow."

"Got it," Wayne had replied, putting his fingers to his lips as if puffing on a joint.

As the darkness had thickened, the faces of those remaining turned to shadows. The trees and shrubs created fascinating shapes and configurations. The guys sat in a circle. In the middle, a C-ration can filled with burning heat tablets offered some light. The darkness hung quietly. There was little noise, except for voices coming from the brigade area.

Little Rod, his voice deep, hoarse, had said, "I seen Peña start to change..." His accent was heavy, and he always called guys by their last names. The shadow from the brim of his cap had buried his eyes. "When Peña transfer'd to join the infantry, I tol' 'em not to do it. In the artillery, Peña didn' see much ac'chion—not 'til he start humpin' that radio. I seen how he kept laugh'n, real scare' when he come to the sessions, seen 'em tryin' to hide it. I could tell; he was scare', sompt'ing in his eyes. He trie' to not cho' it...but I seen it."

"Gimme a break, *pinche*, Rodriguez. You sound like a bullshit *curandero*...don't start that Aztec shit, man," said Alex.

"Okay, Little Rod, Jesse's scared—so all right," Danny had said in his usual levelheaded way. He argued, "Jesse said he wanted to see action, said he was tired of fillin' sandbags and carrying ammo. Got his transfer all right. Now he's with

85

the grunts, and yeah, I'm with you...the bush is the shits. So he's got reason to be scared...common sense, man. Logical as all hell. But you sayin' Peña deserted?"

"Runned off an joined Charlie, *ese*?" said Little Rod.

"A traitor...Peña?" said Danny.

"Bullshit-an-stupid-to-boot. You gotta be a lame mother-fucker to even think like that. Damn Catholics, man, teach you guys all that mystery shit in church. Suckers should a been Protestants," Alex said, looking at Little Rod. "See things the way they are."

Little Rod spoke again, his back against the sandbags, his voice sullen. "*Abra los ojos*, Martínez. Peña's a good dude, no? He got his *vieja* an' his kid. Every time the *cura* come' out to the bush, Peña he goe' to Communion, never misses. The *vato* cracked, *ese*."

"Man, all you suckers go to Communion, too. Big Rod goes into town, beds down with a whore one day and next day he's on his knees and got his tongue hangin' out in front of a priest," Alex interrupted, squinting his eyes, looking annoyed, then laughing.

"Alex, your Protestant ass is going straight to hell 'cuz you don't even believe in Communion. Your buns is gonna cook in Hades," said Danny.

"Eat this! Babyface, asshole." Alex grabbed his crotch and turned towards Danny. "You think you got all the answers 'cuz you read that chickenshit little Bible you carry in your pocket."

"At least I can read."

"Sompthin' had to 'a happen to Peña," said Little Rod. "Maybe he learned that God ain't in the fiel'. Maybe he see that God ain't on our side. Firs' time he carrie' that radio, 'C' Company got ambushed...remember, bodies tore up into thousan' pieces. Peña told us how he smelt the burn meat, arms an' legs that belonged to his friends—blood all over. Said he looked into their dead nasty eyes, like they was alive, but they wasn't. I remember. Peña wouldn't talk about it no more."

Alex had jumped from the box where he'd been sitting. He called to Little Rod in an angry voice, "Shit! what are ya' sayin', Li'l Rod? You sayin' Jesse's the guy the Tiger Force saw out there, that Peña's out in the bush, fighting for the VC? Hell, maybe they made 'em a training NCO and he's in charge of VC recruits. Bullshit! You think a little death's gonna make Gordo run off with them gooks? Gimme a goddamn break already."

"¿Sabes qué, Martínez? One day, ese, you gonna see. You gonna see, an' it's gonna scare the livin' chit oughtta you. Pinche, Woodland Hills, Californio, you vatos spend all your lives with Mickey Mouse y la Marilyn Monroe y John Wayne. That ain't life, ese. C'mon down to the Rio Grande Valley and learn what's it all about."

Little Rod had turned and kept talking, slow, distinct. "How 'bout the time we was in the fiel'? Peña's squad come in out'a the bush. Was the firs' operation after his transfer; he's carry'n the radio. Remember, Ríos, you was there? Before Almas and Martínez was with the batt'ry...was someplace outside Tuy Hoa. Hijo, cómo llovió—en chorros. Ever'thin' was like a sponge. Peña come out the jungle into our batt'ry area...his eyes big...man, like two big ol' hard-boiled eggs. That ain't regular scared. He's soaked, dirty, smelly and he's talking' a hunder' miles' an hour. Had to slow 'em down. Hunder' miles an hour, ese. That ain' reg'lar scare'. Sompth'n happen to Peña, man. That ain't no shit; I seen it."

"Right on! Little Rod," said Danny. "When Jesse come in out a' the rain that day his face was tight, stretched like a drumskin, pale...cold; talked like he was on full-automatic...

head moved with quick jerks, always checking his back. Two hours later—his squad moves out, Jesse goes, rain still coming down. Said they had to find cover before dark. Look like Jesse wanted to cry, man, but he went, no arguing, nothing; went...just like the other dudes in his squad. Right on, Little Rod, that wasn't no regular scared."

"Goddamn, Danny, at least I thought you had some sense. You tellin' me you gonna start fallin' for this *Llorona* bullshit, like these superstitious *Tejanos*," Alex said, getting to his feet.

"I'm tellin' you what I saw, Alex, and I don't know what to believe," Danny said. "If Jesse's so scared, why's he gonna go into the jungle alone an' take off with the gooks? How'd he even know where'ta find them. And if he did find them, they'd prob'ly shoot him first. I don't know, man, ain't logical, don't make sense to me. But it's gotta mean something. Everything happens for a reason. That's how things're planned...part of the whole, you know."

"Here he comes with his gospel shit," said Alex, pulling at the beak of his cap. He turned to David and said, "Tell 'em Davy. Tell 'em what the fuck's up."

David had turned to Big Rod, who always had an answer for everything. Big Rod stared at the ground, a stick in his hand and just kept making designs in the dirt, his cap turned backwards. Little Rod smoked a cigarette, just that orange glow coming from under his hat. Danny sat on a stack of boxes, his hands folded between his knees, like a ballplayer waiting his turn to bat. Alex smoked, taking long, deep puffs, suspiciously eyeing the others.

David told them that he didn't think Jesse had deserted. He figured that was some trippy story, but that's all it was, a story, and he wasn't believing that shit. "Jesse's probably in town, hiding, afraid to come back and get busted."

"That's right," said Alex.

"So?" said Danny.

"It's the only answer, man. Guys just don't run off and join the enemy," David declared. "It don't happen in real life...only in stories, movies. It just don't happen that way."

"There it is!" Alex blurted, throwing down his cigarette, squatting and leaning forward, the light shining against his square jaw and pitted skin. "Almas is right. It just ain't fucking done. Gordo ain't no traitor. He's probably in town right now, ass hung over and wantin' to come back."

Big Rod looked towards the burning heat tablets. He broke the twig in half and tossed it behind him. He'd been unusually quiet through most of the discussion. Jesse was his best friend. They'd gone home on leave together from jump school. Big Rod said, looking to Alex, "You're wrong, *ése* Martínez. Peña went...took off, didn' take nothing but his rucksack an' M-16, went to the bush with them. *No sé cómo, ni por qué, ni dónde. Pero,* he's out there. I feel it. It don' need to make sense, don' need to be *¿cómo dices,* Danny? Logical? I feel it, *ese. Como dicen los gabachos, lo siento en los llesos.*"

"You're bullshitting me, aren't you?" said Alex. "You know what you're sayin' can't happen, Big Rod. It's crazy, whole thing's stupid, bullshit to the limit."

"I know. Sure, but you din't know Peña like I did. He's lookin' for something," Big Rod went on, rising to his feet, "maybe lookin' for us...maybe looking for hisself. Think— remember wha'd he tol' us before he went. He was tellin' us son'thin' about things he hadda take care of."

Danny stood and brushed off his pants. Little Rod stood. The men began to split up and start back to their units. Alex was flustered. He yelled to the two Rods, "Crazy *Tejanos.* Bastards prob'ly take apples and bananas to dead relatives. *Día dee lo mw-er-toe* and all that bullshit. Always gotta make something out of nothing."

II.

David explained to Luz how the commanders from A and B batteries called each of the guys in to find out what they could. It was clear that the officers thought Jesse was AWOL and somewhere in Duc Pho, screwing around. That's what most of the guys in the brigade thought, too: Jesse would come back, get court-martialed, and that would be the end of it. But the way David told it, Jesse had never been in trouble before. He was the one who kept everyone else out of trouble, making sure the guys got back to camp after a crazy day in town or calming them down after a run-in with an NCO or officer.

Two weeks had passed when they heard a new rumor. They were still operating in the area around Duc Pho. A squad of grunts had made contact with a group of VC.

"I swear to Jesus," said one grunt. "The guy looked like a Mexican, wore camouflaged fatigues, sandals—no boots—a black headband.... He carried an M-16, walked point for the gooks."

It was no mistaken identity, so they claimed. One guy said, "I stared right at the Mexican, and the dude just looked at me and fuckin' smiled. Got that, smiled in my goddamn face. Automatics and grenades started going off, and the Mex and his squad slip into the brush, chief...disappered in the trees, smooth, man, like butter...fuckin' butter, man."

Everybody in the brigade was talking about it. The guys who saw Jesse swore that it was a Mexican-American they'd seen out there. "The guy looked me right in the eyes. He could'a shot me if he wanted. I was froze shitless..." was how another grunt put it.

David told Luz that it was insane how the words built and the story spread, but then, as the days turned into weeks, the reports changed into rumors.

The stories about Americans leading Vietcong squads weren't unusual. Everyone had heard them. But the traitors, or Americans-turned-VC, almost always had blonde hair, blue eyes, were tall and thin. Nobody who told the stories ever saw the defectors. Always it was, "I heard this from a friend of a cat in C Company," or, "Hey, check what a dude back in Phan Rhang told me." The stories were really fables or myths, sort of a military anti-war protest. What made the story about Jesse so different was that the guys reporting it were claiming to have personally seen him. Still, not many guys believed it was an American out there, except for Big Rod, Little Rod, and the grunts who said they'd seen Jesse. Danny wasn't sure, said he just didn't know. Alex still thought that Jesse was in town and would be back soon.

David told Luz that he agreed with Alex, but still, there was always a question rolling around inside his head. More importantly, though, David said that he was simply worried about Jesse no matter where he was.

"Things are so crazy 'round this place, guys'll make up anything fer 'musement," Josh Spenser, an Oklahoman, had said. "Could be true, but who in the hell knows fer sure, man."

Two more weeks had passed before the next sighting. "Saw Peña, man." The guys who said they saw Jesse were now using his name, as if they personally knew him.

One night, when they were at their front-area base camp, Big Rod, Little Rod, Alex and David had walked across the brigade area to talk to one of the guys who'd said he'd seen Jesse.

At first the guy didn't believe they were Jesse's friends. He didn't trust anybody because, as he put it, guys were saying that he was making the whole thing up. But after Big Rod told him about Jesse and even showed him some pictures of them together, the guy began to talk.

"That's him, Jim! That's the dude I seen," he said when he saw the photographs. Then he added, "It's the shits, man. Captain tol' me he didn't want me spreadin' no rumors." His voice quivered, and he puffed on a cigarette like it was glued to his lips, smoke clouds coming from his mouth. "But I seen him, and that's him there, I know, big as shit...it was him," he said, pointing to the picture in Big Rod's hand.

The guy's name was John Conklin, from Manhattan Beach, dirty-blond bangs in his eyes, freckles, fatigues that looked like they'd been slept in, and he talked real fast, his eyes bouncing around like he was high on speed. Alex gave his, is-this-guy-for-real look.

Conklin seemed sincere, yet nervous. He told his story like someone trying to convince people that he'd seen a UFO. He said that he and his squad were on an ambush. They had the whole thing set up by nightfall: claymores out, good cover, M-16's, grenades and an M-60 at the ready. He said that it was quiet out there, no noise, nothing. But Charlie never showed.

Since there'd been no contact, the choppers flew out to pick them up the next morning. Conklin described how he made his way out to retrieve the claymores. He disconnected the firing cap, and squatting down low, started to wrap the wire around the curved, green explosive. He said that as he wrapped, he kept his eyes peeled down either side of the trail, and also checked the jungle to his front. And then he saw Peña. Just like that, Conklin said, using Jesse's last name.

"Pee-ña was down in the bush, a Thompson submachine gun pointed straight 'et me. I was goin' for my M-16, but he jes' nods, cool-like, slow...and I know he means for me to not go for it, so's I jes' set there and check him out, and all he does is check me out. I couldn't talk, man, not a shitty word...couldn't yell. It was like...like one of them nightmares where ya' feel suffocated and can't nobody he'p you. Then he moves back, real slow-like, still squatting, like gooks do, an' then I see two other gooks, one to his right, one to his left. He stands up and the gooks stand up and they move backward into the brush, just like that, fuckin'-A,' man, and he's gone."

"Hey, man. If it's Peña, then tell us what he looked like," said Alex, kneeling in front of Conklin, looking into his dull blue eyes.

"Got on gook clothes. Pajamas—black top and black bottoms, cut off just above the knees, black headband...light complexion, about like you," he said pointing to Big Rod. "I guess he's close to five-seven or eight, not too tall...probably 145 or 150 pounds."

"There it is, man! Couldn't 'a been Peña. He's closer to 185, maybe 190," Alex told Conklin.

"Not no more he ain't. Guy I seen wasn't no 180. And when he smiled, he made me feel okay, you know. Even though I was scared and he could'a blew a hole through me, still...made me feel like...okay. Maybe had something to do with those dimples. Big mothers...one on each cheek." Big Rod and Little Rod looked at each other.

"A *vato* coul' loose some weight out there, eatin' rice and humpin' mountains all day long, Martínez," Little Rod said to Alex.

"Man, you dudes ain't never gonna give up...." Alex said.

Conklin kept talking, "Dimples kinda made him look like a kid. But he wasn't bullshittin', man. It wasn't no joke. If I'd a gone for my weapon, he'd a blowed my ass clean away. I can't figure it, man. Gone, just like that...disappeared with those gooks right into the jungle. And nobody else seen it, on'y me."

As they walked away towards their own tents, Big Rod and Little Rod were quiet, but Alex kept repeating, "Man, that surfer was high. Looks like a speed freak. A bunch a bullshit if you ask me."

❂ ❂ ❂

David told Luz that it was nearing February and Jesse had been missing three months. "Maybe we expected a miracle, like Jesse was going to walk into base camp, say 'hi' and tell us about his days with the VC while he packed his bags, getting ready to catch a hop to Cam Rhan Bay where he'd DEROS home. But nothing. It was just another day; besides, by this time we were in Phan Rhang, our huge rear-area base camp, and a long way from where Jesse had last been seen."

David told how the night of Jesse's ETS, when Jesse should've been boarding a plane home, the guys held a session, more of a funeral, in the training area which was at the perimeter of the brigade camp, near the foot of a jungle-covered mountain range. After dark, it was off-limits, so they had to be careful not to get caught.

David described for Luz the sprawling base camp and the secure, easy feeling of the rear area. He also told her that as he had walked to the session, the sun dipping into the horizon, he stopped on a hilltop and sat down and waited a few minutes until it was dark enough to slip over the hill, into the training area.

As he had sat there, he looked out over the Airborne complex. Camp Eagle was the closest thing to home. He had watched GI's lumbering along the dirt roads, some going to the Enlisted Men's or Officers' Clubs, others to the USO and still others just walking like they were out for an evening in some country town. As darkness fell, carefully rationed lights brightened the area. There was drinking and card games, laughing and yelling, tales about families and girlfriends, heroic stories, with a few idiots displaying their macabre trophies. Some guys listened to records in tents, wondering what their friends back home were doing. At the USO, guys who hadn't touched a girl in months would talk to the Red Cross donut dollies and play Monopoly, Scrabble, Dominoes and other games with them, but in their minds they'd be making love to the American women who sat at the other side of the game boards.

David told Luz that he had waited until it was dark enough, then had stood, turned, and headed down the opposite side of the hill. He followed a dirt trail under a canopy of trees and made his way deeper into the jungle. Even though this was the training area and relatively secure, it was still part of the wilderness, and the VC had occasionally sent in sappers and recon squads. As he had approached the jungle clearing, David saw a dim light shining through the trees and brush. Alex and Danny, using C-ration cans and heat tablets, had designed a church-like atmosphere. The flickering blue flames, much like candles, were spread out in a straight line to their front, lifting the darkness so that faces were barely recognizable. All around, the trees, brush and vines hung with a heaviness that leaned more towards enigma than fear.

"Jesus! Couldn't you find any place farther away than this?" David whispered, breathing hard.

"Ah, quit yer bitchin'," said Alex.

Five minutes later, the two Rods arrived, followed by Wayne, Doc Langley, Hector Medrano and another Chicano, a kid named Joey Serrano from West L.A., David's hometown.

"All right, Hector. How you been?" David asked.

"Good, man. But those Marines, some crazy motherfuckers, bro'. Chicanos over there done lost it. Them dudes carve up gook bodies like they were doing a damn autopsy, man...checking out the guts and shit. You should've heard them ooo-ing and ahhh-ing. I saw two dudes playing jump rope with a dude's intestine. Ain't that some gross shit, *ese?*"

"Jarheads *son bien locos*," said Little Rod.

"Check this out," said Big Rod. "I found another of you *putos* from Los Angeles. He almos' started a brawl at the bar."

David walked over and shook Joey's hand. The kid was already drunk, rocking on the heels and balls of his feet. He'd just arrived in-country, had that cherry look about him, new, stiff fatigues, a cone-shaped cap. His eyes rolled around loosely.

"Hey, man! I heard your name before," David said. "I think my old man knows your old man."

"Maybe. Ah..." he burped. "We lived over near Cot-ot-ner," said Joey. "The old 'garra.'"

"Yeah, that's where my dad was raised. What unit you with?"

"The O'Deuce, B-bbb-company, 2nd squad."

"A grunt, huh?" said Danny, shaking his head.

"Big Rod's with the O'Deuce?" said Langley. "You watch over him, Big Rod."

"Shit, I'm on my way home in five days, *ese*," said Big Rod. "Just be cool—¿*sabes*, Serrano? Chicano-cool, and don't make stupid mistakes."

"Where'd you go to school?" David asked.

"Uni-ver—ersity...shit, I need a seat," Joey said, falling onto a log. "How a-about you-ou?"

"Loyola, out near Normandy and Pico."

"Shit, man, tha-at's a long ways froo-om the Westside."

"Cut the mush, man. This ain't no high school reunion. Fuckers think we got all night," Alex said, scowling.

"You tell 'em, Martínez," said Wayne, his eyes red. "There's some good shit happen' at the EM club tonight."

"We'll talk later," David said, looking at Joey, who sat, shoulders slumped, eyes dazed.

David told Luz how other guys wanted to come, but Big Rod didn't want a crowd...wanted to keep it intimate.

The guys had sat on logs that were laid in a semi-circle. Big Rod told everybody to be quiet and said there'd be no drinking, not yet anyway. When David nodded, Wayne reached into his pocket and pulled out a plastic baggie, took off the rubber band, opened up the plastic, and handed Big Rod a stack of joints, each rolled extra thick. Big Rod passed them around and said to light up. Except for Wayne, Langley and David, none of the other guys smoked much, but this night they all breathed in the stinging herb.

The jungle moved in closer, the roots, leaves and trunks swelling. The trees came down on their heads like thick spider webs and the plants weighed against their backs. The joints moved around the circle until the air and smoke mingled into a kind of anesthetized gas.

Big Rod pulled an envelope from his pocket, unfolded it, and began to read. It was from Margaret, Peña's wife. The Army had told her that Jesse was listed as AWOL. In her letter, which made Big Rod pause many times as he read, she wanted to know what happened to her husband. She'd written, "Jesse's mother, me too, we are going crazy. I can not sleep at night. Please tell me where he is. If he has died and nobody wants to say it, I have to know. I wrote the Army but they don't say anything to me. Please, help us. Every day the neighbors ask about Jesus and if he has been found. Tell me what you know. Please answer soon."

After reading the letter, Big Rod gave it to David, saying that since he was the one with some college, he should answer Peña's wife. The other guys agreed. David had hesitated and told Big Rod that he wouldn't know what to say. That was when Hector, who wore purple-tinted granny glasses, said that they shouldn't be moping but celebrating.

"Write her, man," Hector said to David. "Tell her the truth. Her old man split. The dude's got balls. I don't know how, but this guy Peña understands that everything here means nothing. It's all fantasy, a joke, a big fuckin' lie, man. I ain't never met the guy, but I been thinking about him a lot. I heard the stories. I heard that Peña lived in San Antonio, in some rat hole that he could't afford to buy because the bank would't lend him the money. I heard that in the summer when it hits a hundred, him and his neighbors fried like goddamn chickens because they could't afford air conditioning. So now they send him here to fight for his country, for his land! Wow, what a joke, man."

Hector was the first to raise the issue. What the others wanted was to fight the war, get to the rear area, drink, joke and never think about the truth...in Vietnam or about their lives back home.

A bitter argument started. Alex, in his surly voice, said that whatever they have it's better than what other people have. Even if they work the factories and fields, it's better than what people got in Mexico. Little Rod yelled out, "¡*Puro pedo*! We don't live in Mexico. We live in the States. You ever worked the fields, *pinche*, Martínez? You ever lived on the border? If you ain't, *ese*, you ain't seen shit." Somebody else called out, "Our *jefitos* worked to build the States. My old man fought in WWII. My uncle Tino died in some shitty field in Korea. We got rights just like anybody else."

The voices became belligerent, and Hector wanted to know how come Chicanos get the worst duties. Whether it's pulling the shittiest hours on guard duty or going into dangerous situations, if there's a Chicano around, he's the one who gets it.

Joey looked bewildered, searching one face then another.

"Because you bastards don't say shit, man," Doc Langley spat. "Whatever the gover'ment wants to push on you guys, you just take it. Medic in B Company says he gets more wounded Mexicans an' Puerto Ricans than anybody else... think you guys are supermen."

"Yeah, like *pendejos*...we do whatever nobody else wants to do. We don't want to be crybabies, 'better to die on yer feet than live on yer knees...' ain't that what we learn, all that macho shit? So we die left and right while everybody else makes out...." yelled Little Rod, throwing a fist into the air.

Danny Ríos said, "Well, maybe we should start crying."

Little Rod followed up. "That's right, Hector's carnal got his'elf chot up 'cuz nobody wanted to take their turns at the point...walked point for his squad every operation. What good it do 'em? He's dead now. *Pobre* Rudy, man."

"Hey, man..." said Doc Langley. "Medrano was a 'far out' dude. Nobody messed with him. The 'cat' was together, a heavy, heavy dude, man."

Hector sat still, his eyes hidden behind his glasses. There was a moment of silence. Then Alex stood up. He told how teachers insulted him in front of his Anglo classmates. "Shit, I just figured I was a fuck-up. There were a lot of white dudes worse than me, but the teachers didn't jump on them like they jumped on me. Damn, after a while, I just thought I was one of the dumb white kids. But din't nobody kick my ass, no goddamn way."

Little Rod talked about tennis clubs built where the townspeople of Brownsville had once grown produce, about schoolhouses with holes in the roofs, streets still unpaved in 1967, primitive electrical systems for lighting. And they went on and on until they grew into a fury.

Wayne didn't say much, just listened and laughed.

Big Rod pulled out a bottle of tequila. Nobody even asked where he got it. He passed it around. They drank. As the alcohol hit, the voices got louder, crazier. Before long, beer cans made the rounds and nobody talked about Jesse any longer. Everyone talked about friends back home, girlfriends and good places to find prostitutes in Phan Rhang. The session was over. Somebody kicked out the heat tablets, and the jungle, once again, distanced itself from them.

As David told Luz the story, he laughed, describing how Hector and Danny draped Joey's arms over their shoulders and they all marched to the Enlisted Men's Club singing "Land of a Thousand Dances". They toasted Jesse several times, honoring him and wishing him well, and drank until they were thrown out. They staggered along the roads, falling into ditches, looking at the stars splattered against the sky, some of the guys getting sick as they worked their way back to their units. David said that after stumbling through numerous tents, he finally found his bunk, threw himself down, and sank into a dizzy sleep.

The next morning when he woke, David was hung over; so were most of us guys. They went through the usual routines, cleaning weapons and resupplying their units. A few days later, they flew out in C-130 transport planes to the next operation, somewhere outside Chu Lai.

David sat back into the sofa and stopped talking.

"Well?" Luz said.

"That's it."

"That's it? What happened to everybody? What about Peña?"

"After the war he was listed as missing in action."

"They never found him?"

"There were a few nutty stories that he was traveling with the VC. Some guys said they saw him selling fish tacos in the Mekong Delta. Others said he was running drugs near the DMZ. You know, just a big joke, stupid stuff, like he probably started a *mariachi* in Hanoi or owned a burrito stand near Haiphong.

"We felt bad, you know. He was our friend, and the not-knowing was killing us. Actually, Alex claimed to have seen Jesse attacking our unit, but he was in shock."

"Why would he say that?"

"He was hallucinating."

"Tell me."

III.

David continued talking. Big Rod, he recalled, finished his tour and was sent to Fort Bragg where he started drinking heavily, got into some trouble with a prostitute. But because of his war record, they gave him an early discharge instead of putting him in jail. Danny lost half of his foot when he stepped on a mine the size of a handkerchief. He only had thirty days remaining on his tour. He was sent to Yokohama, Japan, where he immersed himself in Buddhist literature. Little Rod re-enlisted and applied for electronics school, but failed the math test. They sent him to Ft. Campbell, Kentucky, where he went back to the artillery for three more years. After two months, he got bored and asked to go back to Vietnam to serve with the First Cavalry. Doc Langley died on Hamburger Hill.

"That was the movie we saw," said Luz.

"There were a lot of Hamburger Hills, not just one. We heard that during a battle, somewhere up north, Langley lost it. He dropped his first-aid gear, grabbed an M-60 from a fallen machine gunner, and charged up the mountain yelling, 'Ya-ba-da-ba-do!'"

"And Joey?"

"He was with the infantry...started running with some Chicanos who stayed drunk most of the time. In the rear area, they were always in the bars. He saw a lot of action, though, came out of the field and headed straight to the bars. He didn't make it home. I looked him up and heard he died of some stomach problem or some strange thing."

"Hector?"

"Einstein, you mean? One smart guy. I guess that's why they made him an engineer. He specialized in electronics, was a whiz at repairing communication equipment. He stopped coming around, hung out with guys in the technical field, other engineers. I never heard from him again."

"So it was just you, Wayne and Alex?"

"Yeah, except by that last month, a lot of new guys started coming around. Shit, Chicanos from all over, Michigan, Nebraska, Kansas City...couldn't hardly believe how many *raza* were there, even guys from the Westside, Manny Cardoza, Beto Alvarez, Joe Esparza. I was getting ready to come home, so I hardly paid them any attention. I played it safe, kept my ground, you know."

"Had you known them back home?"

"I had met Joe Esparza when we were kids. He was from Santa Monica, Twelfth Street. I didn't know Manny. He was from Hollywood, went to Hollywood High School, and hung around that area over there, Sunset Boulevard and all that. His old man was a school principal or something.

"Beto lived close by, but on the other side of town, a place called the Cozy Courts, a lot of poor people there, mostly immigrants. Beto was a real *cholo*, hardcore, always messing

with his hair. In the rear area, he had starched fatigues waiting for him at a laundry downtown. I heard he got killed.

"There was another new guy, Charley Yañez, from up
north, Modesto or Stockton. Stayed to himself, mostly. He
came around a few times, was into history and *raza* politics,
but we didn't want to hear it. He always talked about going to
Europe and Asia. A lot of times had his head in the clouds.
And always talking about 'white broads.' You should have
seen him making eyes at the donut dollies. They loved him.
He was six-feet tall, light-complected, smooth skin, nice looking...could've passed for a *gabacho*, even had an Okie accent.
Got an early discharge."

"Jesse?"

"MIA."

"They never found him?"

"When I got back to North Carolina—that's where most of
us were stationed after Vietnam, with the 82nd Airborne—the
stories were flying, you know, rumors, insane discus-
sions...hard to tell what was true, a lot was hearsay.

"Last year I met a guy, an ex-medic. He told me that
there were quite a few guys who'd gone AWOL. Some had gotten caught up in the Asian underworld, black market, gun
running, stuff like that. They got greedy, some were killed,
others disappeared. A lot of guys got all strung out on heroin,
opium, morphine. They had nervous breakdowns, serious shit,
some lost their minds—vegetables—poor bastards, didn't even
know who they were. The Army couldn't return them to their
families like that, so they stuck them away in desolate V.A.
hospitals around the country, places like the Dakotas,
Wyoming or Montana. Gave them new identities and told the
families that they were missing in action. Bad PR for the military, you know."

"That's absurd! You mean your friend could be alive in a V.A. hospital someplace?"

"Could be."

"So what happened to Wayne, to Alex?"

David thought for a moment. He was silent, and then he said, "Alex got wounded..." He stopped, looked at the beige carpet, the painting on the wall, and began again. "A mortar shell."

"And Wayne?"

David told her that near the end of his tour, the brigade had moved up north and was operating around Chu Lai, replacing the Marines who had moved closer to the DMZ. He described how the monsoons fell—warm streams of water that turned everything to mud.

By that time, David said, he had just returned from R & R in Bangkok and only had four or five days left. His request to remain at base camp his last few days in-country had been denied. The first sergeant, who was new to the unit and did everything by the book, wanted him back in the field. That same day, David was on a C-130, and by early evening, in full combat gear, back in the jungle.

The battery was dug-in on a mountaintop, surrounded by taller mountains and covered in jungle and fog. The clouds floated through them. On the mountainsides and in the valleys below, the infantry plodded through the mud but made no contact.

David said that he stayed pretty much to himself those last hours in the field, watching the fog, the treeline, and keeping his M-16 close by. He stayed with the battery only one night. In the morning his travel orders came through. The first sergeant could hold him no longer. He packed his rucksack and waited for the noon chopper.

He told Luz that Wayne and Alex wanted to throw him a going away party—a short session. Alex had snuck a couple of beers to the field. Wayne had a bag of "weed." The South Vietnamese Army was helping guard the perimeter, and Wayne had bribed an ARVN into letting them borrow his hootch. It was downhill, away from the view of the battery commander, more private.

David said to Luz, "For a second, I thought about partying with them, then said, 'No way in hell'. Sometimes the noon chopper came in early, and if I missed it, I'd have to spend another night in the field.

"'C'mon, damn hippie. One last session, for old time sake,' Alex had said. He only had about a week left.

"'Davy, don't be chickenshit, man,'" Wayne said.

"'No! Count me out,'" I told them.

"We hugged and promised to get together back at Fort Bragg. I watched Wayne and Alex go down the hill to the ARVN's hootch. It was stupid getting loaded in the field, but what the hell...we were kids, partying, every chance we got, even in the jungle."

David said that the afternoon chopper arrived forty minutes ahead of schedule. He helped unload the mail bag and canisters of hot food. He shook hands with the guys who unloaded the rest of the cargo; then he jumped aboard, and the chopper rose, and with it, his excitement. He remembered how his feet dangled over the edge, his M-16 rested on his lap, the battery area shrank, and the jungle sped away as the chopper lifted, angled through the dark clouds, until moments later, the sky brightened and the sun warmed his face and hands.

At the front-area base camp, David turned in his weapons and equipment. He was scheduled to take a military hop out the next morning to Phan Rhang, then to Cam Rhan Bay and back home. David said that he felt like a kid again, and he wanted to skip through the whole area. He looked up old friends and let everyone know he was going home. From then on, he said that he only remembered fragmented images of beer cans, whiskey bottles, an outdoor movie, loud voices, laughing, silence, night—and then a frightened, stuttering voice, breaking through his sleep, waking him as the sun made its way into his tent the next morning.

Tom, a six-foot-seven-inch Montana cowboy, was shaking David's shoulder, his face a blur as David's head cleared. David said that Tom's eyes were bloodshot, like he'd been crying. Tom hadn't cried, ever, even when a Chinook crushed his hand against a water trailer, he'd only made a couple of grunts.

"Almas...Almas," Tom's voice trembled. "The bat-t-tery got hit, early this morning—overrun. Mack, Dabon, and Morrow's dead. Alex's wounded and Wayne's hurt real bad, shot through the chest. I think he's dyin', man. Real bad. I saw them bring him in, 'bout ten minutes ago. Alex wants to see you, Almas...said to tell you it was Peña. Peña led them into the battery area. Come on. I'll go with you to the infirmary to see Wayne. He's real bad."

Luz started to speak but stopped as David told how he had sat up while Tom just kept talking, wildly. "They got Wayne, must've panicked, started running towards the gun sections for help...gooks was everywhere. A mortar got him...from the back. Cox's gone, ripped his fuckin' head off. Blew Dabon inside out, nothing left, couldn't even recognize him. Edis just got choppered in. His right hand's gone, chief, shrapnel up and down his back. I talked to Alex. He keeps sayin' he saw Peña with the gooks. Wayne's really bad, don't look like he'll make it."

"How? When?"

"Come on, man. Alex wants you, at the infirmary."

"What about Peña?"

"Said they saw him, attacking with the gooks."

David looked at Tom's shiny jungle boots and then into his flushed face. He pushed the poncho cover away, put on his boots and rushed through the canvas into the hot sun. Choppers landed and took off, confusion everywhere. David wiped at the dust. He coughed and spat, stood still and watched the chaos around him. He saw Tom walking towards the infirmary but didn't follow.

He looked away from Luz toward the sliding glass doors. "I didn't go to the infirmary. I didn't want to know anything. It was over for me. I couldn't take anymore. I had to get out. I didn't even wait to see Wayne, whether he was alive or dead, or to see how Alex was. I…I ran."

There was a silence.

"I went back to my tent, grabbed my duffle bag, and ran outside. There were people everywhere, hollering, and the choppers came in, one then another, dropping off bodies, enemy and American. I stepped into the dust. A jeep pulled in front of me and stopped. In the trailer were two bodies, Asian, dressed in dark clothing. One guy had his eyes open, staring, seeing nothing. The other's face was disfigured, a clean slit right along his jawbone, the meat exposed, curling over his cheek.

"At the clerk's tent, I turned in some identification cards…paperwork, and got a copy of my new orders. I moved fast and didn't look at anybody, like I was deaf and dumb. The sun was blinding and dust covered everything. I felt shaky, my knees rubbery. I moved through the brigade area, down a hill, across a flat dirt field, where some Vietnamese men, not even aware of the madness on the hill, were loading wood onto a truck. I made it to the highway, duffel bag over my shoulder.

I hitched a ride on a deuce-and-a-half to the airstrip which was a few miles away.

"Inside the terminal, everything was quiet, orderly. There was no rushing, no screams, no dust. I stepped to a wood counter and wrote my name on a standby roster, took a seat in a metal chair and listened to the C-130's, engines whining, tires screeching on the runway. I waited two hours, alone, sitting in that pre-fab terminal.

"An Air Force sergeant called out my name. I walked through the door, across the tarmac, into the hot sun, and boarded a C-130. I remember how the plane lifted, then tilted, and we flew really low...over the mountains. I looked at the jungle but couldn't see through the thick vegetation. Danny's words came to me, 'It doesn't make sense, man, no sense at all...' and I made a promise, right then, that one day I'd go to Clairton and visit Wayne's parents. It's all I could do to keep from feeling guilty."

They sat silent for a minute. Luz reached up and turned on the lamp, lighting the living room.

"What happened to Alex?"

"He was okay, just some shrapnel in the back."

"And Wayne?"

"Didn't make it, but I didn't know that then."

"Have you been to Clairton?"

"No. But I wrote Wayne's parents once, a few years ago."

"Why didn't you go see them?"

"I couldn't."

"You were afraid they'd find out, weren't you?"

"Wayne wouldn't have left me like that."

"You were nineteen-years old, right out of high school. Like you said, just a kid."

David didn't answer.

"You've got to go to Clairton," she said.

He felt her squeeze his hand.

"It was a long time ago. Another life," he said.

"You've got to go see them, for Wayne, for yourself."

"It's over. I just want...."

"What?"

"Nothing."

"To forget?"

"Why not?"

"Because you can't. Call them. Besides, I've always wanted to visit Pennsylvania."

"It's so hard."

"Before the end of the month...call them. We can go this summer."

He saw a determined expression on her face, as if she knew what was best for him.

"I think they've moved. They were both sick. Look, I'm not sure I'm up to it."

"You need to."

Neither spoke. She waited for his answer.

"I'll try to call them sometime this month," he said.

She nodded. "Okay."

The next afternoon when he came home from work, he saw the telephone recorder blinking. He pressed the plastic button. He listened as the tape rewound, then he heard Luz's voice: "Irene and Albert Podleski, (412) 989...7711, Clairton, Pennsylvania, but no address was listed. I'll make the arrangements to go this summer. Love you. See you tonight."

David wrote the number. He ripped the paper from the pad and held it in his hand. Before he left to teach an evening seminar, he wrote a note and left it on Luz's side of the bed. "*Gracias*," he wrote, "Love, David."

EIGHT
POINTMAN
(DANNY RÍOS & RUDY MEDRANO)

Danny Ríos leaned on a row of sandbags and looked across the battery area. Nearby, sledgehammers clanked as men drove steel shanks into the dry earth. Around him buzzed the calls and laughs of artillerymen razzing each other, and the bark of a section chief ordering his men to wipe down a howitzer. The men moaned as they resisted the order. "Get off your lazy asses and do some work," cried the section chief. Danny glanced at the sun overhead. He peered out over the mountains and valleys that lay quiet, covered in green, not a village or human visible.

A squad of infantrymen had made its way into the battery area during the night, slept, rested, and now prepared to slip back into the jungle. Danny recognized Rudy Medrano, a loner and short-timer, a Chicano from Southern California, and smiled as he watched him put on a soiled black sombrero, tightening the leather strands at the nape of his neck. Rudy sat on the ground, his back to a sandbag wall.

Danny studied the other men in the squad who sat beside Rudy, their steel helmets resting high on their heads, revealing young grizzly faces. They waited for the order that would send them from the relative security of the artillery battery, down the mountain and into the jungle below.

Little Rod approached Danny, stood next to him and whistled a loud, piercing screech.

"Goddamn, Little Rod, gimme a break, man," Danny said, rubbing his ear.

Rudy heard the whistle, turned and looked. He saw the two soldiers. Little Rod called to him, jerking his head with a quick upward movement, "Rodríguez! Brownsville, *Tejas*."

Rudy didn't smile. He acknowledged Little Rod's greeting, also with an upward jerk of the head.

Sluggishly, he lifted himself from the ground, a belt of M-60 ammunition hanging across his chest and the heavy machine gun leaning against his muscular legs. The jungle didn't scare him. His mother had once told him never to fear the jungle. From Oaxaca, his grandparents had traveled to Mexicali, where they settled before Rudy's father entered the United States illegally, at twelve years of age, working the fields from Calexico to Marysville, and settling in Mar Vista, where he began his own gardening business.

Stubbles covered Rudy's dark face. His sombrero, stripped of its silver embroidery and decorative cord, was wrinkled from too many operations in the humid Vietnamese brush. Once, when a new lieutenant arrived from the States to lead the platoon, he ordered Rudy to leave the sombrero at base camp. Rudy turned and walked away without even answering. The officer threatened to have him court-martialled for refusing a direct order. Rudy paid the junior officer no mind. Later, the captain who commanded the company had privately told the lieutenant, "Keep off Medrano's ass!" There was no other explanation, and the lieutenant obeyed the senior officer.

Danny heard the squad leader holler, "Okay. Okay. Second squad, let's get outta here. MOVE OUT!"

He looked at Rudy, who removed his sombrero, picked up the M-60, looped the strap over his head, and replaced the hat. The machine gun hung at Rudy's waist. He jerked his shoulders, and his rucksack rested higher on his back. He pulled the sombrero down low on his head so that the brim blocked the sun. The other men stood and adjusted their equipment, ammo bandoliers, grenades, canteens and ruck-sacks.

"Check out how the dude moves," Danny said to Little Rod. "He's so cool."

Leading the infantrymen, Rudy walked through the artillery area, past a howitzer. The other artillerymen watched silently as he and his squad moved through the camp.

He leaped a dirt mound onto a grassy mesa, his sombrero bouncing on his head. Staggering the column, the men disappeared behind a green knoll. A few minutes later, they reappeared far down the mountain, walking through a break in a roll of concertina wire, outside the battery perimeter.

He stopped in front of an eight-foot wall of elephant grass. The temperature hovered at a hundred degrees. He rolled down his shirt-sleeves, secured the buttons at his wrist, fastened the button at his neck, and lifted his collar. The squad members behind him did the same. As he stepped into the razor-edged blades, he put his head down. Using the wide-brim sombrero and the barrel of the machine gun, he divided the grass and began his descent, moving into the green maze until he and his men vanished and all that could be seen was the top of the quivering grass, as if a breeze was passing through.

"Who is that guy?" Little Rod asked.

"Name's Medrano, Rudy, a baa-a-d dude. Got a Silver Star," Danny answered, watching the elephant grass where the infantrymen had disappeared.

"You check out his sombrero?"

Danny laughed. "Won't ever see him without it. Even at base camp, always got it on."

"¿Lo conoces?"

"Big Rod knows him."

"*¿Es un vato de aquéllas?*"

"Don't know him that well, but I hear some Chicano guys are pissed at him."

"Yeah. How come?"

"Wanted him to transfer and join up with them in reconnaissance."

A puzzled expression crossed Little Rod's face.

"Knows his shit, man," said Danny. "Big Rod said those dudes keep buggin' him."

"Hey, Danny, ain't Arnulfo Sevilla in reconnaissance?"

"Used to be...got wounded, a little shrapnel in the ass. Talked himself into light duty. The dude can use a typewriter, so they made him company clerk. The guys in recon listen to everything Sevilla says. Word is out that he's saying Medrano is a punk for not helpin' his *raza*."

"What's that all about?"

"Jealous, man. That's how I see it. Pisses Sevilla off 'cuz he knows Medrano is bad."

"And all the time Sevilla, he's safe behind his typewriter?"

"You got it."

"A bunch a punks, huh?"

"That's the way some Chicanos are. Don't like anybody who doesn't think like them. Narrow-minded assholes, you ask me," said Danny.

"Funny, huh? Medrano wearing that sombrero."

"We all got to do our thing in our own way."

✪ ✪ ✪

Four chinook helicopters swooped down and delivered ammunition for the howitzers. Danny worked the ammo section and helped unload the canisters. When he finished, much of the afternoon had passed. The sun was still high, but it was getting late.

A rifle shot rose from the valley. Some artillerymen walked to the edge of the mountain, squatted and peered into the rice paddies a half mile away. From the mountaintop, they had a clear view of the entire valley. They heard another crack, and another. A machine gun opened up, more rifles, automatics, and there was no distinguishing between individual shots. There was a lull in the firing, but it didn't last. The valley erupted into long bursts of fire, grenade launchers thumped their canisters into the air, and mortars exploded.

On the mountaintop, the artillery gun chiefs hollered, "Fire mission! Fire mission! Battery adjust."

Artillerymen, who were lounging around, flipped on their helmets and rushed to the howitzers. The coordinates arrived, the breech clanked shut. The gunner called, "Fire!" The lanyard was pulled and one of the six howitzers thundered. There was a short echo, a long silence, and a moment later, the round exploded in the mountains, near the valley floor.

Gun number three released a flurry of rounds. Someone ordered a cease fire. Danny left the ammo section, and Little Rod, who was assigned to gun six, walked toward a radio jeep parked near the Fire Direction Center. The artillerymen gathered around the jeep, listening as a voice struggled to break through the static.

The radio operator pressed the button on the side of the mouthpiece. When Danny arrived, he heard the RTO's southern-accented voice shouting, "Say ag'in! Say ag'in!" He released the button and picked up the incoming voice.

"B com...comp...pinned...down..." The static crackled as the voice broke. The RTO placed his ear to the radio. A weak voice pleaded, "Sen...Med...vac...fast...man down...in... se...se...cond sq...uad." The radio operator called to a lieutenant, loud, "Somebody's hit bad down th'r. Jungle's too thick. Can't cut a chopper pad."

The RTO's fingers moved from the receiver to the radio, turning one switch then another, passing messages from the entrapped infantrymen in the valley to the artillerymen on the mountain.

Danny and Little Rod, who put on a pair of sunglasses, walked to the edge of the mountain. They looked into a long, flat valley, filled with rice paddies and surrounded by dense verdant mountains. The infantry fought a short way up one particularly steep mountain, above the valley's perimeter, where the jungle and rice paddies converged.

Little Rod pointed to a farmer and water buffalo moving across a green field. "*Hijo*, check out how small. They look like Chinese letters."

Danny shook his head. "This is crazy shit, man. Dude's are gettin' shot up and that old man's plowin' like there ain't a thing happening."

They watched as a black-clad figure, the size of a fingernail, emerged from the jungle and ran into the open. Carrying something in his hand, the man in black sprinted across a dike. Seconds later, three men dressed in green chased him. As they ran, they fired their rifles. The man racing across the dike collapsed. His body hit the ground, rolled from the dike into a rice paddy, and sank beneath the water. The men in green turned, ran from the dike and slipped into the jungle.

Danny looked at Little Rod, whose eyes were fixed on the valley.

They heard the RTO yell, hands placed at the sides of his mouth, "Chopper comin' in! Clear the landing pad...fast! They're five minutes out and bringin' in a WIA! Prepare to throw smoke, Ammo Section!"

"That's me," said Danny, running towards the chopper pad.

Little Rod followed him to the LZ, a flattened slab of earth chiseled into the mountainside. Two medics and a number of men waited. The sound of an engine drew their attention. Far off, like a fly buzzing, a Medivac moved towards them.

"Throw smoke, Ammo!"

Danny gripped the smoke grenade, pulled the pin, and tossed the canister to the ground. The grenade sizzled, popped, and a cloud of yellow smoke seeped into the sky.

The helicopter neared. An oval-shaped bundle swung back and forth, fifty feet below the chopper's metal belly.

"What the..." Danny mumbled.

Little Rod removed his sunglasses. The chopper closed in.

The limp cargo oscillated at the end of a rope.

Danny placed his hands in his pockets, stood back and watched as the chopper's blades slapped the air and sucked up dust and bits of dried branches. The bundle, a man's body, was wrapped in a green plastic poncho that came loose and flapped wildly. It was tied around the man's chest and waist. The medics stood on the chopper pad, looking towards the sky, their arms outstretched, waiting to catch the descending load. The chopper struggled in the wind. The pilot tried to bring the machine down slowly, but he miscalculated the height, and the chopper dropped quickly, the body slipping through raised hands. It crashed to the ground. First the head hit, twisting the neck, and then the back bent like a bow, until the body rested against the hard, dusty sandbags. The chopper rose, gained altitude, slanted, and sped away.

Danny swallowed and breathed deeply.

A medic ripped at the plastic covering, revealing a man's disfigured face. Portions of his naturally dark skin were charred, crispy like burnt toast.

The medic jabbed a needle into the man's arm, while another punched the chest.

"*Hijo de la chingada*," said Little Rod.

Danny moved in closer and watched the medical team work. Some artillerymen walked away. The body lay still. Needles jabbed the arms and fists pounded the chest.

"Who's he?"

"Done wasted this cat."

Danny looked at the dead man's muddy boots and noticed one untied shoelace. The fatigue pockets bulged. Dark patches of hair clung to where the crown of the head had been. The left shoulder was gone, but the torso was intact. The muscular arms were well-defined, but one hand was missing, cauterized at the forearm.

"Had to be some kind of mine," someone said.

"Prob'ly the pointman. Must've put up his hand or some shit."

Inside the left arm, above the crook of the elbow, Danny saw a homemade tattoo that read, "Angelina, *Por Vida*."

Except for Danny and Little Rod, most of the artillery-men drifted away. The medic who pounded the man's chest, remained kneeling, looking down. Danny saw what looked like a black piece of hard cloth sticking out from under the stiff thigh. He reached down. Someone had tied it to the man's leg with leather string. Danny untied the knot. He stretched the clumped material, working it like a lump of clay, until a torn sombrero rested in his hands. He held it out towards Little Rod, who had a sick look on his face. After some seconds, Danny, slowly, respectfully, tucked the sombrero back under the man's leg.

"It's the pointman—Medrano," someone said.

"They got him, bad," said another.

"Put his shit out to dry."

117

Danny and Little Rod didn't wait to be asked. They immediately moved in to help carry the body. It was wrapped, head to foot, in a clean poncho and tied about the neck, chest and feet. Four men lifted it. They walked fifteen meters from the chopper pad and placed the body behind a sandbag wall, where a helicopter would retrieve it the next morning.

NINE
BLIND IN GRANADA
(CHARLEY YAÑEZ)

I.

Charley Yañez arrived in Granada nine years after his discharge from the U.S. Army and one year after Franco's death. That's how Charley measured time, not by dates, but by events, like the time Salisbury purposely shot himself through the hand just before Christmas, 1967. Charley remembered the incident because he'd only been in Vietnam two months. Manny Cardoza and Albert Alvarez had laughed like hell as Salisbury whined like a hurt puppy. *"Huevos pelu-dos,"* Albert had said.

The most disturbing event Charley saw, though, was on the evening news, 1975. He had watched the last chopper rise from the roof of the U.S embassy in Saigon. Thousands of Vietnamese surrounded the gates. Complete chaos, a wasted effort, Charley had thought, a total waste of life: Jesse Peña, David Almas, Danny Ríos, Alex Martínez, the two Rodriguezes, John Conklin, Doc Langley, Joey Serrano, Wayne Podleski, the Medrano brothers...gone, just like that, some dead, some living, but all memories swept away on the whirling blades above the U.S. embassy, as Sgt. Benavides—officially the last American out of Vietnam—boarded the waiting chopper.

✪ ✪ ✪

Granada sweltered. Summer had started, and Charley helped his roommate load boxes and suitcases onto the Madrid-bound train, the first leg of his trip home to National

City, California. After his friend's train departed, Charley walked outside the station, turned, and saw a woman standing alone, a bulky backpack and scratched leather suitcase at her side. Her blonde hair curled, covering her ears and neck. She wore Levi's and a white, long-sleeved cotton shirt, tucked neatly into the waist. Her brown, Mexican-style sandals and round, wire sunglasses gave her a rustic, Hollywood look.

Charley watched as she rummaged through her bags.

The taxi drivers stopped talking, straightened their black berets, and whistled. She shifted her bags, looking for something.

Charley approached her. "Are you American?" he asked. She was young, late teens, early twenties. He moved closer.

She nodded. "I'm from California."

"Yeah? So am I. A little town outside of Modesto. Riverbank, 'City of Action.'"

"I'm from San Francis...well, really, San Jose," she said, tapping her right foot, her eyes unable to settle on any one place.

"Something wrong?"

"I...I think someone stole my purse. I know I had it when I boarded in Madrid. I've looked everywhere and can't find it. Someone must have stolen it."

"Your passport?"

"Everything was in my purse."

"That's a problem."

She looked away, paused, then turned to him again. "Well, what should I do?" She sighed, and with one hand shielded her eyes from the sun. "I got to Madrid the day before yesterday. I planned on staying in Granada for the summer."

The perspiration settled on his forehead. Unable to think of anything else, he convinced her to return to the station lobby and report her stolen purse, although he knew it wouldn't help. The clerk behind the counter grimaced and shook his head. He tossed his hands around and spoke in heavy Andaluz, sounding more Arabic than Spanish.

They stepped outside. There was little else they could do.

"Today's Sunday," Charley said. "Government offices are closed."

"The police?"

"They'll keep you waiting all morning then tell you they can't do anything."

She placed her hands in her back pant pockets and remained still.

"Don't you know anybody in town, anybody you can stay with?" he said.

"No. I was going to stay in a hostel, you know.... I heard there were a lot of cool people traveling through Europe. I didn't think anything this 'heavy' would happen."

"Cool people?" he said, dryly.

She shrugged and turned her head.

He ran his fingers through his hair, tugging lightly at his scalp.

"I'll be all right," she said, reaching down to pick up her backpack.

"You don't have any money. And without your passport, you can't check into a hotel or pensione. Spain is strict—very rigid. You're like a...a...non-person."

She smiled, unfazed by his words.

"Have you eaten?"

"No, I'm not hungry...busy stomach, I guess."

He looked at her trim, athletic body.

"There's a cafe downtown. We can get coffee and bread..."
He paused.

"Really. I don't want to hassle you. I'll make it okay."

She lifted her backpack, and the strap slipped from the buckle. The aluminum frame dropped and hit her exposed toe. She winced. "Jesus...shit," she mumbled, removing her sunglasses and wiping her eyes.

He grabbed the heavy pack. "You shouldn't wear sandals when you travel. You okay?"

"I guess."

The aluminum had pinched her skin, and a small spot of blood started to form at the corner of her big toe. She reached down and rubbed it.

"My name's Charley Yañez, but most people here call me Carlos...or Sh—arley."

"I'm Magan Finely. Magan, spelled with an 'a', not an 'e,'" she said, standing straight and holding out her hand. Charley took it. Her grip was firm and her hand soft.

"You sure you're okay?"

She nodded.

"C'mon, let's get that coffee," he repeated. "The cafe's not far. We can figure something out for you there."

"I'm supposed to be in South America."

"What?" he said, as he reached for her luggage.

She giggled. "I changed my mind at the airport in San Francisco and bought a ticket to Paris. Been traveling by train ever since."

"That's a pretty drastic change," he said.

"No big deal. Change is what it's all about."

Charley raised his eyebrows and shook his head. He took hold of her backpack.

"That's okay. I'd rather carry it," she said, fixing the strap. She lifted the pack over her shoulders. "You can take my suitcase, though."

"Okay by me. I don't use rucksacks myself."

"Rucksacks?"

122

He laughed. "I mean backpacks."

"Why not? They're so much easier."

"I spent a lotta time carrying backpacks. I try to avoid them."

"I don't get it."

"It's a long story."

A cab driver rushed over, but Charley waved him off, saying, "*Con-yo, tranquilo. Está bien, 'stá bien.*"

They hopped a bus headed for the center of the city.

II.

Beneath the Cafe Granada's white canvas veranda, they talked until noon. Magan laughed a lot, drinking espresso the whole time. She sat snuggled into the chair, both her legs crossed, like a yogi. She was intelligent and perceptive. She told him that she was raised in San Jose but had spent the last two years in San Francisco, living with a friend in North Beach, just hanging out, traveling around, trying to find her "niche."

"Niche?" Charley said, teasing.

She shrugged.

Three buses pulled to the curb. A swarm of tourists stepped down from each bus.

"Let's get out of here," he said as the foreigners, mostly Japanese and Americans, a few Germans, pushed chairs and moved tables.

The smile on Magan's face disappeared.

"Hey," Charley said, "my roommate just moved out. You can use the spare bedroom until you get settled." The words rolled out. He acted calmly, but his stomach turned. "It'll take me a few days to find a new roommate anyway."

DANIEL CANO

"I don't know. I've been enough of a pain already."

"Well, the room's there and nobody's using it, so if you want...." He avoided her glance.

"Well..."

"I don't have many friends," he said, looking at her again. "I'm a bit of a loner, so you'll have a lot of space. You know, come and go as you please."

"I guess it won't be but a little while," she said.

"Right. You'll have your own place in no time."

"Okay," she said, looking relieved.

✪ ✪ ✪

During the next few days, they rode buses through the city and outlying neighborhoods, visiting the Alhambra, the Renaissance cathedral, the Albaicin, Sacramonte, and La Cartuja—where Charley attended university classes during the regular semester. On one of the outings, as the sun went down, they walked near rows of dilapidated, stucco courts hidden away on a far side of the city. Broken glass littered the sidewalk, piles of rubbish filled the corners.

"Who are they?" Magan said, staring at the dark-skinned men in colorful disco shirts, bell-bottom pants, and slicked-back hair, like New York hustlers. She saw children dressed in cheap imitation Levi's and baggy, wrinkled t-shirts. The dark-eyed women wore their hair pulled back tightly. They were dressed in pants and multi-colored blouses.

"Gypsies," Charley said.

She continued watching.

It was getting dark.

"Are they dangerous?"

"Spaniards think so."

"Are you afraid of them?"

124

"No. I tell them I'm Mexican. Everybody here loves Mexicans."

"But you're Chicano."

"That's hard to explain to them; besides, in the end, Chicano is American and they're suspicious of all Americans."

"Do you talk to them?"

"Yeah, I do, in the plazas, where they work, shining shoes, performing, things like that. I'll sit and talk. This is the ghetto. Much different than Sacramonte, where the more popular gypsies live, the artists and musicians."

"Where we went yesterday?"

"Yeah."

"Are these gypsies friendly?"

"They're private."

"That's so wild, but…"

"What?"

"Too bad they don't like Americans."

"Or any whites. They've been treated like shit."

"How do you figure?"

"They don't trust people. They tolerate…because of the money. Yeah, they hustle, because they can't find work. They've been chased from country to country. Spaniards think they're all thieves, drunks. They get treated just like the Indian back home. Don't worry though. You're lucky."

"Why?"

"They love American women…all Spanish men do."

"Because we're supposed to be 'easy,' right?"

He smiled. "Probably. But that's a stereotype. I know that for a fact."

She laughed.

✪ ✪ ✪

One night, after a party in the Albaicin, an ancient hillside neighborhood where many students and artists lived, Charley and Magan arrived home late. She changed into gray sweat pants and a white t-shirt. He invited her onto the balcony outside his bedroom. Barefoot, she stepped into the warm night, sat in a chair, and began asking about the gypsies.

He opened a bottle of Rioja. They drank. He got up and went to the kitchen and returned with a bowl of chilled grapes.

Magan had a joint between her lips. "Hmmm, warm wine and cold grapes," she said, the wrinkled cigarette moving as she spoke.

"You had that on you all this time?"

"Want some?"

"Magan, you're nuts!"

"I could be."

"This ain't San Jose or Paris. It's Spain, next to North Africa. People get ten years in prison for possession, automatic...no bullshitting, no plea bargaining, no writing to your congressman shit."

"Really?" she said, taking out a cigarette lighter.

"The prisons here make the ones in Mexico look like reform schools."

"Well, this is it...last one I got left." She lit the joint, inhaled deeply, then held it out to him.

He took the skinny cigarette from her fingers. It had been a long time.

It passed between them, until it was too tiny to hold. The aroma and foggy sensation raised familiar feelings, images, smells, voices. He drank some wine and thought about his older brother's last letter. "Twenty-seven-years old and still in school," he had written. "You can't escape the war forever." Charley had stopped writing home after that.

He took a book of matches and tore it in half. He set down the matches, took what remained of the cigarette stub and laid it on the upper half of the matchbook.

Magan watched curiously.

He folded the cardboard sheath over the stub and used the matchbook like a holder. He lit the tip.

"I've never seen anyone do that," she said. "Where'd you learn it?"

"A friend...in a place where there was a shortage of rolling paper and roach clips."

He handed it to her. She inhaled. The smoke burned as it rushed into her lungs. "Whewww," she said, coughing.

Music from the cafe downstairs blared. Rock and roll played over and over, the acoustic and steel guitars, melodic voices floating through the streets and into the windows. The image of Albert, Manny and the guys came to him, hanging out at base camp, sitting around, talking about home and what they'd do once they got there. Albert's face came to him clearly, his brown eyes cocky, a crooked smile. Charley made a fist.

"They must really dig the Eagles over here?"

He looked at her some seconds before answering. "Yeah, that's a good band. It beats all that disco shit."

"I didn't think Chicanos were into country rock," she said, teasingly. "The only Chicanos I knew liked 'low rider' music."

"Yeah, well, some'll die for it," he said. "But we're all different, come from different places, have different ideas, attitudes, experiences...." The buzzing in his head made his voice echo, like a foreign sound, distant, as if someone else had spoken.

He drank more wine and became silent, pensive. Often, he thought about the guys, losing himself in daydreams, wondering what had happened to all of them, who had made it

home and who hadn't. As much as he tried, he couldn't keep
Albert's face from entering his mind. Charley was thankful,
though, that the morning after Albert's death, Manny had
stopped him from seeing Albert's body. The sight would have
only made the visions worse, but often Charley wondered how
Manny had dealt with it. Manny had seen Albert up close, had
helped carry his body to the infirmary and to the chopper that
next day.

"Did I hurt your feelings?"

Disoriented, he looked at her.

"I'm sorry," she said. "I just thought..."

He didn't let her finish. "I was remembering, 'bout a long
time ago, a whole other world, when I was a bit younger than
you."

"I'll be twenty-two next year."

"I was nineteen," he said.

"Vietnam, right?"

He eyed her. "How could you know that?"

"I'm a witch." She laughed. "No, not really...you just have
that look."

"What look?"

"Like the vets who hung out in San Francisco, partying,
you know, getting wasted."

He finished his glass of wine and watched her.

"How could you know?"

She shrugged. "What was it like?"

"Why?"

"I want to know, everything."

"Nobody cares. Nobody gives a shit. You can't understand."

"I care, and I want to understand. I think we all have our
Vietnams."

He laughed. "Not quite. Not, fuckin', quite."

128

"You don't know that," she said, nibbling at her lower lip.

He looked at her, a blonde strand resting on her forehead, her green eyes shining in the light.

"I killed a close friend; shot him dead."

"Why?" she asked, no hesitation, no change of expression.

"I was pulling guard and didn't hear him get up to take a piss. I was so deep into my own world that I forgot about the real one. It was late, dark. I just fuckin' panicked."

It was the most he'd said since he'd seen the V.A. psychologist in San Francisco. Charley had relived the scene, at first every night, in thoughts and dreams: the shot, Beto's face, the shadows, the yells, the confusion.

During his first year home from Vietnam, he woke up every night, paced his mother's kitchen for an hour, sometimes two or three, until he tired and could go back to sleep. Still, even now, he woke, occasionally crying out, perspiring, falling back into his pillow, his body shivering.

She put down her glass and touched his forehead, her fingers sliding over his skin.

"It was your fault?"

"I was burned out, exhausted, scared...not concentrating. Yeah, it was my fault. I mean, Beto—that was his name—he should have said something, warned me, but he didn't. Hell, I'd been working all afternoon, a hundred fuckin' degrees... shit. It was everybody's fault, the fucking world."

He stood, but she grabbed him and pulled him down.

"Mine, too, I guess." she said.

He looked at her.

She put her hand behind his arm, pulled him towards her and kissed him. He leaned back and looked at her. She smiled. They embraced, kissed. He closed his eyes. Her skin was smooth under his fingers. A glass fell from the coffee table and rolled on the floor. A child shouted in the street. The jukebox blared. They moved through the room, their arms wrapped around one another, until moments later, the water from the shower slipped down their naked bodies. They laughed, touched and embraced. They stepped from the shower, groping at each other and fell to the bed, their bodies clasped, the beads of water turning to perspiration, Magan touching him in ways he never experienced.

The sun rose, bright and warm, and the passing semi-trucks outside rattled his window. He woke. Magan slept beside him. He studied her hair, her eyes, her nose and mouth. He'd never been with anyone this beautiful. He looked around the room, stark, white, like a monk's cell, except for a dresser. He lay his head in the crook of one elbow. His eyes focused on the other arm, near the shoulder, and he saw, where as an eighteen-year-old paratrooper, fresh from jump school, on his way to Southeast Asia, he'd tattooed a parachute, a skull, and the words, "Death Before Dishonor—Vietnam 67-68." Magan must have seen it. That's how she knew, he thought. "Witch, hell," he whispered to himself, and turned to watch her sleep.

Charley was enrolled in one summer-school class at the old university campus in the center of town, on Avenida Puentezuelas. Each day after school, Magan would join him, and they'd stop at a neighborhood store for food and hike along a mountainside to the Fountain of Avellano, beneath the Alhambra's walls. Their favorite place was near the bell-shaped cement fountain, a patch of grass and oak trees. Here they'd peer across the Rio Darro and the valley below to Sacramonte, where the more popular gypsies lived, in glimmering whitewashed caverns built into the mountainside.

Charley told her this spot was "*campo santo*" to Granadinos who loved literature, since years ago, Andalucia's famous poets, Lorca, Alexandre, Alberti, and Hernandez would meet here to discuss politics and writing.

"Poetry is such bullshit. Pure arrogance, ego, elitist crap, like golf and tennis... sailing," Magan said.

"Not all writers are like that."

"But inside, way down deep, they think like that."

"You never heard of Oscar Acosta, the Brown Buffalo?"

"What's a brown buffalo? What's it supposed to mean?"

"A state of mind, I guess, an identity with something mysterious, something ancient, something powerful, mythic, you know. Maybe it means something different to each person."

"Was this guy a writer?"

"Yeah, from my hometown. He moved to San Francisco, got a law degree, quit his practice and went to L.A. He got caught up in the Chicano Movement, anti-war shit... all of it. He wrote a couple of books, incriminated himself in some crimes, and disappeared."

"Disappeared?" she said.

"Gone, just like smoke."

"Like your friend, Jesse Peña, the guy you told me about awhile back?"

"Yeah. Only I didn't know Jesse. I heard about him. He was one of the old timers, nothing more than a story by the time I arrived in country."

"How could this guy, the Buffalo, disappear?"

"After his last book, he went to Mexico. Said he was going to travel around Latin America, dig up his roots, smoke dope... take it easy. No one ever heard from him again."

"Not his parents?"

"Nobody. Gone, vanished, vamoose."

"And he got away with it?"

"So far."

"Can I become a brown buffalo?" she said, smiling mischievously.

"I don't know. I guess. Maybe it's all in the heart, a part of your roots."

"I don't think so," she said.

"Could be."

"Why're minorities always into this roots thing? Why can't you just be who you are?"

"It ain't that simple."

"Why?"

"It's complicated."

"What a cop out."

"Okay...because who we are isn't good enough. We have to prove ourselves, over and over and over."

"We all have to do that...."

"No, not everyone does. See, our past has been distorted in his books, so...we try to salvage it by looking for it ourselves. Our history and literature aren't present in our school system or correctly described in history books. But your past hasn't been hidden. The history books are all yours. The great writers and painters and thinkers are all yours, their writings and lives preserved by scholars who keep your roots alive every day. Man, how many studies can a dude do on F. Scott Fitzgerald anyway? You see, you take all this for granted. but your history books are full of shit. You've been taught lies about America's history and those lies erase a lot of people, people who've helped build this country."

"Oh, God, Charley. The past is dead...bullshit, live for today."

"You can do that. You're white as a sheet of snow. Whether you like it or not, you're a part of the power structure that makes sure the lies last."

"That's shit. Besides, you're pretty white yourself," she said, sliding her hand on his arm. "And I don't think I've got any power. Maybe that's why I came to Granada, to find some."

"Back home, in Modesto, the past is alive, and the farm owners—ex-Okies who my dad fed when they had nothing—their kids, the media, they throw it in our faces every day. 'Mexicans this and Mexicans that.' They even got us insulting each other...whose skin is whiter? Who's more American than whom? Who's a 'wetback' and who's not?

"I saw white dudes crack up in combat, cry like fuckin' babies, bitch and moan...chickenshits, refuse to go out on operations, refuse to walk the point or pull their share of guard duty, big fuckin' white dudes, giants, whimpering like kids. Still, some of them got promoted or sent to the rear to rest."

"Charley, so what? Okay, there's racism, okay! It's all part of the game. But every group's got its cowards, its heroes."

"That's the point, yeah...some guys pretended to be heroes, but when it came down to showing steel balls, they couldn't cut it. But I saw other dudes, Indians, Chicanos, Filipinos, Puerto Ricans, ready to do what they had to, never weaseling their way out of a dangerous detail...."

"How many white dudes did you see chicken out, Charley?"

"What?"

"How many? Give me numbers. Twenty? Thirty? Five? One?"

"What do you mean?"

"I want to know how many white dudes you personally saw chicken out. Not what you heard, but what you saw."

"That's not the point. I saw enough to confirm my theory that white boys don't have a monopoly on courage. That's how many."

"You sound like the racist, stereotyping everybody, sweeping generalizations."

"You don't see it?" he asked, sliding behind her, placing his hands on her shoulders and rubbing.

"I see it. You haven't said anything new, not to me anyway. I kind of feel like that. Maybe it's because I'm a woman.... We've had to put up with a lot of shit."

"Yeah, I know," he said, looking down at the river, his thumbs massaging her neck.

"You want kids, Charley?"

"I want kids and grandkids and great grandkids."

"A big family, huh?"

"Family's what it's all about."

She sat quietly for a long time, then she said, "And this guy Acosta, the Brown Buffalo...disappeared, huh, just like that?"

"Just like that. Some people say he'll be back."

"I wouldn't guess so," she said.

After all the words, Charley lay back, closed his eyes, and dozed under the shade and warm sun. Magan crossed her legs and looked to the adjacent mountains and watched the gypsies walk the narrow roads as busloads of tourists entered the caverns to see flamenco shows and have their fortunes told. When Charley awoke, she was still sitting, legs crossed, watching the gypsies across the valley.

✪ ✪ ✪

His neighbors didn't complain when they learned Magan was living with him, yet he sensed their disappointed eyes, as if he were disrespecting the barrio. Whenever he entered the market downstairs, the women's greetings were curt, their manner distant. Their children, who often went to Charley's to talk about baseball and football, stopped visiting.

Because he was Mexican, carried the name Yañez, had served in Vietnam as a soldier, a *conquistador*, the Spaniards doted over him protectively, as though he were a lost son returned. Their eyes were the eyes of his grandparents, watching to see how far he'd go, to see if he was more *gringo* than hispano, to see if he would insult the family honor.

Reluctantly, he and Magan separated. She understood.

"It's really cool that these values still exist and that people are willing to stand up for them," Magan had said. Her words drew Charley closer, made him respect her more.

Magan moved in with Katie, a congressman's daughter, a friend of Charley's. Katie had been in Granada a year and was looking for a roommate.

Charley and Magan saw each other almost every day. Mornings, they'd meet at one of the crowded cafes near the university. She'd tell him how much she enjoyed Katie and her friends, but she also confessed that she'd felt "bummed" since she'd moved from his apartment. He told her that he felt the same way.

He'd sneak her into his apartment where they'd lose themselves, at least for a couple of hours, submerged in passion, surfacing dizzy, disoriented, and sometimes bewildered.

✪ ✪ ✪

As summer ended, students throughout Europe flooded into the city for vacations and jobs. Apartments filled quickly. He asked Magan to stay, to see Granada in winter, at its most beautiful, when most tourists were gone.

They were sitting in a neighborhood park, Plaza de los Lobos, when Magan told him her father had sent her a four-thousand-dollar check to do whatever she wanted to do.

"Let's get a place together," he said, impulsive, excited.

"Charley, I don't know."

"With my fellowship money and G.I. Bill, we'll be fine."

"I know. But to live together..." Her eyes were penetrating. She took his fingers. "I don't want to cause any pain."

He didn't really understand. "Look, we can be roommates. We'll find a place with two bedrooms, so we can have our privacy. It'll be like those first weeks."

"Charley."

He watched her.

"I can't promise anything, you know. This is an experience...a trip. I like you, but this...I can't promise. Oh, I don't know. I've got problems, like you. My own Vietnam, remember?" She looked away.

"No promises. If it doesn't work out, it'll be an experience, that's all."

"You say that now, but..."

"I'm serious."

"If I need my freedom, no hard feelings, huh?"

He saw himself in the reflection of her sunglasses, a dim figure, smiling happily, as if nothing else mattered.

✪ ✪ ✪

They found a two-story, 15th Century home in the Albaicin, a mountain dotted with white Arab-style villas and chalets overlooking the city. A long stone's throw across from them was the Alhambra, its walls, towers and turrets rising from the adjacent mountain. Below and to the right, the city of Granada unfolded like a brown carpet and the Vega stretched towards the Mediterranean.

Magan enrolled in classes for foreign students at the Puentezuelas campus. Spanish came to her easily, and her pronunciation surprised Charley. It was as if she'd been born in Granada.

He studied at the main campus, completing courses in elementary Arabic and Arabic linguistics, tedious classes but necessary to his field of study: the Spanish Moors and their impact on the Americas.

He had always studied until 9:00 or 10:00 P.M., sometimes midnight, forgetting everything except the books, the stories, the lessons. But now he looked forward to finishing his work early so that he and Magan could go out, sometimes alone, sometimes meeting friends in the *tablaos* around the city.

Magan wanted to learn everything, to soak up the city. She wasn't like anybody he'd met. They talked about the Spanish language—Castellano vs. Andaluz, about culture, the bullfights, writers, Chicanos, Mexicans, Spaniards, the Arabs, and Vietnam—a subject he had always avoided. But she managed to pull the stories from him, and she'd hear his voice soften, witness his most vulnerable moments.

✪ ✪ ✪

Charley introduced her to a friend, a gypsy guitarist who performed in a local tavern. The guitarist introduced Magan to a flamenco dancer in Sacramonte, who introduced her to a number of gypsy women, dancers also. She was able to gain their confidence and was invited to their homes, something rare among foreigners. She loved Sacramonte and the gypsies who sang, danced, and told fortunes, and she spent much time with them, exchanging English lessons for flamenco lessons.

When Magan started missing school, Charley didn't worry. He always knew where to find her. Afterwards, they'd talk for hours, and she'd tell him what she'd seen and heard, some stories tragic, others humorous. She'd once said, "Before a gypsy woman can marry, her future mother-in-law, the night before the wedding, has to...'check her out'. You know, to make sure she's a virgin."

"Check her out?"

"Yeah."

"How?"

"There's only one way."

"You mean..."

"That's the way."

"And if she doesn't want to?"

"She can't get married."

"That's really extreme."

"Some people take things to the limit," she said, and smiled.

"Be careful," Charley cautioned. "Don't be a crazy *gabacha*, get caught up in things you don't understand. Some people take advantage of innocence. All they see is your savings account."

"You mean, gypsies are thieves and crooks?" she said, poking him in the chest

"You calling me a bigot?" He laughed.

"If the shoe fits..."

"You be cool, that's all I'm saying."

"I've never done a stupid thing in my life," she said, smiling.

He laughed.

"Charley..." she said. "Thanks. I wish my dad had given me advice. He never said anything. Just let me do whatever I wanted."

"Sounds like a kid's dream."

"No. Not really."

✪ ✪ ✪

They never talked about marriage. There wasn't any need. Their new Spanish neighbors, thinking them married, told them what a beautiful couple they made, and why didn't they have any children, and that, God willing, they would have many beautiful sons and daughters.

Magan confessed she'd had an abortion, somewhere on the outskirts of San Jose. There were complications. Later, at the hospital, a doctor told her that she'd never have children.

Charley wanted her to talk about it. After several weeks, she tried but rambled, her eyes teary as she described how her father gave her cash, forbade her mother or brother to help her, and told her to take care of it herself.

"Your own Vietnam?" Charley had said, holding her.

"My own Vietnam."

"That's a shitty story."

"I didn't know whether to tell you or not... you know, you being Chicano, Catholic and all, your ideas about family."

"Look, they've all failed me too many times. Sure, I have my own beliefs, what I value and what I don't. But when two people share what you and I have, what's important is you."

"And children?"

"When it happens it happens."

She shook her head, her eyes on his. "No, Charley. It isn't just a happening. It's life, and life can't be taken, or given like a flower, or a dog."

"I meant that only you are important."

She smiled, yet he detected a sadness in her eyes, as if she knew better than he did.

✪ ✪ ✪

The days slipped by. Weeks became a month, then two. The sun lost its warmth, and a cold chill blew off of the Sierras. There were no more trips to the ocean where the two had swum in a lagoon and camped near the town of Salobrena, beneath the walls of a Moorish *alcazba*.

By November, the trees were bare, the dirt hard, and the cobblestones icy. Charley and Magan were sitting in front of the hearth, the logs burning, when they heard the rains slap the patio. They stepped into the cold and leaned on the low wall. The city's rusted roofs glistened. Across a ravine, the Alhambra's copper walls turned red.

"There'll be a lot of snow," Charley said.

Magan was quiet, then said, "I loved the snow."

"Past tense?"

"I skied every year."

"Why'd you stop?"

"I didn't like the elitist part. I hated being around those people, their alpaca sweaters, BMW's, Mercedes, their tans and superficial laughs. But the skiing I loved. When I was five, my uncle Marlin said I was a natural. I got really good. I loved the speed, the adrenalin rush."

She said that she was also trying to earn her dad's love. She became an expert. By the time she was sixteen, she could keep up with the best skiers on the mountain. Then she saw a skier lose control, hit a tree, and break his neck. She described his blood against the snow, the gawking crowd, and the helicopter airlifting the wounded skier over the trees. She hadn't skied since the accident.

There had been hopes she'd try out for the Olympic team. She had won many local competitions. Her father had arranged the invitations and trials. She refused. She and her father fought. She knew that her name in the papers would have been good for his business, which was already a success. She tried to explain. Finally, her only defense was to say, "The Olympics are for asses, Dad."

Her father had hit her in the face, closed fisted, blackened her eye and fractured her jaw. The two spoke little after that. When she tried to discuss it with her mother, her mother refused to talk about it.

As she spoke, Charley interrupted her. "Let's go skiing!"

"Didn't you hear anything I said?"

"Come on. This is a new life, a new world. Your old man ain't around. Do it for yourself, because you want to, not for anyone else."

They argued. Magan cried.

Charley kept it up for two more days, using every reason he knew. She was weakening. He said, "You made me talk about the war, about that night. Before you, I couldn't do it... didn't want to. Remember, you said I needed to get it out. Now you've got to do the same thing. Go beyond, past your old man's control."

She agreed, nervously, and said, "Okay, but I'll only do it if you learn how to ski, too."

"Me?" he said, thinking about the 14,000-foot mountains he'd seen on earlier trips to Granada's Sierras.

"You," she said.

"Hell with it. All right. Good enough. Just point me down the damn mountain. I'll be hell on skis."

"Yeah, right."

✪ ✪ ✪

It was a Friday when they took the bus to Mt. Veleta, the ski resort. The mountains were steep, white and beautiful. New redwood condominiums spotted the landscape. After some coffee, they headed to the ski rental shop. The boots, bindings and other paraphernalia held Charley to the ice like concrete. He took it slow. "Hey, Magan," he called. "You go ahead. Do it! Don't let me hold you back."

"Hell on skis, huh? Just point you down the damn mountain, huh?" she chuckled.

Charley threw up his arms in mock disgust.

She practiced on the lower hills, weaving and cutting back and forth like an ice skater, elegant moves and a wonderfully supple body. An hour later, she was on the expert slope, a steep mountain, unmarked but for one warning, *"Peligroso."* At the end of the first run, a thousand-foot rock cliff filled the horizon, a deep fissure at its base. Magan raced towards the cliff, made a sharp right with no trouble, and headed down the longest and steepest section of the run. She fell twice, recovered and reached the bottom, laughing jubilantly, throwing her arms around Charley, and riding the lift again.

She skied all afternoon, while he stayed on the lower hills, falling and struggling with skis and poles most of the day. He rode the lift up one time, looked down the mountain, told Magan good luck, then jumped back on the lift that headed down.

Some weeks later, on their sixth trip to Mt. Veleta, two students from the university ski team asked if Magan wanted to join the team. She declined. Her confidence soared at the invitation.

"I've never felt this free in my life," she said. "It's like I want to do everything."

Magan's boldness reminded Charley of himself at eighteen-years old, riding to Modesto on a dare, entering the recruitment station and signing up for the U.S. Army, no fear, just a little nervousness, but wanting like hell to get away from the San Joaquin Valley, away from the peaches, rednecks, Okies, labor contractors, farm owners, racist teachers. He'd go any place, even Vietnam. No wonder Oscar Acosta had vanished. He got as far away as he could, and Charley realized that he and Magan were doing the same thing, on another level.

III.

They visited the Alhambra, the old Moorish castle, two or three times a week. Few tourists braved the cold, icy weather as Magan and Charley did, often alone, donning coats, beanie caps and gloves. They walked the empty halls and courtyards. They sat in the ancient leather chairs and looked out over the fountains and pools, walked the meticulously tended gardens. No matter where they stood or sat, they heard the water, a continuous flow that echoed through the stone halls and sculpted patios. An old gypsy, a caretaker named Bernardo whom Charley had met while taking a seminar in the Palacio de Carlos V, let them wander the chambers and caverns beneath the Alhambra, long tunnels cutting through the mountain, hiding old muskets, cannonballs, secret passages, and locked rooms, some not entered in years.

One evening just after sunset, sleeping bags slung over their shoulders, they sneaked into the ancient Arabian castle. Friends had told Charley that behind some brush and shrubs was a wide crack leading inside. He and Magan crawled through and found their way to the Patio de Los Leones. In one of the Nazari's chambers, they spent the night, bundled in sleeping bags, bodies pressed together, listening to the sighs of the wind and the echoes of a thousand lovers who must have lain there in pain and pleasure throughout the centuries. The incessant splashing of the fountains lulled them into a sound sleep.

✪ ✪ ✪

It was during the following months that Charley first noticed the change in Magan, nothing serious, a slight moodiness, now and then a stinging phrase, a bewildered glance, a long silence.

Without announcement, Magan would leave the house and walk through town, up the mountains and along the river. She visited the gypsies, ancient monasteries, churches, and villages hidden away in canyons outside the city. She followed narrow goat trails and discovered waterfalls and wide, dark meadows.

Charley was busy studying, his mind occupied with the Arabic alphabet and numbers.

Magan explored places he'd never been, vaults and chambers in the Alhambra, deep passages beneath the *Generalife*, the Alhambra's terraced gardens. Once, she had lost her way, and when she didn't return, Bernardo had to go find her.

The old gypsy refused to let her down there again. For days, she pressured Charley to take her, to sneak in at night and wander around.

"There's something important in there. It's a chance to do things we'll never do again," she said, hoping to change his mind.

"No! Bernardo said not to go down there. He might get fired."

"Is it him you're really worried about?"

"What's that supposed to mean?"

"Maybe you're scared, pure fear, nothing more."

He looked at her, trying to see if she was joking. She didn't smile. Her eyes were piercing. "Why're you being so bitchy?" he said.

"If I was one of your guy friends, you wouldn't have said that," she said, standing rigid, immovable.

"Why're you so goddamn mad?"

"I'm not mad!"

"What then?"

She looked at him, her eyes fiery. "Isn't that what it's all about...doing things nobody's done before?" she said, and turned away.

"I've already done that, Magan, remember. I've done something few people ever have," he answered bitterly. He turned and began to walk away.

She rushed to him, blocked his retreat. Facing him, her eyes narrow, she said, "Then of all people, you should under-stand."

"I'm trying. I really am."

"That's not what I mean."

"What then?"

Frustrated, she said, "You didn't kill Beto that night. You killed yourself, your capacity to feel, to get close. He's just your excuse."

He looked at her and didn't respond.

"Charley. I'm sorry," she said, recovering quickly. She moved towards him, trying to put her arms around his neck. "Charley, please."

He raised his hands, as if protecting his face, not allowing her to touch him.

"Charley..."

"Forget it. Let's just forget it," he said, walking to the couch and opening a book.

"We've got to talk. Help me."

When he didn't say anything, she left the room.

✪ ✪ ✪

It was a frigid night, late, and Magan still hadn't come home. Charley went looking for her. He walked to Sacramonte and knocked on the door of a gypsy family, the Riveras. They asked him inside their home—an exotic stucco cave. Magan sat at the table, eating dinner, a child on her lap. She looked composed, comfortable with the environment. Charley looked around. Thick, round logs supported the ceiling. White, textured walls were decorated with floral-colored plates and framed photos of flamenco dancers and bullfighters, their eyes on him, the intruder. He remembered Magan's words about not feeling badly if things didn't work out. Charley smiled weakly, struggled for air, and told Magan he had been worried about her.

"I'll be there soon," she said, offering the child on her lap some food from her spoon.

"Okay. Be careful going home. If you want...I can wait."

"No. It's cool."

"Okay."

Magan spent hours each day at Sacramonte. On Sundays during the winter months, as fewer bus loads of tourists came into the city, the gypsies asked Magan to dance with them, sing songs, and help hustle the foreigners. She was the only blonde gypsy and told the tourists, in feigned, broken English, that she'd been kidnapped from her home in Norway and had been raised a gypsy since the age of four. The tourists listened happily to her stories and enjoyed her dancing, which was improving.

After her first flamenco lessons, months before, Magan had hopped around, clicking her fingers and slapping her feet to the guitars' rhythms and complicated beats. The gypsies had laughed, but they liked her spirit.

As time passed, and she practiced every day, she picked up the slow, seductive movements, the angled head, proud, haughty eyes, and firm, straight body. After a day's show, Magan, her hair pulled back tightly behind her head, wearing a traditional flamenco dress—she liked green with red dots—would collect twenty or thirty dollars, which she gave to the gypsies, telling Charley, "It's their money. I'm learning everything I need to know, like I'm along for the ride."

"Well, you're getting pretty damn good," Charley had said.

✪ ✪ ✪

One day, Magan walked along the banks of the River Darro. She had her sweatshirt tied about her waist, the sun's warmth on her back. She noticed that the brown fields had taken on a pale-green tinge. The sight made her think of melting snow. They hadn't been skiing in a long time, and Magan felt the urge to visit Mt. Veleta.

Charley worked madly to keep pace with the passing semester. He had to go to the archives in Sevilla, so he suggested that Magan go skiing with the university students, who scheduled trips nearly every weekend. She said that if he couldn't go, she preferred to go alone, that she needed to check out some things.

Nervously, she said, "Look, Charley. We've got to talk."

Charley packed a few shirts.

"Wait. Let it wait 'til I get back."

"It can't wait," she said, grabbing a shirt from his hand.

"Everything can wait," he said, leaving the shirt in her clutched fingers and walking towards the door. "Just wait until I get back...all right?"

He took the bus to Sevilla, worked there for three days, and returned to Granada about noon on a Sunday.

When he entered the house, Magan was sitting in a chair, next to the glass doors, looking out at the Alhambra, her bag, ski jacket and trousers tossed carelessly on the couch. He kissed her on the cheek. She turned. He thought she was someone else. She wore heavy makeup, dark lines around the

147

eyes, thick mascara, rouge on her cheeks and red lipstick. Her hair was pulled back tightly, her gaze distant.

"*Cómo-o-o 'tá uté*," she greeted quickly, using the formal pronoun for 'you,' sounding like a gypsy.

He told her everything was fine but he was in a hurry, on his way to see Professor Isleta Moraga and give her some monographs that she asked him to bring from Sevilla. "Let it wait," Magan said. "We need to talk. I promised I'd wait until you got back."

Charley told her he'd be home before dark. She turned and said, "How about a kiss." He kissed her a long time. "Do you want to make love?" she asked.

"I sure as hell do," he said, "but I can't right now. I've got to deliver this stuff. Let's make a date for tonight."

"Tonight?" she said, turning towards the patio.

The house was dark when he returned. He walked through, checked each room, and stepped back out into the cold night.

Under the dim street lights, he walked to Sacramonte, past the white stucco facades built into the mountain. He knocked on a door. A handsome, eighteen-year-old gypsy answered. He stood straight, watching Charley.

"*¿Has visto a Magan?*" Charley asked.

The gypsy said nothing.

"*¿Bueno?*" Charley barked, moving closer.

The man smiled, shook his head, and said in English slowly, as if taunting him, "Yes. She has gone." The gypsy stepped away from the door, but before he closed it, he said, "She iz wis La Katie."

The narrow passageways curved through the Albaicín, and the cobblestones pushed through Charley's hiking boots, and even though he'd walked the streets a thousand times, he stumbled often before reaching the main plaza. He crossed the lighted public square, his shadow moving in front of him, oblong and thin, like an El Greco painting. He made his way up Calle Reyes Católicos, passed brick buildings, monuments, the new Banco de Bilbao, until he came to a barrio called El Realejo. He saw the lights in Katie's upstairs apartment.

He knocked. "She's in the bedroom," Katie said.

"The bedroom? Is she okay?".

"Seems uptight. You'd better talk to her, Carlos."

The bedroom was dim, lighted by streetlights only.

Magan sat in a chair. She faced a window.

He moved next to her, reached down and stroked her hair.

"Magan...you okay?"

Seconds passed.

"Yeah, I am."

He searched for the right words but found nothing. "What's wrong? You sick?"

"Some people might think so."

He was tired, had traveled much and had little patience. He answered harshly, "I don't like playing games."

"I'm pregnant."

He tried to speak, and she watched him closely.

"But...but I thought..." He couldn't get the words out.

"That I'd never have children."

The room shrank. A garble of words raced through his mind. He couldn't react. He wanted to move to her, put his arms around her, but something gripped him, a fear, like the fear he felt the day he saw Albert's body stretched out on the ground, only this time Manny wasn't holding him back. Charley held himself back.

She sensed his confusion and turned towards the window and the glittering lights in the darkness outside.

"Do, ah...you know for sure?" he asked.

"That month, when I got lost in Alhambra, I missed my period. It didn't bother me. I've always been irregular. Then when I missed it again last month, I went to see the doctor. He said I should have a healthy kid since I'm in such good condition," she said, trying to sound pragmatic, controlled.

"Was he positive?"

"He's the doctor."

Charley ran his fingers over his face.

"Look, I don't want to hassle you with it." She'd said those same words when he first met her at the train station.

"Why didn't you tell me sooner?" he said. "If you've known so long, why didn't you say something?" Carefully, he placed his hands on her shoulders.

"I had to be sure. Anyway, I need an abortion," she said. "You've gotta find out where I can get it done."

"In Spain? No chance. We'd have to go to France." He thought a moment and said, "The first abortion nearly destroyed you. Is that what you want?"

She didn't answer.

He paced the room, stopped, then said, "I don't know. I think it's crazy for us to make a quick decision...I...I need some time to think."

"Look, we're not making a decision. I am."

"Can you destroy a life that easily?" he asked.

"That's got nothing to do with this."

"It's got everything to do with it."

"Responsibility? Is that what we're talking about here?"

"Of course."

"Let's just drop it.

"Magan, all I'm saying is that we can't make a quick decision, not now."

"I'm not condemning you, Charley. I just need to get this taken care of. I can't wait," she said, as if making a final decision.

"You're talking crazy."

She spoke quietly, "Yeah, all right, but look, I still can't have a kid."

"What about...us? How about that?" he asked.

"Us?" She laughed, curtly. "That's not important anymore."

"It's important to me."

"Yeah, well, I don't think you really see it. Do you?"

"What...what don't I see?"

She shook her head slowly, "Remember, this is all...a trip, an experience."

He turned from the window and walked to the other side of the room.

"If I have a kid," she said, "I'm finished. All I want to do now is dance...that's all I want, to be the best flamenco dancer in the world."

She waited for his answer then rose from the chair, walked to the window and looked down at the alley below. "I'll have the abortion, get myself sterilized, and get out of your hair."

He stood, hands in his pocket. "Go ahead then, get yourself killed if you want."

"Yes, daddy," she said.

"Bull! You can't lay that shit on me," he said, stepping towards the door.

"Look, Charley...wait!" she called.

He stopped.

"I haven't lied to you or cheated on you," she said. "Think. I told you, when it was time...no hard feelings. Remember? You agreed. Don't make me hate you."

"Magan... what the hell's going on?"

"I need your help. If you won't... well, it doesn't make much difference."

"This is nuts, crazy."

"You don't need me anymore."

"What?"

"I can't be what you want me to be, a wholesome, innocent white chick who's good in bed. It's not me, Charley. I know it, and," she paused, then said, "you know it. There's no way we'll ever be together, so at least be a friend."

"A friend?"

"If you really love me, you'll help. I'm asking you to keep my secret. When the time's right, you'll know."

He didn't say a thing. He stood, shaking his head.

"Please," she said firmly.

"I'll keep your secret," he said, turning the door knob. "If I think it's the right thing to do."

He walked down the hill and through the streets and plazas, listening to the laughter and music coming from the bars. When it got too cold, and he couldn't walk any longer, he went home and removed his coat and threw it at the couch, next to Magan's things. He picked up a pair of castanets that had been carelessly tossed next to her bag. Crudely carved into the dark wood were the words, Gitana '77–'78. He dropped them to the floor, slipped into a lounge chair and tried to forget, to chase her from his mind. He covered himself with a blanket. Minutes passed, an hour. He fell into a slumber, and the images and sounds formed: A lieutenant, CID, the military, FBI, interrogations, the accusations: "Fucking Mexicans, man, barrio warfare in Vietnam... gang shit, cold-blooded murder;" officers entered, exited, a different face, blue eyes, green eyes, a new voice, southern, mid-western accents, questions, threats, the Saigon Stockade, Lea-

venworth—for life; there was no murder, just a stupid-fuck
mistake; more questions, the brigade shrink, asking about
parents, brothers, sisters, sexual habits, religion; then the
pills, a hazy reality, a jungle fog, for days; and the order:
admit to nothing, one slip and hello Kansas; "Son, it was an
unfortunate accident. Forget about all of it. It never happened. A VC sniper done found his mark."

IV.

Magan came home four days later. She apologized for
anything harsh she may have said, claimed the pregnancy ter-
minated, but wouldn't elaborate.
"You're okay, you're sure?" he said.
"It's over. Forget it," she said.
"Did you get an abortion?"
"Let's just say I've got friends in…mysterious places, and
leave it at that," she said, removing his shirt. "I want to make
love."
"We can't do this."
"Yeah. We can."
Magan led him into the bedroom.
She became a lover of many faces and bodies, not one
woman but thousands. He couldn't distinguish between reality and fantasy. Throughout the night they slept and woke,
many times. He dreamed that she was in his arms, and shak-
en from his dream, he woke to find himself clasped to her,
moving violently. And when he thought they were making
love, his eyes would open, and Magan would be asleep, and
the entire room quiet. And when he awoke in the morning, the
sun shining through their bedroom window, he felt afraid.

The days passed. Magan talked about shopping for new sweaters, gloves, books, and furniture. She listed the names of bars and restaurants she wanted to visit. She wrote to her father for another credit card so she could buy *Lladro*, "...bunches and bunches of it." But she never mailed the letter, just like she never went shopping or visited the places on her list. She seldom left home. Instead, she washed windows, walls and scrubbed floors, forbidding him to help. When that was done, she'd slip a tape into the cassette and practice intricate flamenco steps, her castanets clapping, feet stomping, her body in a frenzy, while perspiration poured down her face. She showered so often that each night they'd run out of hot water. After midnight, she'd lie in bed, eyes closed, castanets in hand, clapping out complex beats, well-rehearsed, not spontaneous or improvised.

She wanted to invite some friends for one last ski trip before the best snow melted. Charley was beginning finals and needed to study, but he realized, by her excited voice, how important this was to her.

"It can be our final adventure," she said.

"What does that mean?"

"You know, 'search and destroy,' a mission before the snow melts and...washes away, forever."

"I don't know, Magan," he said.

"Goddamn it, Carlos!" she said, using his real name. "Loosen up, enjoy what we have. Remember the poem in the Alhambra 'Give alms, sir, for there's no greater curse...'"

"I know," he said, "'...than to be blind in Granada.'"

They always quoted it when one of them became too nervous or serious.

"Whaddya say?"

"All right...yeah, let's go."

V.

The red and white Alsina bus followed a rain soaked road that went along the Genil River, the murky water churning against the stone walls as it entered the city. On the crowded sidewalks, people carried open umbrellas and huddled in heavy overcoats.

The bus headed into a walled valley, rocky mountains on either side. The almond, sycamore, and poplar trees stood naked in the moist earth. Every few miles they passed a settlement, white stucco homes, tile roofs, old and tarnished over the years.

As they began to climb the narrow mountain road, the valley's skimpy vegetation vanished. The gradual grade turned into a sharp incline, and the steep ascent began. Higher up the mountain, the clouds moved in, first looming ominously overhead, then dropping down to an arm's length. The bus's engine groaned beneath the tonnage, and the vehicle slowed, and in an instant, everything disappeared, and a dense fog clutched at the windows. To the right of the road was a five-thousand-foot drop. They drove higher.

The bus was half-full, mostly with students going up for a day of skiing. The chattering, laughing voices were now silent. Charley looked towards the front, up the narrow aisle between the seats, curious to see the driver's view. Charley saw nothing but a blanket of fog. He began to perspire, feeling claustrophobic like a night in the jungle.

The engine whined, a high-pitched cry. It was as if they were in an airplane, lost in storm. Charley's imagination drew a vivid scene: the bus's tires losing traction on the slick asphalt, slipping from the roadside, and the huge metal carcass careening down the mountainside, rolling and tumbling, bouncing off the mountain, crushing and coming to rest against the rocks in the canyon below.

Magan put his clammy palm between her warm hands and started playing with his fingers, a smile on her face.

The road became steeper. He leaned back and shifted in his seat. The bus jerked, a tremendous shock that caused a gasp from the passengers. Charley sank deeper into his seat. Magan laughed and clasped her fingers through his. The bus picked up speed, smoothed, then violently quaked, as if caught in a wave. He looked out the window. The fog was silver, translucent, like spun glass, and he could only see shadows through the haze. Another wild motion—a submarine surfacing in a wild sea, and the bus burst through the fog, quickly, angrily, until nothing but white mountains appeared against the blue sky.

"Some paratrooper," Magan said, kissing his cheek.

"I just had this feeling that something was going to happen, like one of us was going to die."

She remained silent.

"I remember hearing about a guy, Joey Serrano. He kept telling everyone that he was going to die, that something bad was going to happen to him."

"And?"

"He was killed."

"Well. We're fine, couldn't be better," she said mechanically, turning from him and looking out the window.

Everyone on the bus applauded, laughed and spoke chaotically, pointing in different directions. Magan leaned over and kissed him again, jumped from the seat and moved up the aisle to where Katie sat.

Charley sighed and looked into the driver's rearview mirror, where he caught sight of the driver's stoic expression. The man drove steadily, both hands on the steering wheel, his eyes on the road.

Magan clicked her castanets and Katie sang, as another friend, a Spaniard with wild hair and eyes, strummed awkwardly at his guitar. Jaime Ortero, a Cuban from Fort Lauderdale, passed around a bottle of wine and they all drank.

As they neared Mt. Veleta, Magan slid in next to Charley. She took his hand and placed it in her jacket pocket, his knuckles resting against her castanets. Squeezing his hand, their fingers rubbing the wood instrument, she turned and looked at him. "Charley...you've really been a good friend," she said, and leaned her head against his shoulder.

"We're much more than friends."

Magan said nothing.

Once on the snow and equipped with their gear, they stretched and loosened their muscles on the low hills near the tourist village. An hour later, they were on the lift, looking down at the red and brown rocks jutting through the snow. Magan didn't speak. The mountains below looked like swirling clouds, not a tree or shrub visible, and in the distance they saw more mountain caps, snow and sky. They rode higher. Magan and Charley had been on this slope many times, and its immensity still amazed and frightened him.

At the top, he slid from the chair and held his hand out to steady her. She stepped down. They moved to where their friends sat, on wooden benches, checking their bindings, and at the same time, razzing each other and asking the lift operator to save one chair going down. They told him it was for Charley, since the first three times on the mountain, he'd descended on the chairs.

Katie shuffled onto the run, pushed off and sped down the first stretch. Jaime followed, then the Spaniard, and two other friends. Like a mechanical chain, one after the other, they raced down the mountain, slicing through the snow, heading towards the cliff and deep chasm, turning sharply, and speeding down the main run.

"Hurry, Charley. Go!" Magan said, pushing him with the side of her pole.

"No, ma'am."

"What? I wanna make sure you're okay."

"Not this time," he said. "Any problems, and I'll be your hero."

"C'mon, Charles. I always go after you."

"No," he said.

"I want to be last," she said, sounding angry. "Now go!"

They argued, but he shook his head stubbornly. She moved close and kissed him on the cheek. "I love you, but people do what's best for them, ya know."

He didn't know how to answer.

"Charley...whoever I am, whatever I believe or do... remember, it's got nothin' to do with you. It's all way before I ever knew you. Remember that...all right? We have had a great time, haven't we?"

"And more still to come," he said.

She smiled weakly, moved to the ski run, and without her usual poking about, she pushed off, the tips of her skis lifting then plopping down onto the snow.

She took off faster than usual, moved smoothly down the hill, her body firm, knees slightly bent. She wore no cap, and her hair streamed behind her. As she picked up speed and moved a good distance ahead of him, he pushed off, following safely behind. He tried to keep his eyes on her, but the slick, rutted trail made it difficult for him to focus. Looking up, instead of seeing Magan, he saw the menacing 1,000-foot rock wall. He knew she'd have to turn soon and head into the valley, away from the cliff and the fissure at its base.

Charley balanced himself, glanced up and waited to see her slow down to make the turn. Instead, he saw snow splattering from her skis, as if she had no intention of turning. She was bent down low, racing faster, slicing right past the main turn and heading away from the run and towards the granite wall and deep scar in the earth.

He yelled, knowing she couldn't hear. Magan skied up a knoll, reached the top, started down, and disappeared, a blur melting into the white ice, gone, out of sight.

He picked up speed, grew nauseated, fell and hit the snow, tumbling over skis and poles. Pulling himself together, he started again, quickly gaining speed. He struggled to keep his balance. He rushed past the turn and sped toward the cliff. One ski rose from the snow, dug itself into the ice and flew from his boot. He stayed on the other ski until his leg crumpled from weakness. When he hit the knoll, he crashed, rolling over several times, the ice rising like smoke. He clawed his way to the top of the knoll, his legs and knees sinking into the snow. Expecting to see Magan on the other side, he saw only her ski marks, lightly carved into the ice. She was nowhere. About fifty yards beyond, over a flat stretch of ice, was the fissure—a deep volcanic crevice.

Charley knelt there. Four skiers came from behind and stopped next to him. When they saw he wasn't hurt, one skied over the knoll, across the snow, to the edge of the abyss. He looked down into the rocky crag and shook his head. Within an hour, police, medics, and a ski patrol arrived.

VI.

El Ideal carried a short account of Magan's death. The newspaper didn't give her name, only identifying her as a young American student. The reporter also reminded readers that Granada's Sierra Nevadas had taken the lives of other inexperienced skiers, some on this very same run. A most tragic accident, the article concluded.

The search party combed the area but failed to find her body in the deep, rocky chasm, so there was no autopsy.

Only the mother came to Granada. She took Magan's things from the apartment as Charley stood and watched. A driver loaded Magan's belongings into a rented car and drove away. There had been few words exchanged.

"My God. This is exactly why I left the States, to get away from shit like this," Katie said later that afternoon, putting her head on his shoulder.

He told her about Magan's pregnancy.

"Why didn't she say something to me?" Katie asked.

"She said that she'd taken care of it. She wouldn't talk about it any more."

"Oh shit," Katie said. "I could've talked to her. Why didn't she say something?"

Charley's revelation bothered Katie deeply. She simply stared at him, and without asking anymore questions, she took him by the arms and kissed his cheek. He thanked her for her help and walked away, not sure where to go.

✪ ✪ ✪

He moved to a new, inexpensive neighborhood, Barrio Amistad, at the edge of Granada's Vega. He gave away most of his and Magan's belongings, furniture, and souvenirs. He let his hair and beard grow and didn't care whether he showered or wore clean clothes. He dropped out of school and stopped reading—even newspapers.

He thought about Magan, but the emotions ran too deep. He tried to forget her, and dredged up memories of Beto

Alvarez and the other guys he'd served with, or had heard about, in Vietnam. The guys would have liked Magan, her fearlessness and sense of adventure.

Periodically, Charley thought about returning to the States, but he didn't have the strength to go home; so instead, he'd sit alone in his apartment, think, and listen to the radio for hours or go to the bar down the street, drink wine and listen to the Spaniards complain about the new government.

He missed Magan terribly, and often thought about the pregnancy, about the child they could have had, and he felt guilty. He should have been more forceful with her, more open, but there were limitations with his ability to express himself, and he didn't know why he hadn't been able to overcome them. Sometimes he hated everything about himself.

One afternoon, a small box wrapped in brown paper arrived for him at the university. A friend delivered it to his house. It was postmarked Sevilla.

Charley tore the wrapping and opened the cardboard flap. He tilted the box and a pair of castanets fell into his hand. "Gitana, '77-'78," was carved into the wood. Magan had them in her coat pocket the day she died. He stuck his fingers into the box, feeling for a note or card. There was nothing. He slumped into a chair, keeping his eyes focused on the living room window. He turned the castanets around in his hands several times, fingering the etched letters.

At first perplexed, he started to reconstruct everything Magan had talked about and places they had gone during the last few months. He took out calendars and diaries, remembered events, bus trips, hiking trips, lunches, dinners, nights out with friends, dates, times and places, jotted notes, jarring his memory, analyzing his and Magan's last conversations, especially about the pregnancy, her exact words.

He stopped drinking, took control of himself, and over the next few weeks, returned to Mt. Veleta. He spoke to members of the ski patrol and asked if a person could ski to the fissure and exit the mountains by an alternate route. They told him "yes," but it would be a long, arduous walk and why would anybody want to do it.

He packed some hiking gear and returned. The trek from the mountain, down narrow rocky paths and deep valleys, took five grueling hours. When he returned home, he was exhausted and stayed in bed one day to regain his strength.

When he told Katie, she called him a basket case. "Take it easy, Carlos. You're still upset, in shock."

"She's alive, Katie. I know it," he said. "She sent me the castanets she had that day."

"Anybody could have sent those. I've sent all kinds of stuff. I hurried so much I didn't even put a note, just figured people wouldn't care who did the sending, only that the stuff arrived. Now go get some rest."

During the following days, he returned to Katie's, insisting that Magan was alive.

"Carlos," Katie said. "First, a long time ago, you told me that Magan was acting strange, remember? Then you said she was pregnant, but somehow became unpregnant. Now you're telling me she's alive again, cooked up some imbroglio to get away from her father, away from you and live with the gypsies...that what you're telling me?"

"I went up there, Kate, to Mt. Veleta. I made the climb down myself. Listen to some of the things she said before we went skiing that day...."

He pulled out a notepad and started to read.

"Charley...stop!"

He said, "Okay then, listen. This is how she did it. She skied to the fissure and stopped, turned and skied a short way to where she met someone who guided her out...."

"Charley!" she said, rolling her eyes.

"The snow wasn't that high," he said. "They climbed the rocks, down through a narrow pass, between two boulders, a five-hour hike to the main road. I did it. I know."

"You're 'off,' Charley, freaking out. Go to church, talk to one of your priests. See a doctor. Stop drinking. Let the thing go. Magan was my friend, too, and...goddamn it, I don't want a lovesick boyfriend ruining my memories of a beautiful person."

He then realized that nobody would ever take him seriously. Maybe Katie was right. Perhaps he was sick, emotionally distraught...too much shit for one lifetime.

✪ ✪ ✪

He stopped seeing Katie. He stayed to himself, more than ever before. Saturdays and Sundays, for weeks, he would go to Sacramonte to watch the gypsies perform, hoping to see Magan. She wasn't in Granada. He took a job teaching English in a private girls' school. During breaks, he'd take buses to *fiestas* throughout Andalucía and Extremadura, looking for her.

He had heard lots of strange tales. There was the one about a Berkeley grad studying at Salamanca, who left school and moved in with an old couple and lived on their farm raising goats somewhere outside San Sebastián, where, the story went, he stayed for ten years. There was the one about the kid from Minnesota, who shaved his head and carried a haversack, a sword sticking out the back. He followed the novice bullfight circuit, waiting for a chance to break into the *novilladas*. There were the stories of the women, American exchange students who had run off with the gypsies, traveling in caravans through Sevilla, Cordoba, Ronda, Malaga, up to Toledo and Madrid, following the *fiestas*. He and Magan had talked about all of them.

Fifteen months after Magan disappeared, during *Semana Santa*, in a hilly, green pasture outside of Sevilla, Charley saw a young blonde woman wearing a yellow and red flamenco dress. She was performing on the back of a flatbed truck, powerful concert speakers at either end of the stage. Three guitar players strummed wildly as hundreds of people watched. Her work was exquisite, precise, and she captured the dissonant sounds of the *cante jondo*, her movements uncanny, perfect. Charley tried unsuccessfully to move through the crowd. Spellbound by her performance, he stopped, unable to get any closer. He couldn't discern her facial features. She moved delicately and fiercely, twisting fingers and hands as a feather floats, then in anger, she jammed her heels into the wood of the truck, the clapping of her feet timed with the resonating guitars.

When she finished, the audience erupted with shouts and applause. She stood, arms outstretched, rigid, her chest heaving, perspiration dripping. Charley asked a boy, a young gypsy, if he would take the castanets and give them to her. "Tell her thank you. Tell her I understand and that now we're both free." The gypsy pushed his way through the crowd, stretched his thin arm out to her and handed her the wood instrument. She leaned down and listened to the boy's words. Standing straight, she stared at the wood instrument for a long time, raised her head, looked out over the crowd, turned in all directions, smiled, waved, and quickly stepped from the stage. Charley fought to get closer, but he was too slow and lost her in the confusion.

TEN
RUBBER MAN
(THREE WITNESSES)

They grabbed him by the arms and tied him to a bamboo fence. The bloated body hung rigid, straight, like a life-sized balloon doll. Half his jaw had been shot away. His eyes were shut, his mouth a twisted grimace. There were bullet holes in his arms and chest, round punctures, like dark splotches. His torn black pajamas hung loosely.

David Almas and Danny Ríos sat on wood boxes and watched. Bear, a stocky West Virginian, and Mack Brun, a skinny guy from Alabama, paced off twenty steps from the corpse. Two more guys came up from behind. They moved close to Bear and Mack. Somebody pulled out a buck knife. It was huge, shiny. Bear flipped it, point to handle, two or three times. He grasped it between his fingers, pulled back his muscular arm and threw the knife—hard. It moved in a straight line, twirling. The knife point hit the body and bounced off. Bear looked at the others, then laughed. "Whoa!" was all he said.

Wayne Podleski, wearing no shirt and smoking the stub of a Camel cigarette, walked up and sat next to David. "What's the haps?" he said, his shoulder lightly brushing David's.

David gestured towards Bear and the others.

Brun ran for the knife and picked it up. He stepped back a few paces and threw the blade even harder than Bear had. The sharp metal hit the man on the arm. The knife tore a chunk from the body, ricocheted, banged against the dead man's head, then careened over the fence. Someone pulled out another knife. "Le'me try this one," the man said. He threw it, hitting the man on the stomach. The blade bounced to the sand. They all laughed.

David looked at Wayne and shook his head.

"Fuckin' hillbillies," Danny said.

"Have a try?" Bear said to David, holding out a knife.

"You got no fucking sense, Bear," said David, leaning back, arms folded across his chest.

"How 'bout you Podleski?"

"Get the fuck out of my face, you stupid motherfucker," said Wayne, the sun reflecting off his blond hair and round, plastic sunglasses.

"It's a dead gook, man, like a dead dog or cat," said Brun.

Bear held the knife out to Danny.

Danny looked Bear in the eyes, turned and spit on the warm sand.

The dead boy was no more than fifteen or sixteen years old, Vietnamese, dark hair, tanned skin, almost looked Mexican. The night before, he had set off a flare while trying to explode a claymore on the artillery's perimeter. The guys on the outpost had opened up on him with machine guns, rifles and grenades. After the firefight, they walked out and searched the bushes. His was the only body they found. They dragged him closer to the perimeter and dropped him near outpost number two.

When the guys woke in the morning, they all rushed out to look at him.

"He's just a kid," someone had said.

"Fuck that! He was trying to blow us away."

They had left his body there until noon. That's when Bear and Brun had tied him to the fence.

They were operating just outside a village near Phu Bai. As the American soldiers threw knives, the villagers walked past, going about their daily business, eyes looking straight

SHIFTING LOYALTIES

ahead, pretending not to see. They knew the dead boy. Most likely, he was a village son.

Bear walked up to the body and picked up his knife. He stepped back a few feet, raised his arm, ran forward and lunged, striking the boy in the chest. The tip of the knife cut the boy's skin but didn't go in very deep.

"Like rubber, man. Just like rubber," said Bear.

"That's some spooky shit. Let me try," said Brun.

He grabbed the knife, walked up to the boy, and plunged it into the boy's stomach. Again, only the tip entered, and Brun's hand shot back, as if he'd hit a wall.

More guys came forward to try.

"Like fuckin' shark skin," someone said. "Rubbery as hell."

"Shit, we got two more nights camped here. Let's warn these gooks not to be messin' with us no more," said Brun.

"Yeah, man. I'm fer that," said Bear.

"Help us."

David and Danny didn't move.

Wayne stood, his bare shoulders sunburned. He lit another Camel, took a deep drag, coughed. "You put that knife in my hands and I'll throw it at your fat ass, Bear," said Wayne, smoke curling from his nose and mouth.

"I'll cut yer fucking heart out, you dope smokin' Yankee," said Bear, smirking.

Brun and the others cut the body from the fence. They dragged the boy along the sand. When they came to the only road leading into the village, they tied a rope around the boy's ankles. They tossed the other end of the rope over a light post. The four pulled on the rope. Slowly, the body rose from the sand. They tugged. When the boy was about six feet in the air, dangling, they hitched the rope to a wooden slat and walked away, back to the artillery battery.

"This is what happens to bastards who fuck with us," said Bear as he passed David, Wayne and Danny.

"You're fucked up, Bear," said David.

"Weak stomach, Almas?"

"Not like your weak brain," Danny shot back.

"A sorry excuse for a human being," said Wayne, spitting bits of tobacco from his mouth.

"You been spendin' too much time with them Meskins, boy," said Bear. "Make yer Yankee ass soft...like them."

The Vietnamese—women, old men, and children—walked past the body. No one looked at it. It hung there, turning dark, disfigured, until about three in the afternoon. The blistering sun beat off the leathery skin. From their hootch, David and Wayne heard the battery commander holler, "Bear!"

"Yes, sir."

"Get that gook down from there before I court-martial your sorry ass."

"Just trying to teach 'em a lesson, sir."

"Cut him down—you sad excuse for a paratrooper."

"Yes, sir."

"And bury him."

"Sir?"

"You heard."

"Yes, sir."

Wayne crumpled an empty pack of cigarettes and tossed it towards a hole they'd dug for trash. He reached into his rucksack and pulled out a new pack. David looked at the can of ham he was warming. The grease bubbled over the round slice of meat. He picked up a piece with a plastic fork and chewed. He wasn't very hungry but ate it anyway. Wayne coughed and lit another Camel.

"You smoke too much," David said.

Wayne playfully slapped him on the back of the head. "This sure is a fucked up place, ain't it," he said, and continued smoking.

ELEVEN
THE GARDENER'S SONS
(THE MEDRANOS)

It was a narrow, triangular-shaped park located off Sunset Boulevard near Beverly Hills. Neighbors came by each day, some to walk their dogs, a few to throw frisbees, and others to lie in the sun—aluminum reflectors beneath their chins and quarter-sized cotton pads on their eyes.

Two men, both about thirty or so, sat on the grass, not far from their new Ford pickup. Chrome lawn mower handles stuck out the back, but no other tools were visible. One man poured wine into plastic cups. The other placed deli sandwiches and salads on paper plates.

The men were tanned; they wore Levi's, plaid flannel shirts and work boots. The tallest, stoutest of the two had a full beard and combed his light brown hair into a ponytail, like a lumberjack. The other was thinner, with short hair combed straight back and a carefully trimmed mustache. For gardeners, who had already spent half the day on the job, their clothes were surprisingly clean.

They stared as a blonde woman, nicely made up, walked by. She wore a yellow crop top and white shorts, tight, exposing her long tanned legs and flat stomach. She walked two white poodles, fashionably groomed, on a braided leather leash. The man with the beard and ponytail nodded. She smiled confidently, and returned the gesture. Their eyes followed her as she crossed the lawn, walked under a row of eucalyptus, and headed towards Sunset Boulevard.

The two men talked about how the Mexican and Central American immigrants were taking over the gardening businesses in the area. There was no bitterness in their voices, just concern. Their conversation moved from one topic to another, an idea, an incident, a joke. Then Victor Medrano, who wore the ponytail and spoke in a deep, assertive voice, mentioned the Vietnam War, Canada and two dead brothers.

"I should've split to Oregon when I had the chance," he said.

"That was a long time ago," said the other, Roland, Victor's cousin.

"I still think about it," said Victor. "I could've bought a little farm right outside Medford. Some 'bad' country out there."

"You couldn't have left your mom and dad, 'specially after Hector died," said Roland.

"Yeah, shit. Rudy's death...whew, put my mom in the hospital. When that tight ass'd sergeant came to our door to tell us about Hector...goddamn near put my mom over the edge. She ain't been the same since. You seen her, kind of just walks around."

"And your dad?"

"The Bossman? He really went through some changes after Hector died. Had big plans for Hector, used to say that after the Army, Hector was going to Cal Tech, be an electrical engineer. My brother was always messin' with stuff, taking apart watches and lamps, always fixin' shit."

Roland was silent.

"My dad hasn't said nothin'. Ten years an' not a word about it. Like it didn't happen; just holds all that shit in."

"Don't seem right, two brothers killed in one war."

"Yeah, well the government knows who to take and where to find 'em. A year after Hector died, they changed the law about brothers not serving in a combat zone at the same time."

"They could've took you, too?"

"Naw, I was married and had a kid. But, I wouldn't 'a gone anyway. Bunch a macho shit. Medrano or not. They'd 'a had to find my ass in Montreal or Ontario. I'd 'a gone to Mexico to beat the draft...ah, it's all a bunch of bullshit, man," Victor said, looking towards the street, watching the cars drive past.

He changed the subject and began complaining about the price of gas and the long trip to dump trash, an hour drive away—two hours in heavy traffic. He did most of the talking.

Roland listened, agreeing and tossing out a question now and again. He said, "So, wha'd your dad say 'bout you cuttin' what you send Bart for medical school?"

"Disappointed. It don't matter, though. I'm just a disappointment overall," Victor said, touching his full beard. "You know...I didn't go to the war. I was just a dope-smokin', woman-strokin' Chicano, never amount to much, no hero stuff here. I ain't like Rudy. Fucker was a pointman, and I think he dug all that shit."

"There ain't no heroes, just dudes stuck in tough spots lookin' for a way out," Roland said, chewing on his sandwich.

"My dad remembers how pissed I was when my brothers got drafted. I told 'em, fuck it, don't go, play sick, split to Mexico, or Canada. Me and the old man had some tough words. He said we had to show pride. Mexicans don't run. 'What about the people we work for?' I told him. 'Their kids don't have to go to no war.' My brothers died and them kids up in Holmby Hills were partying, dropping acid all day long. What kind of shit is that?"

"Medical school must be expensive."

"I told my dad I couldn't keep sendin' two hundred bucks a month to baby brother Bart. That's a lot of dough, maybe seventy-five or a hundred's more like it. I got my own kids to support. Shit, Catholic school's getting expensive."

"What'd he say?"

"Said I was the oldest, so it's my responsibility."

"Yeah, your old man can be tough."

"Why you think his friends call him the Bossman? Got a successful business, owns apartment units, two houses. Most of his friends ain't got shit."

"You just gotta tell him."

"I don't know. The old man's like, perfect, so he wants everybody to be perfect, and I'm a fuck-up, any way you cut it. In his eyes I just don't measure up." Slowly, Victor shook his head. "Whenever he looks at me, it's like, like I feel he's looking for my brothers in me. Like it ain't me he's seeing. He knows I could've done the Vietnam thing, and he'd 'a been proud. Ya know, it matters what he thinks about me. I try to pretend that it don't. For all these years I've pretended, but it matters."

As they talked, a pickup pulled in behind theirs. It was old, a '53 or '54 Chevrolet, and like theirs, clean. Gardening tools stuck out all over, organized: hoses hanging on wood posts, rakes, shovels and hoes standing side by side, a wooden tool box attached to one side.

"It's him," said Roland.

"Yeah, that's right. He said he'd come by for lunch."

Victor put on his biker sunglasses, gold wire-rimmed, shaped like the eyes of a fly.

Inside the pickup's cab, an old man rummaged around. His keys slipped from his fingers. Anxiously, he reached down and picked them up. Then he picked up his blue Dodger cap, placed it on his head, and stepped down from the truck. He was short, overweight, and swayed as he walked. He greeted the men and put down a brown lunch bag. He removed his canvas apron, folded and placed it neatly on the ground. He wore khaki trousers and shirt.

173

"Why don't you two make your lunches? It's cheaper. Save yourself some money," he said, eyeing the deli containers.

"Sit down, Pop," said Victor, annoyed by the comment.

The old man reached into his bag, pulled out a bulk of tin foil, slowly unwrapped a burrito, folded the tin foil twice, until it was a small square, and put it into the bag. As they ate, they talked, mostly about the weather and business, until Victor said, "Listen, Pop..."

"What's a matter?"

"About Bart, well..." Victor paused.

"*Mira*," said the old man. "I need to tell you something, first." He paused. "And I want my nephew to hear it, too."

Through the blue hue of his sunglasses, Victor saw a twitch at the corner of his father's face, a vulnerable tic he'd never seen before.

"It's something, maybe, I should have tol' you a long time ago."

The old man wiped his chin with a napkin and looked at his son. He drank water from a plastic container.

Victor waited. "What's that?" he said. He shot a look to his cousin then looked back at his father.

The old man said, "Was before the war." He hesitated, raised an eyebrow and continued, "The big war." He coughed. "The one in Europe?..."

Victor nodded.

"You never asked me why I didn't go fight."

"I figured you was maybe too young or something."

"No. I wasn't too young," he sighed. "That's umm, that's why I'm telling you. It started with a car. See, some guys had junker cars, nothing to show off...."

"A car?"

"Yeah."

Victor looked at his watch.

"But I wanted something nice, something that would make people turn. Maybe I was too proud? ¿*Quién sabe?* Anyway, my father, your grandfather, was against it. I had to drop out of school to work; let's see, must'a been around 1939. I planned to go back to school, but by '41 I was still working and, *bueno*, I never went back to school."

Victor picked at the grass, his eyes on his father.

"I worked two jobs every day, seven days a week. My father said I had to give him all my money from my day job, every penny, even overtime pay. Sometimes he go down to where I worked to make sure I was there. And I did, I gave him all of it. But the second job—that money was for me. I wanted a car, and I would work to get it. Maybe seem stupid to some people…a car, a piece'a metal and glass and rubber. To me, no-sir-ee, it was more. It was in my mind all the time, day an' night.

"My father said I didn't need a car, and by rights I should give him at least half the money I earned from my second job, since I was living in his house, eating his food. I never argued with him, never talked loud to him, so I gave him some of the money, *poquito*, just to make him leave me alone. Respect was a big thing in those days. Nobody talked back to their fathers, see. Still, I put some money away, put it in a jar and hid it under the house, next to a concrete piling."

The old man stopped talking and drank some water. A breeze rustled the sycamore leaves. He looked up for a moment at the trees, and his eyes descended and rested on his son, who was chewing on a dried twig.

Victor turned to Roland, gave a slight shrug, puzzled, then turned back to his father, wondering what this was all about.

The old man drank more water, wiped his forehead and began again, "Ooo, did my father get mad when he learn' that

175

I was keeping some of the money from him, called me *desgra-ciado*. I had to sneak whatever I kept. And I worked, some-times thirteen hours a day. The first job was in a factory. A good job. I carried car parts from the outdoor docks to the line workers who packed them into boxes. Heavy parts, cars in those days were all metal and steel, no sir, not plastic like today. When I finished carrying parts and my feet felt like pins going through them, they'd make me sweep and clean the place up. I was the youngest, so I got the dirtiest jobs.

"In the afternoons and at night, I would work at the building material yard, right there in Mar Vista. Hardest job I ever did do. All evening and night, I lifted fifty-pound bags of cement, one on each shoulder and stacked them up. I carried lumber, cement block, bricks, tile, you name it, I carried it.

"On my mother's grave, I swear, so help me God, I used to get home so tired I couldn't eat. Sometimes my mom, your grandmother," here he made the sign of the cross over his forehead and then kissed his cross-shaped fingers, "would come into the room I shared with my four younger brothers. She begged me to give up my second job. Sometimes she'd cry and I remember feeling her tears wet my arms. I wanted to quit. Lord how I wanted to. But now the car I wanted to buy was more than just a car. My father said I could never do it, never be able to save the money. But I'd show him. My mother would pour alcohol over my shoulders and back and rub until I could feel the electricity in her fingers burn my muscles. I could hardly take it, but when she finished, I could sleep and most of the pain was gone.

"I did this for, oh, a couple'a years."

Victor moved around, impatiently. He listened but kept wondering—the point, what's the point?

The old man took off his blue Dodger cap and scratched the few strands of hair he had on his scalp. Carefully, he replaced the cap and continued. "Mr. Jenkins, the boss at my second job, saw how hard I worked. Every two weeks he gave me a bonus, nothing much, but everything helped. My dad didn't think I'd last. When I'd get home at about nine or ten at night, he'd be sitting in his rocking chair, listening to his radio. His eyes would follow me from the front door to the kitchen and from there right into my bedroom. I'll always remember the crooked smile on his face, an ugly smile...ooo, *bien feo*.

"Some weeks he wouldn't even go to work. Why should he? I brought in plenty. The rent was cheap. The food, too. My mom yelled at him. He didn't care. She was careful, though, to not be disrespecting him. I remember one time he hit her, open hand. It was like a whip cracking, and I ran at him. I was only ten, maybe. He apologized. Said it would never happen again. 'Mexican men never hit their women,' is what he once told me. I know he was embarrassed. We all cried. My mom stayed in her room for three days. I suppose that's one thing I can say about him. He never hit her again.

"But I loved him, you know. He was my father. There were others worse. Still," he said, as an afterthought, "some who were much better, too. Even though he scared me sometimes, I always wanted to be around him. He'd chase me away, like one of those dogs, you know, the ones the owners kick and leave outside in the cold, hit them with sticks and sometimes don't feed them. But those dogs come back, even if it's for only one little pat, for them it's enough. That was me. Until I grew older, then I hid it, pretended to not care. But I loved him. Even in the end.

"Anyway, I went on like that for a long time, working two jobs, giving my dad most of the money and saving some for myself. But I knew the time was getting closer. I knew I had almost enough for my car, so, I started looking around.

"I went to all of the car lots in town. Ooh, in L.A. in those days, everybody was selling cars, or land. I wanted the car. The land I'd get later.

"Funny how all of the cars I liked I couldn't afford and the ones that I could afford I didn't like. I'd take a Sunday off from work and take the bus to where I could catch the streetcar, and I'd go downtown. I walked all over L.A., looking. Sometimes I saw cars that looked pretty good, but I wanted to be sure. The car I bought had to be perfect, worth all the suffering I had put on myself.

"I went to Long Beach and Wilmington, San Pedro. You got to remember, in those days that was an all-day trip. Not like today, a short drive on the freeway. Sometimes I would leave early in the morning and not get home 'til late, then get up at five and go to work. Ay, your grandfather would get mad at me, call me names, say I was stupid.

"One day, he didn't get mad anymore. Just like that. I couldn't understand it. I was glad, though, but at the same time, a little worried."

The next words he said slowly, "It's sad when you can't trust your own father."

He stopped, then began again. "About this time, my cousin, Chepo, comes over. He tells me about this old lady who his dad works for. She lives in Beverly Hills. Her husband died and left her his 1930 Ford. She couldn't drive, so she tells Eladio, Chepo's dad, that she wants to sell it; does he know anybody? Chepo and me jump on the bus and go to her house. She's waiting for us at her front window, a window as big as the wall of a normal house. When we walk up her driveway, she comes out and pats Chepo on the back. He introduces me. What a beautiful woman. Even though she was old, she was pretty. I still remember her eyes, brown and so big...and her skin, soft like cotton balls. Anyway, she walks us to the garage in the back, and I am getting nervous. She says to me not to get my hopes up because it's probably not much, not the kind of car a young man would want. She had trouble opening the garage door, so Chepo reaches over and tells her to let him do it. The doors creaked, but Chepo got them open. It was dark inside, a big, big garage, and there way in the back in the shadows, was the most perfect car I ever did see. Black, dusty, but still, the shine came through. It had a visor over the windshield, sparkling chrome, and the inside perfect as a living room, not a scratch on her, not a seam tore or out of place.

"I told the lady about all of the junk yards I been to, the car lots, the private owners...but never did I see a car more beautiful than this one. She smiled and asked us to go inside her house.

"When we walked inside, I felt sad because I knew that I wouldn't be able to afford it, even if she gave me a break on the price. A car like that...

"We sat in her kitchen and she gave us some coffee. She talked, but I had a hard time listening because I kept looking out the window, into the garage.

"Then she says, 'I want you to have the car.' Just like that. I got scared because I knew I had to tell her I only had three-hundred dollars, and I knew she'd have to change her mind. In some of the car lots I went to they wanted three-hundred dollars for scrap metal with wheels. But before I could tell her how much I had, she said that she knew I would take care of the car. It was special to her husband. I took the money out of my pocket and put it on the table, embarrassed, and I told her that was all I had. She looked at it, took two hundred and gave me a hundred back. She stared right into my eyes and smiled, nice, just like she knew what I was thinking. I started to argue with her, tell her it was worth more, but she put her hand up, like a princess, no...a queen, her eyes so kind, and—what's the word—passion, filled with passion, just like me, and she said, 'Not another word about it.' She just asked if we could stay with her for a little while.

"I talked a lot, but I had trouble concentrating. She wore a white dress, soft material, laces all around her neck. And I remember a shiny pin, one of those Jewish stars, perfect, like a diamond. I told her about my jobs and how I saved and worked. Sometimes when I talked, she would close her eyes, reach over and touch my hand. Forgive me for saying this, but no woman ever, not even your mother, made me feel what that lady's touch did. I can't ever forget that. Her hand was so soft and warm. And when I looked into her face, her eyes closed, lightly, her hand slowly moving on my hand, small squeezes, and it only lasted about a few seconds, and to me she became young and beautiful...."

Victor and Roland sat still, hearing nothing but the old man's voice. Nothing else around them mattered, not their work, not the park, the other people, the trees, or birds. The movement of his arms, his fingers gripping the water bottle, his head tilted to allow the water to flow inside him, was all performed with a delicate precision. The water bottle back in its place, the men sitting and waiting...he began again.

"I drove that car around town like I was a king. Wherever I went everyone turned, and it wasn't me that I cared about, oh no, not me, but the car. The car had a spirit, a soul... *ánima*, you know, something more than me. Call it safety, maybe security...*¿quién sabe?* maybe it was just love. But it was more than a car."

"I stopped working the second job, so I was free half-day Saturdays and all day Sundays. I would drive through Santa Monica and Ocean Park, along the promenade, down to the Venice boardwalk, and even the *Americanos* would stop and look, like if the car wasn't rolling on the street but maybe a foot off the ground. It was like everything ugly in my life had been washed away, like going to confession *¿sabes?* And I had done it right. I had obeyed, respected my father's demands, even if I didn't agree with him.

"My mom was happy for me...and proud. She never rode in the car...too embarrassed, she said. It was too nice for her. But I could tell that she gave me a new respect. And my dad ...well, he didn't change, said nothing but had that crooked little smile on his face, like he knew something I didn't.

"A few months later, maybe a year, after I bought the car, my dad's brother, Evaristo, came from Mexicali to visit with us. Every night my father and Evaristo would stay up talking and laughing. My uncle had only visited us twice before, and I liked him. My father had supported him while he stayed with us. He owned a neighborhood store in Mexicali and he didn't have much money, but he was a good man and treated his family good. Still, when I watched how my father acted, I knew something was wrong, but I couldn't figure out what.

"My uncle stayed with us for about a week, and the day before he is to go back to Mexicali, my father decides to throw him a big dinner. That's not like my dad. He doesn't throw nothing for nobody, ever. He invites the relatives and neighbors who live around here and tells them to bring their kids. My mother cooks for two days, and I really got suspicious when he hired a trio to play music. It was a Saturday and there must'a been a hundred people in our backyard, laughing and dancing, eating...kids running around, men joking. Then I knew. My dad probably wanted me to drive my uncle back to Mexicali, and he was softening me up. It's summer. Mexicali's a hundred and twenty degrees. It's seven hours from Santa Monica.

"Anyway, I was happy. I had washed and waxed my car that morning. My father didn't ask me to help with anything...

that was kind of suspicious, too. The party was good. I liked the food and I drank a couple of beers. So... if I had to drive Evaristo, I guess I would.

"In the middle of the party, my dad stops everybody. He hollers over and over, '¡Atención! ¡Atención!' puts his hands around his mouth and turns to different parts of the yard, '¡Atención!' Everyone is quiet and my dad goes to where the trio is playing. He calls his brother up, and says for him to come close, then he calls me up, and everyone is watching. I'm scared because I don't know what he wants me for. Evaristo doesn't know what's going on.

"Well, my father starts slow at first, then he goes and makes a big speech about how his brother is so special to him and how he has struggled to make his life successful in Mexicali. He goes on and on, and I get moved by his talk and by my uncle's struggles.... Then my dad says that he wants to make a very special gift to my uncle, one that will stay with him all the days of his life, and he turns to me and in front of everyone says, 'I am asking that my son, Alfredo, search his heart and perform the action of a hero and give to my brother, his uncle, the gift of a lifetime, the gift of a new car, so that Evaristo and his family can support themselves and will not have to walk the streets for the rest of their lives. And my brother can return to Mexico, his head high...' He kept talking, but I didn't hear nothing after that. I think everyone thought that we had talked about it already and that the whole thing had been a plan. Everyone started clapping and cheering. A few men jumped close to me and patted me on the shoulder. My father had beaten me."

As the old man's voice dropped, the hum of cars increased. He paused, then began again, "My father had that crooked smile on his face. In front of all the people, he held out his hand so I could give him the keys. I looked at my mother.

She looked scared. It was a shock to her. She only shook her head, and then she left the yard and went into the house. I waited, just for a minute. The people quieted down and my father's hand stayed in the air. I wanted to turn and walk away, leave him like that, in front of his friends, in front of his brother and children, his hand stretched out, waiting. I could see a look of fear cross his eyes. For just one second, he didn't know if I would do it. But you see, it wasn't really him that I would be disrespecting, but the family. He was just a bad part of a good thing.

"I reached into my pocket and pulled out the keys. I dropped them into his hand. Everyone cheered. '¡*Una ranchera!*' my father hollered. My uncle hugged me, and he said, '*Hijo*, you come to Mexico and stay with me whenever you want. Always, you have a home.' And the trio played, happy and loud.

"I went into the house and walked past my mother who was in the kitchen. All my brothers and sisters followed. My mother called out to me, but I didn't listen. I took two brown paper bags and packed my clothes into them. My mother came into my room and cried, telling me not to leave, that I shouldn't break up the family. I kept packing, took my jacket from the closet and told my brothers to divide the rest. I walked into the living room and my father stood close to the door with Evaristo and one of my father's *compadres*. They were happy, smiling.

"'What's this?' my father said, surprised that I would try to leave. I wanted to call him a son-of-a-bitch, a *gran cabrón*, *hijo de la chingada*...but I held myself back. I looked at him like he was the filthiest person in the world, and everyone saw it in my eyes. 'Apologize!' he screamed at me, 'Apologize!' He grabbed me by the wrist, tight, but I yanked, and he almost fell to the floor. I pulled free. My uncle Evaristo and the *com-*

padre reached out to stop my father from falling. He knew that with me gone, there would be no more money, and I could see a panic in his eyes.

"I walked past him, and as I did, I heard my uncle say, 'The boy didn't know about the car...' but my father ran out onto the porch. 'Alfredo! Alfredo! ¡*Si te vas, nunca vuelvas... nunca!* ¡*Oigame!*' But his words stayed in the air and I walked down the sidewalk and turned onto the next block. I wasn't really sure what was taking place inside me. Such deception I couldn't understand. Was there no loyalty at all? Maybe in that moment I learned that loyalty meant nothing, that each of us must watch out only for ourselves and nobody else. I remember that as I walked, my stomach turned, and I wanted to throw up, but a few minutes later, it was strange, like lightening striking, I felt lightheaded, and I was really happy... happy that everything had happened like it did...no more strings, no more ties, everything cut. I knew that I had been a good son, and now I was free. Yet what would the lesson cost? I knew part of it was his last words, that if I go I could never return."

A man in a jogging suit, a Doberman pinscher by his side, ran by the three men. The old man got to his knees.

"That's what you wanted to tell me, Pop?" Victor said, suspiciously, a wry smile on his face.

"Partly."

"What? More?"

The old man's voice shook, and he spoke slowly, as if confessing a grave sin. "The war came. My friends were getting drafted, some joining. I was confused, remember? Like you, when your brothers went to Vietnam. Anyway, I knew the draft would get me, and I thought about what I should do. I felt that pain, the pain my own father had placed in my chest, and I got bitter, and I chose not to wait for my draft notice, so

I went to Mexico and there I lived with my uncle, Evaristo, until 1945, working in his store. That's where I met your mother."

His next words were nearly mumbled, as if disgusted with himself. "When the war ended, I returned."

Victor took off his sunglasses.

"You dodged the draft?"

The man nodded, stiffly, mechanically.

"Why now? Why didn't you tell me?"

"To save you from what I've suffered."

"Suffered?" Victor's voice was loud.

"My punishment, my sentence. The lives of my two boys. They gave this country what I refused to give."

"What?"

"Loyalty."

"That's bullshit, Pop."

"*Hijo*, it's the truth."

"Rudy and Hector made their own choices, how they lived and how they died. That had nothing to do with you. A lot of people didn't go to the war, any war, some just had their parents fix it up for them, honorable draft dodgers."

"Only God knows," said the old man. He rose to his feet, picked up his trash, and listened carefully to the tone of his son's response.

"All these years, and…" said Victor.

"I'm not what you think I am."

"Okay, and now what is it that you want me to do?"

"Didn't you hear the story? Do whatever it is you must do."

"And what's that?"

"They took my two boys. Now two boys is all I have left. I won't lose you because I'm a selfish old man. Not like my father lost me. Whether you help your younger brother as I think you should, or not, I will love you, always, the same. You do what you know you must."

Victor sat, looking up at his father.

"I've got two more houses to do before dark. You both be careful," said the old man, walking to his truck.

Victor watched his father's truck turn onto a winding street, hedges, trees, and shrubs hiding the mansions on the hill.

"He carried that inside for all these years," Victor said.

"Maybe he didn't think you'd respect him—if he told."

"Of course I'd respect him. He's my old man."

"I guess that's the only important thing...respect."

"Come on, let's get out of here. It's getting late," Victor said, smiling.

The two cousins picked up their trash, got into their truck, and drove into the Hollywood hills above Sunset Boulevard.

TWELVE
BAPTISM

They were in the rear area for a short break before the next operation. Little Rod approached Danny and told him not to believe it, that Conklin was just bullshitting, "*Tomándote el pelo.*"

"Drinking my hair?" Danny responded, not familiar with the Spanish phrase.

"You know?" Little Rod said. "He's pulling your leg, teasing you. Man, you guys from Califas can't speak Spanish for shit, huh?"

"Why would he bullshit?" Danny asked, ignoring Little Rod's remark.

"*Tú sabes como son estos gabachos*, always lying, making up shit, gold brickin'—lazy bastards, do anything to get out of duty."

Alex walked up, beads of water rolling down his shoulders, a towel wrapped around his waist, his wet hair sticking to his forehead. "Man, these saltwater showers are for shit.... So what's happenin' with you guys?" he said, shaking out his hair and slapping at his ears, trying to unplug them.

"Conklin asked Danny to baptize him," said Little Rod, an unlit Pall Mall bouncing between his lips.

"Do what?" said Alex.

"Said he wants to be Catholic," Danny said, watching for Alex's reaction.

"Ha, you shittin' me?" Alex responded, turning slowly and walking towards his tent. "The dude's probably just bullshittin' you."

187

Danny and Little Rod followed. "That's what I tol' him," said Little Rod.

"Came up to me a little while ago, looking raggedy-assed, like always, like he's been sleeping for twenty hours in his fatigues."

"All wrinkled and shit, huh," Alex said, laughing.

"That's Conklin," said Danny.

"*Gabachos* got no pride in theirselves. Don't care how the fuck they look," said Little Rod, whose spit-shined jungle boots glistened.

"The stuff about Jesse Peña messed with Conklin's head more than it did us," said Danny.

"That's just because Conklin swears he seen Peña," said Little Rod.

"Man, don't start that shit again. Jesse's AWOL, and when he comes back, they'll throw his ass in jail. It's his own fault," said Alex, running a comb through his hair.

"I think Conklin's serious. He really wants to be baptized," said Danny. "When he asked me to be his sponsor, Conklin's eyes got all watery, his face looked kind of sad. Said he'd been taking catechism lessons from the chaplain. Every time we come from the field, he heads straight for the chaplain's office to study. The chaplain told Conklin that he needed a godfather. Asked me if I'd do it."

"Why you?" said Little Rod.

"'Cuz I'm Catholic. We're both from California, says he feels comfortable with me. Besides, he didn't know who else to ask."

"You're gonna fuckin' be Conklin's godfather?" Alex said, a smile at the corner of his mouth. He reached into his tent and pulled out a clean pair of starched fatigue trousers. He shook them, then put his right leg in first. "You're serious about all this?"

Danny smiled.

"If you're lying, I'll kick yer ass, Ríos."

"I swear to God. Why'm I gonna be lying?"

"To squeeze our nuts, that's why?"

"One thing about *pinche*, Danny. He don' lie," said Little Rod.

"Yeah...still sounds screwy to me."

"Conklin said he invited a bunch of dudes to the baptism. Everybody turned him down. It's all set for tomorrow night... in Phan Rhang. He wants you guys to go."

"At night! In the city? With gooks all over the place. Nothing but fuckin' Buddhists, man," said Alex. "I ain't going. Shit, I wanna party, not go to church."

"Conklin said the chaplain told him there's a basilica downtown, been there since the French were here. They're baptizin' a bunch of people, mostly Vietnamese."

"And you got permission to go into town at night?"

"As long as we get escorted by the chaplain."

"Well, fuck. I'm staying here an partying. We only got a couple of days before we're back in jungle," said Alex, tucking his shirt into his pants and rolling up his sleeves to his elbow.

"*Orale*, Danny. You're gonna be a cracker's *padrino*. *Qué gacho, ese*," said Little Rod.

"You gonna go, Little Rod?"

"Naw, *ese*. I'll be partying with Martinéz."

"You guys are punks, man."

"You're the godfather, man, not us," said Alex.

"I'll ask David and Wayne; maybe Doc Langley will go."

"Conklin ain't won no personality contests lately, Danny. Ain't nobody give a fuck about watching that speed freak get baptized," said Alex, taking a cigarette from Little Rod.

✪ ✪ ✪

The church was filled with Vietnamese, married couples, teenagers, children, grandfathers and grandmothers, many wearing dresses and suits, some of the women *ao dais*. Two priests said Mass; one was the American chaplain and the other a Vietnamese Monsignor.

The place reminded Danny of the cathedral in San Francisco, though not so large. Everything was here, the side chapels, statues of the Virgin and saints, stained-glass windows, Stations of the Cross, sculpted pillars, flickering candles, a painted cupola. He listened to the familiar Latin. An organ and choir hummed at the rear of the church.

Conklin stood next to six Vietnamese, both male and female. He was the tallest. Danny stood to Conklin's right.

A rumble of heavy footsteps caused Danny to turn. Through the entrance walked David, Wayne, Big Rod, Little Rod, Alex, and Doc Langley. They took their seats in the last row. Danny smiled. Conklin didn't turn to look.

Alex, who wasn't Catholic, watched as the congregation stood, knelt, sat. He tried to follow, became confused, and decided to sit through the rest of the service.

The two priests walked from the altar, down the steps towards the assembly and through an opening in the railing. They said prayers, first in Vietnamese, then in English. The Vietnamese priest, who was young for a Monsignor, smiled at Conklin and the others.

Conklin bowed his head and closed his eyes. His arms hung at his sides. The American priest nodded, a signal for the sponsors to place their right hands on the shoulders of the people to be baptized. Danny could feel the bone in Conklin's shoulder. The smell of incense permeated the church. The American priest spoke in halting Vietnamese and made the sign of the cross over each person as the Vietnamese priest sprinkled water on their foreheads. When he reached Conklin, the Vietnamese priest said, in perfect English, "Do you, John Conklin, renounce Satan and all his evil deeds?"

"Yes, Father," uttered Conklin, his chin to his chest.

"Do you, John Conklin, promise to follow the teachings of Jesus Christ and the holy Catholic Church?"

"Yes, Father."

"My son, I baptize you in the name of the Father and of the Son and of the Holy Spirit...."

Conklin lifted his head as the chaplain placed drops of water on his forehead. Danny turned to see. Tears ran in shiny rivulets down Conklin's cheeks. Danny squeezed his friend's shoulder. Conklin dropped his head again. He whispered, "Amen."

The congregation applauded as the priests and communicants turned and walked down the main aisle. The organ played. Danny walked behind Conklin, hemmed in by the rest of the people who followed them out.

In the warm night, a burst of camera flashes lighted the darkness. The Vietnamese families and friends were embracing and shaking hands with the newest converts. Conklin stood alone.

David approached him first, said congratulations, and shook his hand. The other soldiers did the same. Conklin smiled and thanked them all for coming. They all rode back to Camp Eagle in a 3/4-ton pickup, went to the EM club, and partied until midnight.

✪ ✪ ✪

Two weeks later, near the end of his tour, Conklin told Danny that he had "extended" for six months. Danny told him not to do it, that he'd regret it. They argued, but Danny could see there was no use pursuing it.

191

Conklin received an immediate thirty-day leave, the standard reward for extending a tour. He flew back home to Manhattan Beach. At the end of his thirty days, Conklin didn't return.

Six months passed and he was still AWOL. The word in the brigade area was that the CID had seen him in San Francisco. He had grown a beard and long hair. He was wasted on acid and weed.

"It'll be just a matter of time before they ketch his ass," said Wayne.

"See there. He set us up. The whole thing was a bunch of bullshit," said Alex.

Danny just shrugged. He wasn't so sure.

They didn't hear from Conklin again. Back at Fort Bragg, a year later, there was a rumor that he'd been caught and sent to Leavenworth, but nobody could confirm it.

THIRTEEN
THE WAY CHARLEY YAÑEZ TOLD IT
(JOEY SERRANO)

The order was to "jump" or lose our fifty-five dollars a month allotment. Joey Serrano didn't like it. "Vietnam's no place to practice jumping," Joey had said, refusing the beer Green held out to him. It wasn't like Joey. He never refused alcohol.

"We ain't practicin'," said Green, taking a sip from the can. "It's a matter of economics—fifty-five bucks worth. I ain't about to lose mine. That's one reason I went Airborne: fifty-five-dollar jump pay, plus fifty-five combat pay, and a hundred and six base pay. Whoowee. I'm a settin' pretty."

"Buy your ass a lotta cornbread, huh, Green?" said Manny Cardoza, laughing.

"Shee-it," said Green. "Buy you more tacos to stick in yer greasy belly, Cardoz-ass."

Joey wasn't listening. "I don't like it," he said. "Shit, we might get ambushed out there. I got this ugly feeling."

"No way," said Green. "The whole brigade's gonna be jumpin'. That's damn near...what? Three-thousand dudes. Who's gonna ambush that many crazy bastards? Don't worry about it. It'll be a gas."

"I just got this feeling, that's all."

Joey complained all week, complained until the night before the jump, convinced something was going to happen to him. He didn't know what, but he felt it, like an omen...a straight-out shitty feeling, and he wouldn't touch a drop of booze, even though we could see he wanted it.

"You'll be okay, *ese*, *vato*. Pretend you're a bird, floatin' on pretty wings, sailing over the Nam," said Albert Alvarez, who

193

had a talent for calming guys down, as he did after Hector Medrano blew himself up trying to booby trap a trip flare by using a grenade. The guys who heard about it couldn't believe the thing had blown Hector into a million pieces.

"Hector knew the chances, man. They told 'em not to try it. Always experimenting an' shit, trying to do stuff everybody knew was dangerous. God's will. *Asina lo quería Dios*," Albert had said, philosophically, as he struggled with his own demons. He himself was trying to give up his own vices, even curbing his urge for drugs. But his appetite for women zoomed: at base camp Albert spent every spare minute with the prostitutes. One time, to make curfew, we had to drag him off a gorgeous Vietnamese woman, pulling him by the legs. All the way back to camp, Albert kept insisting, "I had her going, man. She was loving it." Manny finally had to shut him up by telling him that while he was doing it, the woman was chewing fish, finishing her dinner.

"I'm telling you, Beto. I can feel it inside. Something's gonna happen to me. Maybe my chute won't open or I'll hit a tree...." Joey said.

"We're jumping in a rice paddy. There ain't no trees," said Albert.

"All right, then maybe I'll hit a dike, or drown in the sludge."

"Come on, Serrano. Those paddies ain't but a few feet deep."

"I don't know, man. I never felt this way...never, and I don't like it. If I don't die, I might end up a cripple, like my uncle Maimonides."

"What kinda name's that?" someone else had said.

"Greek," said Manny.

"Sounds Italian," said Albert.

The fear was in Joey's eyes and voice. We all looked at each other as he spoke. We smiled, thinking he was trying to make us nervous. Joey did things like that. We all did—teased until we scared ourselves silly, like when Ricky Jiménez asked Bobby Pacheco before their first operation, *"Ese* Bobby, you scared?"

"Naw, what's to be scared about...." Bobby had said, his eyes round as ping-pong balls.

"Shit," said Ricky, "I bet I couldn't push a needle up yer ass with a bulldozer, ah?"

They had both laughed.

✪ ✪ ✪

The next morning before dark, they trucked us to the airfield outside Phan Rhang. It had been a long time since any of us had jumped. After an hour's refresher course, sharpening us up to the finer points of the "blast," we loaded up our shit, put on our chutes and boarded the planes.

"*¡Orale!*" yelled Albert, who was only about one hundred and thirty pounds. "Airborne! Paratroopers *por vida.*"

Carrasco, a sergeant first class, about three-hundred pounds, a twisted, gritty face, a World War II vet, hash marks up and down his sleeves, passed by Albert and growled, "You little shit. You wouldn't make a pimple on a paratrooper's ass."

So, there we were, inside the belly of a C-130, a thousand and two hundred feet above the jungle, lines of C-130s coming in over the drop zone. Westmoreland had sold it to the press as a combat jump, and we were loaded down: weapons, full combat gear, all one-hundred pounds of it, and the area they'd chosen to drop us was as secure as the Vatican.

My unit was in a plane located somewhere in the middle of the formation. We were all standing, lined up, checking our equipment, the red light glaring at us, wind rushing through the open door, the jump master checking out the drop zone. Green light. We leaped, one guy after another, no hesitation, slapping the static lines and jumping into that three-hundred-mile-an-hour prop blast, bodies twisting like leaves in a hurricane. We descended over those rice paddies, miles and miles of them, green checker boxes, parachutes filling the sky. I hit the ground...soft soil, softer than the drop zones back at Fort Benning, like landing on a mattress. There were gooks all over the place, carrying baskets of shit, selling sodas, beer, bread, souvenirs, war medals, NCO patches, chrome jump wings, CIB's, even a few prostitutes running around telling guys they could do it in the tree line, take no more than a few minutes.

The sky was full of chutes...madness, chaos, guys coming out of the sky, hitting the paddies, and falling through straw roofs. Platoon leaders were running around, yelling, "C'mon! get yer asses off the DZ. Take up your positions on the dikes." We ran from the paddies, dragging our chutes, placing them on the dirt roads where vehicles came by and loaded them all up, easy, no sweat.

They grouped us by battalions. Some guys later said they caught sniper fire, but I didn't hear a thing. We slung our M-16s, adjusted our rucksacks and marched back to base camp, right through the middle of a good-sized town. It was WWII relived. People lined both sides of the road, waving, throwing flowers and paper streamers. We threw kisses, chocolate bars, and we waved, just like we were walking down the middle of Fifth Avenue.

That night, after supper and all the excitement was over, we all met near the edge of the battery area. When I arrived, everybody was quiet, sullen.

"What the hell's up?" I asked.

"Joey," somebody said. "They fucked up his shit, man."

"What're you talkin' about?"

"He hit the ground, A-OK, laughing, you know, happy to be safe."

"And?"

"Some gook broad came up to him, carrying a load of sodas and beer, you know...cold, ice water dripping from her basket."

"Yeah, so?"

"Joey bought a beer. Tiger Piss 33, man."

"He did what?"

"A damn stupid mistake."

"I thought he stopped drinking."

"Me, too."

"Stupid...stupid."

"The shit had Drano in it. Didn't get him right away. I heard that when he started walking, he fell out, straight to the ground, holding his stomach."

"Is he dead?"

"Not the last I heard."

"He'll be okay, though...huh?"

"Naw. The doc says he's gonna die, ain't no way a dude can live through that. Probably already dead. Just a slow way to go ¿sabes? Internal bleeding and shit like that. Probably dead already, poor Joe, man."

"See there, he knew it. Told us something was gonna happen. That's some scary shit, man."

That's how Joey died. None of us saw it happen, not really, but that was the story going around the brigade area. We never saw Joey again, but Manny Cardoza did. He went back to the States to escort Joey's body and to report to the family what befell their kid, except he was ordered to say Joey died of

197

stomach problems, sickness, and not to elaborate or give
details.

The thing about Vietnam was there were a lot of ways to
go. Sometimes when you thought you were over the hump,
knew you were safe, had it "dicked," that's when they'd get
you, *puta madre*...put your shit out to dry, like they did Joey
Serrano. Only, he was expecting it.

FOURTEEN
FIVE DAYS IN THAILAND
(DAVID ALMAS)

David entered the hotel lobby. A porter took his duffel bag. Another man tapped his shoulder. "You want taxi? Number-one driver."

Before David could answer, the porter gently pushed him through the throng of noisy American soldiers. "Room 445," called the clerk, who stood behind the marble registration counter. The chattering voices were confusing, chaotic. "Fill out form," the man said, hollering above the din. He slapped a card and pen on the marble counter and turned to another soldier. David scribbled his name, unit, place of service—Chu Lai, Vietnam, and handed the form to the clerk, who then gave him a set of keys.

He couldn't remember ever being in a luxury hotel before, couldn't really remember being in a hotel at all. He looked at the lushly carpeted staircase that led to private conference and dining rooms. He could see through the glass doors and into the restaurant, white table cloths, glasses and silverware spread on each table. Palm trees and ferns rose from corners. Plush couches and chairs decorated the lobby. Mural-sized oil paintings hung on the walls. David looked at his key.

"Hey, Almas. This is really something, huh?"

David turned. It was the soldier he'd met at Phan Rhang while waiting for the flight to Cam Rhan Bay. Both soldiers had chosen Bangkok for their R&R. David had heard the Thai women were beautiful. Other guys had chosen Kuala Lumpur, Australia, Japan, Singapore, and Hong Kong.

"Can't hardly believe it," said David, looking around at the chaos, the teenage soldiers calling out to each other.

"What room you got?" the soldier asked, straightening his plastic glasses.

"445."

"I got 440. Must be right down the hall from you. Wanna meet downstairs later and get a Coke or something?"

"A Coke?" David said, a taint of sarcasm in his voice.

He stared at the freckled-faced paratrooper, who resembled Alfred E. Newman.

"Henry, look. All I want to do is take a two-hour bath and sleep, all night long," David said, hoping to discourage the young man from hanging around.

The soldier looked at his watch. It was 8:00 P.M. "Hey! You can sleep. Me, I want to see everything. I'll call you later, see if you change your mind," he said, turning and walking away.

"Yeah, sure," David said, hardly believing the innocent-looking soldier was a grunt, attached to the 502nd infantry, the O'Duece, that prided itself with the motto, "Widow Makers."

Once inside his room, David threw his bag on the bed. He walked directly into the bathroom and filled the tub. The steam rose to the ceiling, condensed into drops, grew heavy, and dripped down the walls. He kicked his clothes into a corner. He dipped his toes into the water and shuddered, delightedly, then sank in slowly, one inch at a time, until finally he lowered himself all the way in. He lay still, afraid to move, afraid to lose the moment. When the burning water had lost its edge, he dunked his head underwater, surfaced, and let out a loud, grateful yell.

He lay there for an hour. The steam cleared. He looked at the porcelain, the tile, the gold water faucets and handles. A knock startled him. He stood, dried, and wrapped the towel around his waist. The knocking continued. He stepped across the carpeted room, leaving a trail of damp footsteps. Through a wall-length window he could see the darkness stretched across the sky.

"What, man?" David said, as he pulled open the door, expecting to see Henry, the bespectacled paratrooper.

"Hello. My name Mr. Dom, best chauffeur in Bangkok, maybe Thailand, huh? I show you town!"

"Sorry, I can't use a chauffeur."

"Sure, you can use! I take you best restaurant and bars in town, show you pretty girls, good music."

"I only got twenty-five dollars on me. I'm staying around the hotel tonight."

"Nobody stay around hotel. Everybody go to bars. You got personal check? You need to cash? No problem."

David was suspicious.

"Tonight you no pay me. You go downtown. Have good time. Tomorrow I show you where you cash check."

"I...I don't know."

"Sure you know. I wait you downstairs."

David stood at the door. Soldiers passed, talking loudly, laughing, wearing civilian clothes, and crowding around the elevator.

"You see, everybody going for good time."

David turned, his eyes scanning the room, the dresser, chairs, lamps, couch, and queen-sized bed. He thought about Alex and the guys in the field, somewhere outside Chu Lai. He knew no one in Bangkok.

He breathed deeply and looked at the man before him, a stranger, a foreigner. David's room was silent and lonely. He had planned on sleeping, but now the isolation crowded in on him. "All right. Gimme twenty minutes," he said.

The man was smiling as David closed the door.

He put on a pair of khaki pants and a blue pull-over cotton shirt. He was about to slip into his black G.I. dress shoes but changed his mind. At the bottom of his duffel bag was a pair of wrinkled brown loafers. He decided to wear those.

As David stepped from the elevator, he saw Henry sitting on a green-cushioned chair.

"Change yer mind?" said Henry, even more innocent in his civies, like a college student. He wore dark-blue chinos and a Madras shirt. His face was flushed, red, his freckles sparkling, probably from rubbing too hard in the shower.

"I take two you...." said Mr. Dom, walking towards them.

Henry turned. Mr. Dom stood a little over five feet tall.

"This is our driver for tonight, Mr. Dom," said David.

"Hi-ya," said Henry, shaking the man's hand.

The lobby wasn't crowded, not like earlier. David noticed Anglo and Asian businessmen dressed in dark suits, briefcases by their sides. There were a few Asian women. They wore evening dresses, sedate colors but tasteful, expensive. They looked like celebrities, aloof, indifferent.

Dom led them to the car, a white Plymouth four-door. He sped down the wide, crowded boulevard, dodging the slower traffic, while talking about the Bangkok nightlife, girls and sights. David sat quietly, staring out the window at the night, the trees and buildings.

He had been in Vietnam eleven months and one week. Three more weeks and he'd be on his way home. He hoped they wouldn't send him back to the field after his R & R, not with only two weeks remaining on his tour.

He listened to Dom's squeaky voice and wondered how much the wily driver would charge. David couldn't remember ever taking a taxi. As a kid he'd taken a bus everywhere. Nobody used taxis, couldn't afford them, and besides, in L.A. everyone owned cars.

David had left a five-hundred dollar check in the hotel safe. His mother had withdrawn it from his savings and sent it to him a week before. He hoped the money would get him through the five-day leave. Some guys, he'd heard, had spent as much as a thousand to fifteen hundred.

Dom turned onto another boulevard. It was crowded, bright, and the traffic slowed to a near stop. Henry smiled and looked around. Everywhere colored lights were flashing, cars honking, and people hollering on the crowded sidewalks. David sat up, resting his arm on the window jamb. Smoke rose from the outdoor restaurants.

"I'm glad I left my room," he said, barely moving his lips.

Dom found a parking spot and quickly pulled in.

"I wait here. You go long you like," he said, pointing to the brightly lit nightclubs and cafes.

"Wow!" Henry whispered as he stepped to the sidewalk.

Other than the cheap, pre-fab bars in Vietnam that smelled of sex and sweat, David had never been in a nightclub. He was twenty, still too young to drink in the United States.

They entered a club. Sparkling lights—reds, blues and greens—flashed around the door. It was a cavernous room with a long bar, bottles of alcohol from floor to ceiling, hundreds of tables scattered about, mostly filled with young Americans.

On stage, an Asian woman in a tight dress and high heels, bellowed in a lusty voice, "Here comes your nineteenth nervous breakdown." She sang with no accent. The organ vibrated a rhythmic line as the bass pulsated and the walls boomed. The electric guitar spun a high-pitched whine and pierced through the voices, cat calls and clinking glasses.

A hostess escorted David and Henry to a table where they ordered drinks, David a rum and Coke, Henry a Pepsi.

"Man, you drink a Pepsi and you go sit somewhere else," David said, tapping his foot to the rhythm and looking at the crowded dance floor.

"I don't drink."

"Well, you're drinking tonight."

The waitress, wearing a flesh-grabbing mini-skirt, waited, smiling at David.

"What do I order? I hate the taste of booze," said Henry, removing his glasses and wiping the lenses with a hankerchief.

"Bring him a screwdriver," David said.

There were women everywhere, standing along the walls, walking between the tables, sitting on guys' laps. Many looked like starlets, beautiful, long legs, flat stomachs, small shoulders, silky hair. Above their breasts, pinned to their dresses and blouses, were numbers, identifying them as bar girls—prostitutes who had regular medical checkups, a precaution against V.D.

David eyed Number 6, a tall, thin woman whose hair was bobbed. She reminded him of an Asian Natalie Wood, smooth skin, seductive eyes. She wore tight bell-bottoms and a striped tank top, her bare shoulders shining beneath the flashing multi-colored lights. She danced with a muscular American, his blond hair cut short. He wore a Hawaiian shirt, the sleeves rolled high to show his hard biceps. The woman moved slowly, her hips swaying, her shoulders straight, feet sliding smoothly.

David sipped his drink, unable to take his eyes off of number 6.

Women came to his table. At first he was too nervous to dance. After a little time—and two drinks—they coaxed him to the dance floor, their hands warm, comforting. He closed his eyes, arms close to his sides, hands turned into fists, mov-

ing to the rhythm of the Harlem Shuffle. When he slow
danced, he felt the firm, curved flesh under his hands, the
skin next to his cheek. The women pushed close to him, slipping a leg between his. When the music finished, he turned
away quickly and returned to his table and drank more, gulp-
ing down each drink and crushing the ice with his teeth.

Henry also danced, moving clumsily. He drank four
screwdrivers and talked incessantly, confessing his virginity.
He told David that he'd never had such a great time. It was a
night he'd never forget.

When the eyes of Number 6 met his, David was dancing
with a bleached-blonde woman. Number 6 was dancing with a
different soldier. David smiled, his head dizzy from the liquor.
Number 6 smiled and continued looking at David.

When the song ended, he returned to his table. Henry was
chattering with an older woman, who wore glasses and a dress
too small for her chunky body. David sat down. Number 6
stood behind him. He turned. She smiled, more beautiful up
close.

"I think you didn't notice me," she said.

"Oh, I saw you. But I thought you were with that other
guy."

"No. Tonight I don't work. Tonight I just dance. My night
off."

"Can I buy you a drink?"

"Thank you, no. I must go...finish for night."

David was puzzled. He hesitated, then asked, "You'll
come back another night?"

"Tomorrow my night off. I come back night after dat. You
come see Kim?"

"The night after tomorrow?"

She nodded, smiling and looking directly into his eyes.

"Ah, yeah, sure, okay. I'll be here."

"Very good."

She turned and walked away.

David laughed. He kicked Henry in the shoe, excited by his good luck. Henry signalled, one thumb up.

David turned to watch Kim disappear into a back room. He vaguely heard Henry say something about wanting to travel to Jupiter, a dream he'd always had as a kid, that one day people would live there, maybe before the year 2000. David shook his head.

The band played a slow song. A woman asked David to dance. He took her to the dance floor. She held him closely, rubbing his back with her hand. She laughed, holding onto his arm.

Back at the table, he swallowed another glass of rum. His vision blurred. His mind dulled. Again, he danced with the same woman and held her tightly. She breathed lightly on his neck, her warm breath moving down his shoulder. She looked into his eyes. David smiled. He noticed the number, 78. She was older, maybe thirty, a youthful body, thin, firm. She wore yellow pants and a pink sweater. She asked where he was staying. He said the Parliament Hotel.

"You want Chakra?" she asked.

He swallowed and nodded, shyly.

She took his hand and led him from the dance floor. She whispered something to a man, a tall Asian who wore a mustard-colored suit.

It was 3:00 A.M. Henry wasn't ready to go back to the hotel.

"How long you staying?" David asked.

"Oh, 'til the night runs out."

"Be careful, man."

"Affirmative," Henry said.

Dom met David and the woman on the sidewalk. "Car over here," he said, pointing.

The traffic was light. Dom spoke to the woman in Thai. David sat back and closed his eyes. She took his hand. The night was peaceful.

✪ ✪ ✪

The knock at his door the next morning startled David. He sat up, rubbed his eyes and looked at his watch. 11:00. He heard the shower. The knock continued, a loud banging. He looked for his pants. The room was clean, not messy as he'd left it the night before—clothes hanging over chairs, duffel bag tossed in a corner, shoes in a pile.

He walked to the closet. His clothes were on wood hangers, neatly organized, shirts all facing the same direction, pants carefully folded, his duffel bag placed neatly on a stool. He scratched his head, pulled a pair of Levi's from the hanger, put them on and opened the door.

Dom stood there, smiling.

"Dav-eed. Good morning. You come now. We go see Bangkok. Go cash check. I show you Number 1 place."

David nodded. "How about a bank?"

"No, no. Bank charge big-time fee. You go with me. I show you."

David fumbled, "I...ah, well. I don't have all that much money, not for a full-time chauffeur."

"You don't worry. Mr. Dom cheap. I stay with you all day, drive you everyplace. I pick you up in morning, bring you home at night."

"How much?"

"Twenty-five-dollar-a-day, twenty-four-hour service. I show you good time."

David studied the short man. His smile was genuine, intelligent. There were wrinkles at the corners of his friendly brown eyes.

David had heard stories of G.I.'s getting "rolled," especially in places like Tokyo and Singapore, guys getting beaten, killed, their money taken.

"I don't know," David said.

"You check hotel management. Ask about Mr. Dom. They give good reference. I chauffeur many year."

"I believe you...twenty-five a day, huh?"

"Pretty cheap."

"Give me thirty minutes."

They shook hands.

The woman walked through the bathroom door. She was dressed, her make-up applied. She was older than David remembered. She smiled enthusiastically and walked to David, kissing his cheek.

"We go now. I take you breakfast?"

"No thanks. I have a lot of business to take care of."

Her excitement waned.

"Chakra stay with you, take good care of you, be your woman for week."

Images came to him, the alcoholic stupor, a blurry haze, her arms and legs wrapped around him.

"I don't think so. I have friends I need to see."

"I go with you. I number-one tour guide."

David didn't want to argue.

He showered and dressed. There was no need to shave. He had no beard.

The woman sat waiting. She had made the bed and placed his shoes neatly against the closet wall. As he buttoned his shirt, he glanced at her, remembering more clearly the night before, her naked body pressed against his, an hour of kisses, his body melting into hers, the jolting sensation, the disappearance of pain, and the staggering warmth.

Her nose was flat, her eyes round, light brown, like walnuts. Something about her was sad, tragic, and he wanted no tragedy in his life, not now.

When they entered the lobby, Dom stood and came towards them. She held David's arm. He tried to wriggle free, but she held on tightly. Dom looked at her, then at David.

"We go," Dom said.

"Wait a second," David said, pulling his arm free, signaling her to wait. He moved a short distance and whispered to Dom, who looked over at the woman.

The chauffeur smiled and nodded. He walked to her, his hands flapping like a bantam's wings. Dejected, she looked at David. When Dom finished, she walked towards the glass doors, waited for them to open, and walked outside into the heat.

$$\text{❂ ❂ ❂}$$

From the main boulevard, Dom turned and raced into an alley. Brick and concrete buildings shaded the asphalt. He slowed, spun the steering wheel, and entered another alley, darker than the first. He drove fast, whizzing past trash cans and discarded boxes. David touched his wallet, relieved it was still there, the five-hundred-dollar check tucked safely inside.

"They honest businessmen. Take care of you," said Dom, keeping his eyes on the narrow street, dogs yelping as he passed, children standing close to the walls.

David perspired. He wanted to tell Dom to go to the bank instead, fee or no fee, but he was embarrassed that he might insult his host.

Delivery vans parked near the walls. Drivers unloaded boxes and packages. Old men, haggard and disheveled, smoke rising from their cigarettes, lined one doorway. Dom stepped on the brakes and parked the car next to a row of rusted barrels. He stepped out. David opened the back door and stepped into the alley.

He joined Dom, who stood before a black steel door. Dom knocked. The bang echoed. He peered into a square glass at eye-level. Again, David touched his wallet. The door opened. A tall, muscular Asian man stood staring at them, his face bitter. He wore a blue suit, gold shirt, and brown tie.

"You cash check for my friend...." Dom said.

The man smiled. He opened the door wider.

David looked up and down the alley. Dom entered the building. David followed. The three walked down a dim, narrow hallway. On either side, neatly stacked wood boxes reached the ceiling. One bare light bulb dangled from a frayed cord.

They came to an entryway. A coarse gray cloth separated the rooms. The man pulled back the thick material and entered. Dom held out his hand and motioned for David to go next. David paused, the man looked at Dom, and stepped inside. The bright lights surprised him. When his eyes adjusted, he saw rolls of silk fabric, reds, greens, yellows, golds, and blues. There were glass shelves displaying jade figurines, elephants, wizards, jaguars, snakes, and Buddhas. There were mahogany carvings, elegant sculptures, sets of gold and silverware, sculpted trunks and chairs, antique lamps and jewelry, glass case upon glass case. Customers, speaking German, Italian, Swiss, Japanese, and different Asian languages, browsed, holding up various objects.

The Asian man motioned to David. Dom pulled out a stool from beneath a glass case. David sat. A woman asked if David wanted a beer. David nodded. She placed a glass in front of him.

He held it up. "Not too generous with the liquor, are they?" he whispered, wrapping his fingers around the tiny glass.

"Hello, my friend! Hello," said an older Asian man, smiling, his white hair shining. He wore a dark suit. He was clean shaven, handsome, probably in his sixties.

Dom stood, respectfully, and shook the man's hand.

The man gave a slight bow.

"Well, well. May I see your check?" he asked in perfect English, a British accent.

David handed the man his check.

"Ah, yes, Bank of America, internationally stable, locally honored. No problem here. I will return in a few moments."

David rose from his seat.

"No, no. Remain sitting, my friend. Look at the merchandise. Enjoy your beer...and remember: probably you will never visit Thailand again. It is your opportunity to buy quality gifts for yourself and your loved ones. Make yourself at home," said the man. He turned and walked to another room.

David sipped the beer. It was strong, and he hadn't eaten. His head buzzed. He looked around the room, took another sip, and smiled, happily. He saw a Seiko watch inside the glass case. He'd never owned a watch, and asked to see it. The clerk nodded, reached into the case and placed the watch on a velvet pad. David picked up the watch.

"How much?" he said, sipping his drink.

"Twenty-four dollars, top quality," said the clerk.

"I'll take it."

David pointed at a silver ring, the sides engraved with lines like delicate thread, a black star sapphire set in the middle. He tried it on. "Yeah, this too," he said, winking at Mr. Dom, who patted David on the back.

David hadn't ever bought anything for himself, except a couple of Ritchie Valens' albums and some 45's, but never anything expensive.

"How 'bout gift for your mother?" asked the clerk.

"Like what?"

"Ah, look." The man reached to a shelf, took down a finely sculpted mahogany box and placed it on the counter.

David looked at the hand-carved designs, faces and flowers. The clerk opened the box and the goldware gleamed, spoons, knives, forks, a setting for twenty-five people.

"Yeah, how much?"

"Twenty-eight dollar."

"Wrap it up."

The clerk beamed.

"And how about those elephants?" said David, pointing to three miniature teak carvings on another shelf. "And that head, too," he added, showing the clerk the bust of a youthful Buddha.

"Ten dollars for all," said the clerk.

"Okay."

He turned to Dom. "Man what'd they put in that drink? I'm fuc...I mean feeling great."

Dom shrugged, "Maybe little opium, huh."

"Whew. I don't doubt it."

He bought a silk *ao dai* for his sister, a jacket for his father, and he was about to buy a suit for himself, when Dom pinched his arm. "You buy plenty already. Remember you got to ship stuff home...big cost."

"Yeah, that's right," he answered. "I don't wear suits anyway."

"How about silk suit, pinstriped?" the clerk asked.

"No, that's fine. I just need to ship it all home."

"No problem."

The clerk handed David a mail delivery form and an ink pen.

The man with the white hair returned. He placed five one-hundred-dollar bills on the counter. David took one and gave it to the clerk. The white-haired man smiled when he saw David's purchases.

"One day," said the man, "you will look at your gifts and remember Thailand. Once-in-a-lifetime experience, my friend."

"You'll mail it—all?"

"It will arrive to..." He picked up David's form. "2627 Vance Street, West Los Angeles, 90025, before you arrive there," said the man smiling. "God be with you, young soldier."

David and Dom left through the back door. Motor bikes were parked in the alley, next to the buildings. Young men made deals, passing objects—boxes, packages, bills—back and forth. Garage doors flew open, revealing homes inside, couches, tables, chairs, throw rugs, and children sitting around eating, laughing, chasing each other. Mothers swept the floors and fathers stepped into the alleyway to throw trash and sweep the street. David smiled at a boy who played with a string and sticks. The boy also smiled.

"Where we go?" Dom asked.

"You decide," David said giddily, hopping into the back seat, sitting low, as if he were cruising in Santa Monica.

Dom drove into the jungle, some miles outside Bangkok. He passed farms and plantations, towns and villages. Palms and banana trees clung to the roadside, the asphalt highway cutting through the thick foliage like a black vein.

An hour later, Dom stopped at a Buddhist pagoda where orange-clad monks and tourists, cameras hanging from their necks, walked among the trees, halls, and fountains. In the

213

center, a gold Buddha, twenty-feet high, sat cross-legged, an ominous grin on his lips. Siddhartha, David thought, staring at the peaceful saint, remembering the novel by Herman Hesse, the one his teacher had assigned for English class during David's first year in college.

Outside the pagoda, Dom bought two bowls of soup and handed one to David. The vendor stirred the warm liquid in a metal cauldron that was attached to a wood cart.

David sat on the pagoda's stone steps and savored every spoonful of soup, which was red, spicy, and reminded him of his mom's *albóndigas*.

When he finished, he walked alone along a jungle path beside a creek. Palms, orchids, philodendrons and ferns hung over the water. He thought about Alex and the guys. He hoped that the doctors wouldn't amputate Danny's foot. He thought about Jesse Peña, and wondered if he'd ever return. If captured, Jesse would be sent to Leavenworth. No woman was worth that, even if Jesse was in those warm arms every night, which had happened to a lot of guys who'd gone AWOL; some even got married, running off with Vietnamese hookers. Would Jesse ruin his life, give up his country, his family?

David placed his hands in his pockets and peered into the water, listening to the rush of the current, the dribbling and whooshing sounds of the breeze and stream. A green parrot with yellow breast and bent beak looked down at him and screeched, the cry echoing and disappearing in the brush.

Once inside Dom's car again, they drove along the narrow jungle road. David saw a row of bamboo structures, some stores, and a bar. He asked Dom to stop. The two stepped to an outside table where David ordered a cognac and a beer. Dom drank a Coke. Before he left, David finished three shots and two beers.

"You have good time?" Dom asked.

"A *toda madre*," David answered.

"What that mean."

"The world's beautiful."

He reached his hotel room at 3:15 P.M. He fell asleep and woke at 5:30.

Earlier he had noticed a massage and sauna parlor adjacent to the hotel. He brushed his teeth, washed his face, and walked next door.

She was the shortest and prettiest of the women. She sat on a bench with five other women, their shapely legs exposed beneath short, white smocks. They chattered when they saw David. One giggled. David whispered to the manager, who walked to the woman, leaned down and spoke to her. The woman, who was in her early twenties, smiled, rose, stepped to David, took his hand and led him through an open door, down a freshly painted white hallway, and into a carpeted private room. It was furnished with a green upholstered armchair, divan, glass coffee table, and a raised leather massage table covered with a fitted white sheet.

The woman walked to a sunken bathtub and opened the faucets, both at the same time. The hot water steamed. David remained still, noticing the painted, tiled walls and ceiling, blue flowers on every fourth tile. His hands hung by his sides. He watched her slow, graceful movements.

She touched the water with her long, slim fingers, turned and walked to him. He wanted to wrap his arms around her and pull her to him, feel her lips press against his, her small, curved body in his arms.

"You plenty tired, huh?" she asked, as she unbuttoned his shirt.

"I don't sleep much."

"Shiu make you feel better," she said, slipping his shirt from his shoulders. "You no have too much hair. American soldiers have lots hair. You look like Thai man." She giggled and ran her hand over his bare chest.

He smiled, embarrassed.

She tugged at his belt. His knees stiffened. He sucked his lower lip and turned his head towards the opposite wall. His zipper opened. Her hands were on his legs. She pulled down his underwear and trousers in one quick movement. She slapped his calf, playfully. He turned slightly, excited, ashamed. She led him into the tub, where he sat in the hot water, steam rising to the tiled ceiling.

As she bathed him, her fingers touched each part of him, washing carefully, professionally, and when she touched his inner thighs, she spoke, asking him about his home, girl-friend, family. She did nothing sexual or embarrassing, but cared for him, as if she were his friend.

Shiu dried him and guided him to the table, where she massaged his toes and feet. The perspiration poured down his forehead. Her fingers were like sparks.

He lay on his stomach and closed his eyes. She spread ointment over his shoulders, rubbing his spine, buttocks, legs and calves. She rubbed, kneaded, pushed, pulled, even got up on the table and sat on his buttocks, her bare legs touching his skin. She rose to her knees and slid over his back, pushing gently against the back of his rib cage, along his spine. David breathed hard and placed his forearm over his mouth, smoth-ering his sighs. She hummed, her voice a single-stringed Asian instrument, one he'd heard often over village radios, an exotic melody, mystical, dissonant yet harmonious, enigmatic like a Mayan wood flute.

When she turned him over, she placed a square towel over his thighs and stomach. Sitting on his legs, she bent down and pushed the bottoms of her palms along his chest, circling his nipples, lining his collarbone and neck. David clenched his teeth. He looked at her dark, curled hair, loose strands falling alongside her ears to her shoulders. Her neck was long, narrow, and smooth. He pulled her down to him. She gasped, surprised, smiled, and kissed him, hard. He ran his hands over her cotton smock, down her legs. She pulled away, breathing hard, looking at him, confused, excited.

"No. No can do. Massage only. You be good boy," she said, sitting up and continuing her work.

"Shiu, you're so beautiful. I've never made love to a beautiful woman, ever."

"Ah, not true. You Number 10 butterfly," she said, teasing, one eyebrow rising, her eyes on his.

"What's that?"

"My girlfriend see you at bar last night. You dance plenty girl. Not go home alone. You take friend. You butterfly."

"Butterfly?"

"You see too many flower. You want to go to all flower, not stay on one," she smiled.

David laughed.

"Let me take you on a date."

"No can do," she said, continuing the massage.

"I no bar girl. I massage girl."

"If I pay your boss what he wants, will he let you go with me?"

"You need talk him. He no like girls working outside business."

"Shiu...."

"Sorry," she said, shrugging.

She placed her hand on David's forehead, lay on his body and kissed him. They kissed, deeply, like teenagers on their first date. Minutes passed. They breathed hard, their bodies together, the pulsing rhythm mingling. David reached down, placed his hand on her bare thigh, beneath her smock. Her hand caught his.

"No joke. I can not do more. You nice, almost look like Thai boy."

"What if I talk to your boss?"

"No, you no talk. He get angry me."

"I need to see you again."

"I like you," she said, as she wiped the remaining ointment from his body and dressed him.

He looked at Shiu, at her powdered cheeks, oval eyes, curled lashes, the high school girlfriend he never had.

"I'll see you again," he said.

"Butterfly, please, no come back. You get away from here. Find bar girl, have fun. Soon, you go back Vietnam, forget Shiu, forget Bangkok. I massage you no more, please, butterfly."

She moved close and kissed him, long and softly. Then, she opened the door and led him back to the waiting room where he paid the manager and left.

✪ ✪ ✪

That night, Dom drove David and Henry back to the club. They each drank six shots of cheap tequila and three bottles of beer. David looked for Kim but didn't see her. Other girls asked him to dance. David declined. Shiu was all he talked about. Henry sympathized. He told David about Eileen McGill, the high school prom queen and varsity head cheerleader.

"Didn't even know I existed," said Henry.

"A dream love, un...unreal, something that can't happen," said David, slurring his words.

"Rodger that. I mean, at lea...east I should have told her how I fe...elt," said Henry.

218

"You should've laid it on her."

"She would've laughed in my face."

"A bitch, beautiful or not. She was a bitch."

"Ya th...ink?" Henry asked, stumbling over the last word.

"If you're sure she'd laugh in your face, she's a bitch."

"Whooo, I'm dru...unk. Let's get out of here."

David downed his last shot. As the music blared, he and Henry walked outside into the warm, musty air. The sidewalk was crowded, mostly G.I.'s and bar girls.

"You go home now?"

David turned. Mr. Dom stood there, smiling.

"What time's it?" said David, trying to see the blurred hands on his new watch.

"2:25."

"No, I'm hungry," said Henry, leaning against a wall, the red lights from a neon sign lighting his face.

"Me, too. Shit, Mr. Dom, I ain't ate nothing but that soup you bought me."

"Okay, good restaurant. Come I show you."

At the outdoor restaurant, they could see the cooks working, smoke rising from the woks and pots.

"I go back to car and wait," said Dom, pointing to the car.

"Lemme buy you som...omething to eat, Mr. Dom." said David.

"Oh, no, no. I already eat, while you and Henry inside drinking."

"C'mon, join us," said Henry, pushing his glasses off his nose, his eyeballs wandering.

The driver laughed, waved, and went to his car.

David looked at the cooked food, four or five different pots full.

"Man, that stuff right there, looks like *chile colorado*, stuff my grandma used to make," said David.

"Chili what?"

"Never mind. I'll order for both of us," said David, grabbing the counter to steady himself.

He pointed to the food, raised two fingers, and paid the cashier.

"I want to know everything about this world before I die," said Henry.

"Let me have two beers," David said to the cashier.

"Two beer!" the man called, reached into a refrigerator and handed David the bottles.

David gave one to Henry. They both drank.

"What's there to know?" said David. "One day we're here, next day we're gone."

"There's more to it than that. We're all here for a reason. I want to know what it is. Why're we born? Why're we raised by the people who raise us? Why aren't I black...or Indian...or Metzkin, like you?"

David squinted and looked at Henry suspiciously. "Look here, there ain't no answer for that shit. It is, and that's it. We are what we are and there ain't no use asking why. Just make do. Live each day for today, let tomorrow worry about itself."

A man in a white apron, shirt, and cap handed David two plates. David gave one to Henry. The food smelled of garlic, cooked honey, and chile. David put a forkful in his mouth.

"Man, this is some good shit. I swear to God, it tastes just like Mexican food."

"I don't know. I never ate Mexican food. This tastes okay...a little spicy."

"You need to move some of them cells from your brain to your taste buds, man."

Henry laughed.

"What's that shit you're eatin'?" said a goliath, redheaded American, looking at Henry.

"I don't know what it's called," Henry said.

"We bought it right here," said David, stepping aside and pointing to the kitchen.

"Gook food! You fuckers're eatin' gook food," the man said, staggering on the sidewalk, bumping into another man, who passed by, among the crowd.

"It tastes pretty damn good to me," David said, shoving more into his mouth.

"Come on, Marty, let's go," said another man, slapping the redheaded soldier on the arm.

"Anybody that eats gook food is a gook-lover."

The man was a foot taller than David and heavier by fifty pounds.

"Man, then why don't you go find some meatloaf and potatoes and leave us the fuck alone," David said, putting his plate on the glass counter, keeping his back against the wall to steady himself.

The redhead stared at David, then at Henry. "Shit," he said, "I'm going back to Tay Ninh tomorrow. We made contact everyday for the past month...every fucking day, man." The man's eyes softened.

"Here brother, take a drink," David said, handing the man his beer.

The man reached out. "Thanks." He drank and handed the bottle to David. "Every fucking day, contact," he said, then turned and stepped into the crowd. "Take it easy," he said. The words seemed to come from all the soldiers on the sidewalk.

"Yeah, you too," David called.

"We can analyze that guy," said Henry. "He's scared, so he needs to take it out on someone else, someone different than he is, so he's taking it out on anyone with slanted eyes.

Pressure, man, an' heaps of it. What's it all about, David? That's what I want to know. What the fuck's it all about?"

David finished his beer. He reached out and took his friend's empty bottle. Henry's eyes were glazed, his freckles bright red. Wrinkles crossed his forehead.

"I don't know, man. It's life...that's all," David said.

"But if we can figure it out, we can control it."

"Can't control the wind, man, or the ocean."

"We can make it work for us, stop bad things from happenin', or make them happen differently, for our benefit."

"Henry, you're too far out there for me, brother, way too far. C'mon, I'm tired as hell. Let's find Mr. Dom and get our asses to bed."

Henry turned and looked at the people, a carnival crowd, Coney Island on a Friday night, the voices, the hollering, the laughing, the calling; Asian music echoing in the night, cars honking, Thai women hanging onto American arms—servicemen in civilian clothes, post-pubescent children playing a role, a pretense, each night sleeping with a different woman, suckling foreign breasts, plunging against female thighs—boys gritting their teeth, crying out at hotel ceilings, at jungle skies, at shadowy trails, at hidden weapons, and at shattered lives.

"No, you go ahead," said Henry. I want to walk around a bit. I'll take a taxi later."

"Henry, it's late, man. Dudes get rolled out here alone, ripped off, killed."

"Here or...back there...what's the difference?"

"What's that mean?"

"Nothing. I'll see you in the morning," Henry said, and drifted away.

✪ ✪ ✪

As he stepped from the elevator, David looked around the lobby.

Mr. Dom sat in a chair, closed the newspaper he'd been reading, and walked to David.

"You sleep pretty late, huh? Almos' 1:30."

"Yeah."

"Where we go?"

David hadn't thought about it. There were no tours, nothing planned. Most of the guys started for the bars, drank all morning and afternoon, returned to their rooms, slept, and hit the bars again at night.

"You don't worry," said Dom. "I take you see Bangkok."

"Yeah, all right," David said, an ache at the base of his neck.

Dom drove through the main boulevards, pointing out stores, hotels, and other new businesses. David thought about Shiu, her eyes, her mouth, her laugh, and her voice. He told Dom about her.

"No, not good place to find girl. Too expensive. Massage okay...boom boom bad. Owner tough man, like Mafia man. Keep close watch on girls, afraid of V.D. Shiu beautiful woman. I know her little bit. Very, very expensive."

"I've got money. I'll pay what he wants."

"Not good idea, ah. You maybe get Shiu in deep trouble," said Dom, his eyes studying David in the rearview mirror. "You don't look good?"

David leaned back and looked out the window, seeing nothing. "No, Mr. Dom. I feel pretty bad."

Dom drove through the city, past monuments, gardens, hotels, and businesses. He pulled into an alley, not far from the river. He drove slowly until he came to a group of boys playing soccer in the middle of the alley. He pulled his car to one side and parked.

DANIEL CANO

David opened his eyes. "Where are we?"

"This my house. You come in…rest."

It was a garage, two levels. The living room faced the alley. David noticed the couch, the carpet, the chairs, the black and white television that was placed on a dark wood dresser. Three young children played on the floor. Behind the living room was the kitchen—stove, table, chairs, and refrigerator. A wood cabinet held the dishes and glasses. Above the kitchen was a loft.

Dom's wife, wearing a simple dress, her hair pulled back in a ponytail, stirred pots over the stove. The aroma filled the small room.

"You rest," Dom said, pointing to the couch.

He spoke to the woman. She moved to David. Her teeth were pushed a bit forward. Her eyes were friendly, kind. She smiled and said something David didn't understand. He stood and shook her hand. She motioned him towards the kitchen. A child held a toy truck out to David. The child made a noise, imitating a car engine. David took the truck, slid his hand beneath the wheels and made a louder noise. The boy laughed.

"Come, time to eat," said Dom, pulling a chair from the table.

"Oh, I don't want to be any trouble."

"You don't be trouble. Come and eat."

David sat. The children smiled at him. They ate fish soup, rice and cooked chicken. The children spoke. Dom translated as best he could.

After lunch, David sat and played with the kids on the floor, building bridges with crudely cut blocks of wood. Dom helped his wife in the kitchen.

"You still tire', huh?" said Dom as he looked at David's lowered eyelids.

"I'm okay."

"You come with me."

Dom led him up the stairs. There were two double beds, a dresser, and a varnished crate used as a table. A soothing shadow covered the loft. There was no window. A fan turned gently, blowing a stream of air across the room.

"You lie down, short rest. I wake you in little while."

"Naw, I'm all right. Thanks anyway," David said, glancing at the bed, the breeze cooling his scalp.

"You rest, really, it okay."

David sat on a bed. It was soft. Slowly, he removed his shoes. Dom went downstairs. David lay back. It was like being home again. He closed his eyes and slept.

It was late afternoon when he awoke. Outside the sun was still bright. The alley outside Dom's house was busy, children playing and vendors pushing carts along the street. David walked downstairs. Dom turned. He and his wife had been on the couch, talking.

"I need go store," said Dom, smiling. "You go with me."

"Sure," David said, then turned to Dom's wife. Not knowing how to thank her, he bowed, as he'd seen Asian people do in movies, and he said, in English, "Thank you very much. I feel better, very good, very good."

Dom translated.

The woman smiled, also giving a slight bow.

"My store pretty expensive," said Dom. "Prices in Bangkok too high."

"Dom, is there a PX around? I can get anything I want, and cheap."

Dom smiled.

An hour later, they returned to Dom's house, carrying six bags of groceries, plenty of American canned foods and cartons of cigarettes. David insisted on paying.

On his way back to the hotel, Dom saw a young woman sitting at a bus stop. "This my friend. Okay I give her ride her house?"

"Yeah. Fine," David said, sitting up to look out the window. When the woman saw Dom's car, she rushed forward. They spoke in Thai, quickly, chuckling between lines. She opened the door and stepped inside, sitting in the front.

"This David," Dom said to her.

"Hello, David, I'm Mayon. Glad to know you."

David nodded to her. "Glad to know you."

She was dark skinned, a round nose, full lips, and mischievous eyes, like a naughty child.

"Mayon," Dom said, "she a whore." He laughed, loudly.

"Not whore. I work hard," she said, slapping him on the shoulder.

David smiled awkwardly, not sure what to say.

They drove along the river. Sampans, canoes, boats with oddly shaped sails, flat barges, and cargo ships floated with the current. The sun was a vibrating orange ball.

"She make G.I.'s happy. She a good whore. Number 1 in bed."

"Sure I good, best in business. Customer love me."

"Lot experience."

"I know business."

"Her... ah, how you say—big, like barrel," Dom said, slapping the steering wheel. He laughed, turning his shoulder to one side.

"Oh, you dirty man." Mayon punched his arm. "Mayon not so big. I make plenty men happy."

David watched them as if they were brother and sister arguing over a silly topic.

"See," she said to Dom, "you make David embarrassed."

Dom pulled alongside the road and parked next to a house built on stilts over the river.

"Come, you visit with Mayon," she said, stepping out and opening David's door.

They crossed a wood walkway that led to the house. The bamboo walls were waist-high, netting and canvas reached to the ceiling. There was a main greeting room and two bedrooms. From every room, the river was visible.

An old woman sat in a wood rocking chair next to a table.

"This my grandmother," said Mayon, introducing her to David.

He moved close and shook the woman's hand. She smiled, her teeth stained red from years of chewing beetlenut. Dom stepped to the woman's side and kissed her on the cheek.

"You want something to drink?" Mayon said to David. "Beer? Whiskey?"

"Whiskey."

David and Dom sat at the table while Mayon walked into one of the other rooms. When she returned, she wore a shiny, green shift buttoned at the neck. Her brown hair rested on her shoulders. She handed David a glass filled with liquor. She gave Dom a Coke and opened a beer for herself.

David asked many questions, about her family, about the house, about school, and about living in Bangkok. Sometimes only Mayon answered; sometimes Dom spoke. An hour or so later, Mayon took David into the bedroom. She opened her closet. "Look. Presents from American G.I.'s."

Rows of colorful dresses, suits, and shoes filled the wall-length wood armoire. She showed him her drawers, filled with sweaters, blouses and pants.

"Pretty good, huh?" she said, proudly.

"I've never seen this many clothes in my life," said David.

"Dom!" she called, then turning to David said, "Come we sit on, how you say, ah, patio."

She took David's hand and led him though a screen door to a patio covered by a bamboo awning. He heard the sounds of the river, the water rushing against wood and steel hulls, propellers slapping through the current, whistles blowing, people calling from boat to boat.

Dom carried David's drink. Mayon's grandmother brought a platter covered with cooked seafood and brown rice to the table. David thanked her. Mayon served him a plate. The sun dipped, only the upper half shining in the eastern sky.

"Thank you for letting me come here. Your home is a beautiful place," David said.

"You come back any time," said Mayon, rubbing David's shoulder. "You good friend Dom, good friend mine."

After the sun disappeared and they'd eaten, Dom announced that it was time to leave. David thanked the grandmother, who laughed excitedly.

"I never bring customer my home," Mayon announced.

The old lady said something and giggled.

"She say you cute guy, look like Thai boy," said Mayon.

✪ ✪ ✪

David stepped from Dom's car to the sidewalk. People entered and exited the hotel. A taxi driver honked.

"What time you want me pick you up?"

David looked at his watch. "How about ten. That'll give me time to shower and rest."

"Okay, sure, ten."

Before he entered the double-glass doors, David looked at the building next door, an extension of the hotel. He knew that Shiu was inside, working, her hands spreading ointment over the naked body of another American soldier. David wanted to see her. He read the words Oriental Massage printed over the front door.

The air was hot, humid. He stood still. Limousines and buses edged past, the engines rumbling and exhaust clouding the air. He looked down at his shined shoes. They reflected the evening lights. Again, he stared at the white building, his eyes on a lighted upstairs window. He waited to see if a silhouette appeared. Nothing. He turned and entered the hotel lobby.

After his shower he poured a glass of whiskey, took a long drink, and lay naked on the bed, his body sinking into the mattress, the soft bedspread rubbing his skin. He ran his hand over his bare chest. Tonight he would meet Kim and bring her back to this bed. It would be his second woman. He sat up and gulped his drink. The liquor burned his throat and rushed to his head. He saw Shiu's face, her smile, her eyes.

He finished his drink and poured another, the liquid rising halfway up his glass. He drank, taking two swallows, coughing, his nose burning. He lay back, hands by his side. His thoughts flickered, rushing from idea to idea, vision to vision, from Shiu to Kim, to Mayon's home, the river, the sunset, the alley where Dom lived, the children, his first night with Chakra, her small breasts and body. He slept.

A few hours later, he sat up, his vision hazy. He called Henry's room. No answer. He dressed and slapped lotion on his face just as Dom knocked. They walked outside together. The night air, though warm, refreshed him.

✪ ✪ ✪

Kim sat at David's table. He drank too much. They danced. The colored lights shone against his face. He blinked and shielded his eyes. His head whirled. The American men all looked the same, big, light-haired, loud. He wasn't aware of

Kim's beauty, or her thin, curved body. She was a woman. He danced, held her close, and squeezed. The hours passed. She laughed, her eyes cocky, professional. He drank, one shot then another.

In the early morning darkness, they walked to the car, Kim steadying him as he staggered limply. Dom drove them to the hotel. They went to his room and fell to the bed. She tried to slow down his wild fingers, lips, arms. He fell back exhausted, staring at the shadows on the ceiling.

"You drink too much," she said, her head on a pillow, her eyes on him.

"No," he breathed, panting, his head dizzy, "I'm okay. Just need a rest. I can do it."

"Too much drink no good."

"Too much drink okay," he said.

She whispered something he didn't understand. She slid her hands over his shoulders. He rolled on top of her. The moon's reflection entered the room, a bright ray crossing the carpet. Kim lay still. He finished and apologized. She rose, dressed, took the money, said goodbye and went away.

After the door closed, David lay awake. He watched the semi-darkness inside his room, the dawn outside his window. His eyes and head throbbed. He tried to remember Kim's face, her body, but there was no memory. He pulled a pillow over his face, held it tightly, turned in his bed, locked his knees, pushed them to his stomach, and listened to crickets and running water, the jungle's silence, Jesse Peña's chuckle, and Danny Ríos's yells. He ran to the toilet and fell to the floor, wrapping his arms around the cold porcelain, and he heaved, coughing, spewing forth everything in his stomach, until he could hardly breathe, and his eyes watered, and he wiped away everything with a rough towel, dropped into the bed and slept. The sun rose, another burning day, and the heat woke him, sometime late in the afternoon.

✪ ✪ ✪

When David stepped into the car, Dom sensed his anxiety. Without asking, he drove to an outdoor restaurant where he made David eat soup, rice, and drink a lot of water. From there, Dom drove David downtown, to a movie theater. He parked on a side street.

"What's here?"

"Oh, good American movie...James Bond."

"Movie?"

"I want to see. Don't get to movies too much. You take me, huh?"

"Man, I don't feel like a movie."

"You go movie back home?"

"Not too much."

Dom looked disappointed. "American movies, number one," he said.

"Movies are for old people who got nothing better to do. You know, married people, couples...those types."

"You take Mr. Dom see James Bond."

David didn't care enough to argue. "Man, all right, let's go."

Thirty-foot movie posters, mammoth advertisements, decorated the sides of the tall, modern theater, Sean Connery and an Asian woman hanging onto him, mini-helicopters flying around his head, a volcano in the background.

You Only Live Twice, David mumbled, reading the marquee above the theater.

The ticket line stretched three blocks down the busy boulevard, and a crowd swarmed the entrance to the theater.

As the people stood in line, they ate lunches and talked excitedly, some having waited all afternoon.

"Dom, this is for shit, man. I ain't gonna wait in this line."

"No worry. You give me money. I take care everything."

David reached into his pocket and handed Dom a bill. Dom walked into the center of the crowd. David stood in the shade and watched the line push and swell as the theater doors opened. Five minutes later, Dom returned, smiling, waving two tickets over his head. He called to David, and they entered the theater, walking past everyone.

"How'd you do that?"

"Oh, no problem. I tell them you big-time American Army officer visiting Thailand."

They sat in the balcony, first row. Dom went downstairs to buy candy. When he returned, the theater was filled, the audience buzzing. The lights lowered. The projector clicked. The screen brightened, newsclips and advertisements brought cheers. The feature film started. The voices were in English, with Thai subtitles. David was back home. In the darkness, he forgot about Thailand, Bangkok, Vietnam, the 101st Airborne.

Nancy Sinatra crooned the theme song, "You...only... live...twice...or...so...it...seems, one...life...for...yourself, and one...for...your...dreams." The American music was laced with Asian instrumentation, flute and lyres, delicate, dramatic, melancholic. Only the characters on the screen mattered, James Bond, handsome, strong, stereotypically European, the British secret agent in Japan, investigating the disappearance of a free-world missile. The movie transported David away for two hours, into the love, the drama, the mystery and humor of Hollywood.

When the film finished and the crowd erupted in applause, David had forgotten where he was. Slowly, the house lights brightened. He heard the voices. There was no language, only a jabbering sound, homogenous, ubiquitous. He got ready to go home. He straightened his back and shook his head vigorously, and he heard his dog tags rattle. He shivered, and remembered where he was.

"Good movie," Dom said.

Surprised, David looked at the foreign face, slanted eyes, wide smile.

"Really good."

The movie stayed with him, the love story between the Asian woman and James Bond, the conflict with the villains. He could see the love scenes and he heard Nancy Sinatra's voice and the music, subtle and beautiful.

David asked Dom to take him back to the hotel. Dom nodded. He sped through the traffic and talked about the movie, David half-listening. In front of the hotel, Dom pulled the car into a parking spot and turned the key. The engine died.

"Dom, I want you to go up there and get Shiu for me."

Dom turned towards David, hanging one arm over the seat.

"Not good idea."

"I don't care how much they want for her."

"She owner girlfriend."

"You weren't in that room when we talked, Dom. She likes me, a lot, and I like her. If I could, I'd take her back home with me."

"You marry Shiu?"

"Yes."

Dom smiled. "David, all G.I. feel that way 'bout Thai girls. G.I.'s here for five day, then go back war. You all fall in love quick with Thai girls. You not love girls. You confuse love with freedom from war. Shiu not whore, not like other girls."

"I'm not like other guys. Sometimes I feel Thai. Look at me, my face, my eyes, my skin color. Do I look American?

Maybe I am a Thai man. All I know, Dom, is that I've gotta see her again, and not in that place."

The driver was momentarily silenced by David's words, and David had no idea why he'd said them.

"How much money you have?"

David thought. "Two hundred."

Most girls went for ten dollars, all night.

"You sure this what you want. Shiu won't be happy 'bout this."

"Whatever it takes."

Dom opened the door, stepped out and leaped to the sidewalk. He strutted towards the massage parlor. David waited.

Twenty minutes later Dom returned, his face wet, his eyes nervous. He got back into the car. "Okay. One hundred. You pick up at 10:00 tonight at massage parlor. Tomorrow morning Dom pick her up at 7:00, take her home."

They walked to the hotel room. David gave Dom the money.

"Go have dinner, Dom. Come back at ten."

"Okay," Dom said, and left.

"Dom," David said. "Thanks."

The door closed.

○ ○ ○

Shiu was sitting on a couch when David entered the massage parlor. She wore a lime evening dress, her white neck and shoulders bare. The hem was cut slightly below her knees. Her hair curled down to her shoulders, waved bangs touching her arched eyebrows. Five other girls, wearing their white smocks, sat on padded seats. An older man, dressed in brown slacks and a tan long-sleeved shirt, stood at one corner of the room, his arms crossed. He glared at David. The man turned to Shiu and nodded. She rose and walked to David.

They turned and walked through the door.

They rode the elevator downstairs. Neither spoke. When the doors opened, David placed his hand on Shiu's lower back, nudging her forward. She moved quickly, as if to avoid his touch.

"Shiu, I had to see you," he said.

She didn't answer.

They walked past American soldiers in uniform. The men stared at Shiu. One whistled. Europeans, men and women, stood on the sidewalk waiting for a limousine. Their heads turned as she walked past.

David's throat tightened. He perspired. His heart pounded. He saw Dom's car and led her to it.

"You Americans think you can buy all things you want," she said, looking straight ahead.

David swallowed and wiped the sweat from his eyes.

"I tell you not see Shiu again. Why you not listen to me?" she turned towards him, her eyes hard.

"I thought you liked me," he said, his voice soft.

"That why Shiu not want see you again. In two days you go back Vietnam. I not toy. I not bar girl."

"We can talk, Shiu. Nothing else. We can go to dinner and talk. Then Dom can take you home," he said, stopping and facing her, looking directly into her oval eyes.

"You already pay for Shiu. Do what you want!"

Dom opened the car door, and they both sat in the back.

He drove through the outskirts of Bangkok, passing suburbs. Palm trees lined the curbs. He drove along the river, past docks, homes, and warehouses. He stopped at an outdoor restaurant, built on a pier, overlooking the river. Dom waited in the car as David and Shiu stepped to the street and walked to the restaurant, where a waiter, dressed in a white coat, seated them. The restaurant was crowded, and David was the only American.

The waiter spoke. David looked at Shiu. She said nothing. David spoke, but the man didn't understand. The waiter looked at Shiu. They waited. She looked into David's eyes for a long time. Silence. David held his breath. Finally, Shiu spoke to the waiter. He returned with two glasses of cognac. They sat quietly.

David looked at the people around him. He heard Japanese, French, Vietnamese and Thai. The waiter brought a basket and set it on the table. Inside was cooked shrimp.

"You give too much money for Shiu. Make boyfriend mad. How can he say 'no' when you want pay so much money?"

"I'm not rich, Shiu. Before the Army, I worked taking care of rich people's gardens. After Vietnam, I'll go back to college and get a better job. The money I brought to Thailand...well, I've been saving it all year. I know it's a lot. It's a lot of money to me, too. But I saved it for one reason, to come here and have a good time. I never thought I'd meet anyone like you. I'm sorry if I made things bad for you and your boyfriend."

"He my fiancé," she said, taking the glass in her hand and raising it to her lips.

Quickly, David grasped his glass, raised it, and held it close to hers.

She looked at him.

He said, "I hope you're happy, Shiu. I hope you'll always be happy, forever."

She didn't speak.

They drank.

David placed his glass on the table. "If he's your fiancé, why did he let you come with me?" David asked, taking another drink.

"Hundred twenty-five dollar lot of money in Thailand."

"A hundred and twenty-five?" David said, setting down his glass. Dom told me one hundred."

She wrinkled her forehead, a confused expression crossed her face.

"Who paid the extra twenty-five?" David asked.

"Maybe your friend."

"Oh, man," David said, turning toward the entrance of the restaurant, seeing Mr. Dom sitting in the car, parked along the street. The glow from his cigarette shone behind the steering wheel.

"He good friend?"

"Yes, but I would have given anything for one more time with you. And if I was your boyfriend, I wouldn't let you go with anybody, not for all the money in the world."

She smiled. "Life very hard in Thailand. Americans not understand Asian people. My fiancé sacrifice. Right now he feel terrible."

"Shiu, he seems so old for you?"

"Old? Old not matter. He take care of Shiu. Shiu take care of him."

"What do you feel for him?"

"Feel?"

"You know…feelings, happiness, love?"

She looked at him strangely, as if he'd said something ridiculous. "Feelings not important. People happy one day, sad next day. One day laughing, next day crying. Cannot live by feelings. Live by need, by what he give me and what I give him."

David leaned back. He wanted to ask her about sex with an older man but didn't want to insult her. From time to time, a man from another table sneaked a look at Shiu and David. Except for his clothes, David might have passed for an Asian. His skin was olive, a near-bronze sheen from the Vietnamese sun. His hair was straight, although shorter than the other men. His eyes were almond-shaped, and he wasn't too tall. There was something about his Chicano face, an expression, not Indian, not Mexican, not American, something in between, a blend of three cultures, a humble arrogance, confidence, and sincerity.

"You not talk like other Americans," she said, leaning forward and looking into his eyes.

"My grandparents were from Mexico. In their country there was a civil war, so they left and went to live in the U.S."

"Mexico?" she said, savoring the word, the sound, her lips touching slightly.

"I'm what is called Chicano, part Mexican, part American."

"But you fight war for Americans?"

"I'm an American, born in Los Angeles...."

"Hollywood?" she laughed.

He smiled. "Close by."

"You like Shiu?"

"Very, very much."

She winked at him.

David paid, and they left through a side entrance, walked down a wood path, and strolled along the river. The moon rose slowly, only half of it shining. They were silent. Both breathed in the night air, the smoke of wood fires, and the aroma of cooked fish and tea.

It was near midnight when they reached Dom's car. He sat up. David opened the back door. Shiu moved in first and David after her. The three talked as Dom drove back to the hotel. Sometimes they all spoke English, sometimes Shiu and Dom spoke in Thai. After a short exchange between Dom and Shiu, she turned to David and smiled.

A warm breeze rushed through the back window and rustled David's hair. Shiu sat next to him. He moved his hand hesitantly and placed it over hers. She took his hand, coupling their fingers together.

In front of the hotel, David opened the door. He was about to tell Dom that if Shiu needed to leave, he'd understand, but as David stepped out Shiu followed.

Dom said something in Thai and looked at his watch. Shiu nodded.

"I be back at seven," he said.

David's stomach fluttered. He looked at Shiu, sadly. She smiled, took his arm and led him inside the hotel. They heard music coming from the lounge. American servicemen staggered through the lobby, and Asian women, dressed in tight, bright-colored dresses, clung to the men's arms and leaned against their shoulders.

David took the stairs, and stepped slowly, nervously. Shiu held his hand. When they reached his door, David pulled out his key and fumbled with the lock. The key turned, the door opened, and Shiu walked inside. David took a deep breath, wiped his brow, entered, and closed the door behind him.

Outside, the moon was high and the light brightened the room. David reached for the lamp, but Shiu stopped him. They walked to the bed and sat down.

"What you want from Shiu?" she said, clutching David's hand. "After tonight, you no see Shiu again...promise?" she asked.

David looked at her, for a long time, then answered, "I promise."

"Okay, you tell me...what you want me to do?"

He touched her shoulder, ran his hand down the back of her arm, over her small elbow, and said, "I want you to pretend," he hesitated, swallowed, "that you have great feelings for me. I want you to pretend that this afternoon, you and I were married, your family was there and my family was there. We all had a wonderful time, and Shiu and David are going to be together always. This is the first night. I have never been with another woman, and you have never been with another man. We are in love."

She looked at him, turned her head slightly, to get a different angle, a different view of his eyes, then she kissed him, and said, "Tomorrow, we go to river, buy house, on water. I know man who sell house cheap, big house, plenty room for children."

Then, she placed her arms around his neck and they fell back against the soft bedspread.

✪ ✪ ✪

David woke a little after 8:00, dressed slowly, and went downstairs for breakfast. Although the hotel's restaurant was crowded, he talked to no one, ate alone, and read the Hong Kong edition of the *New York Times*. The print slipped past him, forming no images or ideas. He looked at the photos. They held no interest. He left half of his breakfast, walked outside, and dropped the newspaper into a trash can. He wished he was back in Vietnam.

He walked out of the hotel and through the grounds, past tropical foliage. The birds and parrots screeched and yelped, the sounds echoing dully in the humid air. He walked along a narrow dirt path lined with ferns and came to a boulevard where he walked, wandering around for two hours, sitting to rest at bus stops and park benches.

David had given Dom the morning and afternoon off, and wasn't expecting him until evening.

He hopped on a bus and held out a handful of change. The driver picked some coins, and David took a seat. In the center

240

of town, David walked the crowded sidewalks, stopping to look at window displays, seeing nothing other than a blur of clothing, women's apparel, men's suits, children's clothing. He walked through department stores, and was sickened by the replica of Sears, May Co., Penny's, and Broadway. He thought: is this what the war is about? To force America on the rest of the world? The cheap clothing? The junk?

He rushed out of the store and found a bus stop. He asked which bus went to the Parliament Hotel. People tried but didn't understand him. He looked into their faces and he heard the voices, chattering, high-pitched.

"Parliament Hotel? Parliament Hotel?" At last, a woman, a college student, directed him to the right bus. He rode for an hour, passing poor neighborhoods, wealthy suburbs, arid, grounds with sparse vegetation, heavily landscaped areas, and when he thought he was completely lost, the Parliament Hotel came into view. He stepped from the bus, walked to the hotel, passed servicemen—new arrivals just beginning their R&R's—and he ran up the carpeted stairs, four flights, skipping every other step. The sweat poured off his body, soaking his shirt and underwear. He pulled off his clothing, walked naked through the room, stood at the window to cool off, but perspired more. He turned on the shower, cold water only, which came out tepid, and he stood beneath the stream, washing with soap and a rough cloth, scrubbing hard, until his skin burned, and he threw down the cloth, which slapped the tiled wall. He didn't know what to do. He had to keep his mind off of Shiu. His head was burning, and he raced, holding onto himself, until he could hold it no more, and Shiu's face came as a clear vision, a perfect image, and he turned off the water, dried himself, fell into his bed and slept.

✪   ✪   ✪

241

The loud knock woke David. He struggled to rise. He wrapped a blanket around himself and shuffled to the door.

"Who is it?"

"David, it's me. Henry. Come on, guy, last night. Let's get out and do her up right."

David opened the door.

"Where the hell you been these last couple of days?" Henry asked, walking into the room.

"Me? You're the one who took off. Shit, I thought somebody killed you and took your money or something," David said, rubbing his eyes. "What time's it?"

"Eight-thirty, almost dark. Think we should eat before we go out?"

"Man, I can't eat. Whyn't you pour a couple of drinks while I get dressed."

Henry walked to the dresser, picked up a bottle of whiskey and poured two glasses. He handed one to David. They toasted,

"To night Number 5," Henry said.

"To all nights," David answered.

They drank.

"So where you been, you crazy nerd?" David asked.

"I got me a girl...two nights. Took me to her house, and we stayed there, in bed, damn near the whole time. I took her to the PX and bought her all kinds of stuff for her house, then took her downtown and bought her dresses and shoes. It was like going to heaven." He got a sad look in his eyes. "She got another date tonight. But, I'll tell you," he said, happy again, "it was good while it lasted."

They finished the bottle. Dom picked them up at 10:30 and took them to get some food. They ate very little, then went to the club.

For David, everything was dense, hollow. People were figures, shadows, irrelevant, no connection to anything real. Kim saw him, came up and kissed him. They danced once. Two other women came to him. They knew it was his last night. One woman sat on his lap. He laughed and kissed her neck, but he didn't invite her home. Henry danced, like a robot. The waiter brought more liquor and David kept drinking. In the darkness of the bar, David saw Chakra standing in a corner, next to another woman. She saw David and smiled. He motioned her over. She came forward and sat at his table. She was older than the other girls, more experienced. Henry brought over another woman.

The hours passed. It was time to leave. David asked Chakra to come with him. She accepted and made arrangements with the manager.

She slept with him and stayed the entire night, holding him closely, as if he were her son, comforting him, knowing there was something hurting inside.

The next morning, they showered and made love again. She helped him pack his bag. He took his uniform from the closet and put it on, his jump wings shining over his left breast pocket, his name tag ALMAS over his right pocket.

At noon, they walked downstairs arm-in-arm. In the hotel lobby, many soldiers, all in uniform, had women on their arms. Chakra held David tightly. They walked into the sunlight, the heat pressing against them. Dom was waiting. David had already paid him, but put an extra fifty dollars into his hand. Dom gave him a business card and invited him to return to Thailand. David read the card:

Mr. Dom

Professional Chauffeur

Parliament Hotel

Bangkok, Thailand

He placed it in his wallet, shook Mr. Dom's hand, then they embraced.

Chakra kissed David on the cheek as the buses pulled to the curb. David smiled and thanked her. The soldiers filed onto the buses. David took a window seat, near the middle of the bus. He looked out at the crowd of soldiers, all in summer khakis. He saw Shiu standing alongside a tall Air Force lieutenant. The officer held her by the waist, close to him. She wasn't smiling. David opened his window. Shiu looked at the buses and her eyes found David. They stared at each other for a long time. She smiled, slightly. The officer bent down and kissed her. She rose to her toes and kissed him, then she stepped back and stood with the rest of the women. The lieutenant boarded the bus.

The engines groaned, kicking up dust and exhaust. The first bus pulled away. As David passed Shiu, he glanced at her. She didn't look at him. He heard Chakra call his name. Many of the soldiers waved as if they were leaving behind wives and families. David sat back in his seat. Mr. Dom honked as the bus lumbered along, moving away from the hotel exit and into the main thoroughfare, heading towards the airport where the men would catch a C-141 military transport back to Cam Rhan Bay, and from there, another hop to wherever their units were operating.

FIFTEEN
PURPLE HEART
(DANNY RÍOS)

It was late afternoon, the first day in position, somewhere in the mountains outside Nha Trang. Everything was nearly set up, sandbags filled, howitzers in place, hootches up.

David Almas, Wayne Podleski and a couple of other guys from the ammo section sat in the sun, leaning against a pile of sandbags. They watched as the gun crews sauntered down to pick up rounds for the howitzers.

The ammo section always built the ammunition dump forty to fifty yards away from the howitzers. That way if an enemy mortar or rocket hit the main cache of ammunition, the howitzers and gun crews would be spared. On the other hand, the ammo section's hootch was set up right next to the ammo dump. A direct hit, and the ammo section would be wiped away, clean, no mess, gone...probably just leave a big hole. The guys didn't ponder it. There was no remedy. They had to be near the ammo dump in case a fire mission was called and shells were needed. They'd be there to distribute the shells quickly.

"Come on, David. Get off your lazy buns and load us up," Danny called, laughing, as he and his friend, Emile Jackson, a tall, African-American from South Carolina, approached.

"Short as you are Danny, those rounds oughta jump up on your shoulders by themselves," David said.

"How much time you got left, Ríos?" asked Wayne, a shovel handle resting on his shoulder.

"He's short, brother, so short he makes me feel bad," Emile said, slapping Danny's back.

"Thirty days," Danny said, grinning. "I'm so short I can sit on a dime and swing both legs."

Most of the guys had their shirts off. As usual, Danny wore everything buttoned up, shirt tight at the collar, shirt sleeves down to his wrist.

Emile whispered something to Danny and they both laughed.

"Well, you guys gonna load us up or what?" Danny said.

"Hold your goddamn horses," said David. "We've been unloading shit from choppers all morning. Check out all those sandbags we filled. An' look at them stacks, straight as arrows, twelve-hundred rounds. Ain't even hardly had a chance to finish our hootch."

Danny and Emile looked at the hootch behind David, Wayne and another member of the ammo section. They'd dug out a square, three-feet deep, enough room to sleep six men. Three sandbag walls surrounded the trench. One more wall and a roof still needed to be set in place. Three shovels and a pick lay at David's feet. Wayne held an empty sandbag in his hands.

"We don't have all day," Danny said. "Short as I am, I'll be back home by the time you get off your butts. Isn't that right, Emile?"

"There it is," answered Emile.

He and Danny both laughed and moved close to the stacks.

Inside the ammunition dump's sandbag walls, there were three rows of projectiles, each row stretching about fifty feet in length, slanted at the ends, flat on top, the round, black canisters stacked neatly, one on top of the other, tight as bricks. The entire dump was protected on three sides by sandbags, five rows, four-feet high. One end stayed open for easy access by the gun sections.

"Which row you want us to take it from, chief?" Emile called.

"First row is all H.E.," Wayne answered, a lighted cigarette at the corner of his mouth.

Danny picked up the first round and placed it over Emile's left shoulder, balancing it like a log. He reached down and picked up the second round and placed it over Emile's right shoulder. The sand and gritty surface of the canister scraped Emile's skin.

"Only one more. I ain't about to kill myself today," Emile said.

"Come on now, Jackson," one of the guys sitting next to David said, "you usually carry five of them things."

"Not today, bro'. Too damn hot out here."

Danny picked up the third canister and placed it behind Emile's head, horizontally, resting on top of the other two canisters. Emile tightened his grip on the ends he held in his hands. At a quick glance, he looked like an ox with a yoke over his neck.

"All right, Almas...or you, Podleski, get off your lazy asses and load up my partner so we can get outta here," said Emile.

"Hey, Jackson, you and Ríos there been getting a little chummy, ain't you? Ya know what folks say about intersegmental relationships," said a soldier, leaning against the ammo-section hootch.

"That's the trouble with ignorant people," said Emile, smiling, "have a hard time understanding simple things in life. And the right term, ass breath, is interracial, stupid shit."

Four more artillerymen walked down the hill towards the ammo section.

"Goddamnit, Almas. Get off your ass an' load us up, you lazy son-of-a-bitch."

It was Alex Martínez and some of the guys from gun number two. "There're four of you—plenty to load yourselves up," said Wayne, who rose to his knees.

"Kiss my ass, you goddamn Polish-sausage eater," said Alex, lowering his eyebrows, flexing the arm muscles. "Get your ass over here an' give us some ammo or we'll make you start humping this shit with us."

"Tell him, Martínez. You tell him," said Emile, still standing with the rounds over his shoulders.

"Martínez," said Wayne, wiping long strands of hair from his eyes, "you talk a big game but you ain't shit."

"Goddamn it, Wayne. Just get off your ass and stop flapping your jaws," said Alex. "The rest of the battery is coming down to pick up their ammo, too. Now, get over there and load Danny up."

Everyone turned to look at Danny who had stepped past Emile and was walking to where David sat.

It wasn't an explosion exactly, not like the earth-shattering sound of a mortar or grenade that kicks up dirt, sucks at the air, and makes breathing difficult. This was more of a pop, a quasi-bomb, like a prank, a war joke, a Vietcong tease. It lifted Danny a foot into the air, or maybe it didn't lift him at all. He might have jumped, perplexed by the rattle of dirt beneath his feet, the smell of sulfur stuffing his nostrils, the splintering boot, splattering flesh. Nevertheless, he reeled backwards and his face turned white, ashen. He screamed, "God, Emile...God! What happened? Help me! Help!" Then he hit the ground, flat on his back, writhed, and kept crying out Emile's name.

David stood up. Alex stared.

They had heard the pop, like a blasting cap. From their view, Danny's body fell as if he'd slipped on a wet floor. His arms flew out, fingers stiffened, legs crooked. He hit the ground, hard, his back thumping, smoke and dust rising around him. He reached for his foot.

"Emeel! Emeel!"

The heavy canisters dropped from Emile Jackson's shoulders. They crashed to the ground. He stared at Danny, who was now reaching out for someone. Nobody moved. Emile stepped away, slowly, confused, his feet moving backwards, dull, sluggish, putting space between him and his fallen comrade.

Danny lay alone moaning and crying for help.

Finally, David and Wayne leaped up and ran to his side. Alex turned and ran towards the gun sections, yelling, "Medic! Medic!" still uncertain about what had happened.

Danny tried to rise. Wayne held him down. David talked to him. "Take it easy, Danny. Shit, man. It's nothing," he said, looking at Wayne, both trying to figure out what happened.

"Is it bad, Almas? Huh? Is it bad?"

David looked at Danny's foot. The boot had blown open at the toes, shattered like a piece of glass, black leather shreds, blood and flesh, an empty space where his toes had been.

David turned, something slimy crawling up his throat. More guys came running down the hill. Emile stood ten yards back, hands at his sides, eyes wide, lips clenched.

Doc Langley followed Alex. They sprinted to the ammo dump, down the hill, a stretcher in their hands. A crowd hovered over Danny. Langley yelled at them to step aside. He worked on the foot, talking calmly to Danny the whole time. "A million-dollar wound, Danny. A Purple Heart and a plane ticket back to San Francisco, champ."

Choppers were still bringing in supplies. Ritchie Oyas got on the radio. A Medivac swooped down and waited on the chopper pad, a short way from the ammo dump. They put a blanket on Danny, carried him to the chopper, and lifted him aboard. The "dustoff" rose, the tail higher than the nose, and quickly sped away, across the mountain ridges, heading to the forward area base camp, near Nha Trang and the South China Sea.

The battery commander ordered the artillerymen to comb the area, look for anything suspicious. Sgt. Emerson found the first one. He held it in his hand to show the others. It was triangular, green, the size of a handkerchief folded over.

"What is it?"

"A mine."

"What the fuck kinda mine's that?"

"U.S. made. Uncle Sam's finest. We fly over gook areas and drop them like we're droppin' candy. They fall into the grass...hard to see 'em. Kids is always stepping on them. They'll blow when some weight is placed on 'em. Won't kill you, just take your foot off if it gets you in the right place."

"Gook areas? Wherever the gooks are...we are."

"Yup."

By the time the sun set, covering the sky with violet light, they'd gathered a dozen more.

"That's it?" asked the First Sergeant. "You guys checked every place? Just keep an eye where you're walking."

"Hey, Top," someone asked the first sergeant. "Is it true these things are ours...I mean U.S. made?"

"Yeah, but all the ones we found have been buried a few inches under the ground, covered over carefully, real nice-like. That means Charlie got a hold of them and set 'em up. All the ones we found were like that, buried, so a man's footstep will set 'em off."

The veteran NCO walked towards the battery. Stepping up the dirt incline, he turned his head and called back towards David and the others, "The gooks do shit like that, tricky bastards. We fight our wars fair, out in the open. It may be war, but you gotta play fair."

"He fuckin' serious?" Wayne said.

"Goddamn right he is," said David.

SIXTEEN
THE VETERAN STORYTELLERS
(JOEY SERRANO'S UNCLE)

The burning wood sent crackling embers into the dark sky. Light reflected off the faces of the three men who sat near the fire. Maimonides Serrano poured wine into a jar, leaned back on a torn couch, and listened to a friend's recollections of World War II.

To Maimonides, the war stories created vague images of his nephew Joey, who a lifetime ago had believed that fighting in Vietnam and coming home a hero, a proud veteran, would make him courageous in his father's eyes.

As his friend's words hummed in the chilled air, Maimonides blew at the smoke that floated his way. He thought: Joey had been so young, barely eighteen, just old enough to buy cigarettes and not old enough to buy a beer.

Maimonides remembered once, just after Joey had entered the Army, Ruth, his mom, had received a studio portrait of him wearing his Army uniform. Proudly, she displayed the photo on the mantel over the fireplace. A neighbor had come to visit the Serranos, and upon seeing the photograph said, "Hey, did Joey join the Boy Scouts or something?" After his death, Ruth had removed the photo from the living room.

Maimonides sipped at his wine and looked at the man who was talking.

Serrucho Bravo had just finished his second story, bragging about the Bronze Star he should have received on D-Day. He reminisced, "We los' a lotta guys that day, Cordelio Figueroa from San Angelo, Texas; Fabio Escobar—let's see, yeah, from Demming, New Mexico; Mack Delgado, from someplace in Nebraska; Jimmy Navarrette from Fresno...."

On the opposite side of a chain-link fence that separated Maimonides and his friends from the street, a bearded, shaggy-haired man pushed a shopping cart along the dark sidewalk. Two dogs, like burly shadows, walked alongside him. The man started through an open gate towards the fire but stopped.

"Yup, I guess war was exciting," said Maimonides, turning to look at the man with the dogs. "Never did much before the Army took me. First time I ever got to travel, ride airplanes, an' ships, and tanks.... Remember them old towns, Fourcaville, Anzio, Nijmegen, Bastogne? And the women, *hijo, qué buenas*...the bars, the music...Paris was something, wasn't it?"

Still looking towards the fence, he said, "Who's that guy?"

Serrucho looked at the man, but turned back, "Don't pay him no *'tención*. Probably just a deadbeat. Paris, huh?"

"Home wasn't ever the same after that!"

Kicking a piece of wood closer to the fire, Serrucho said, "Too bad about Joey."

"Yeah, so damn young. Weren't too many guys in WWII that young. Did you know my brother wanted him to join the Marines? Joey went Airborne because of me, 'cause he heard I was a Screaming Eagle."

"That Vietnam war was a bad war," said Govinda Samaniego, a short, stumpy man who was part Mexican, part Hindu with hair like a cotton ball.

Maimonides burst out, "You call that a war?"

No one spoke.

Bitterly, he continued, "How many G.I.s died in Europe steppin' on poisoned stakes, booby-trapped soup cans? What kinda war's that?"

"Joey was a good kid. Remember when he used to come to the bar looking for Herman? Christ, he must'a been no more'n five-years old when he started coming there," said Serrucho.

"How'd he die?" asked Govinda.

"That guy's still standing there," said Serrucho, looking backwards towards the gate.

"He looks all messed up," Govy said, chuckling.

"Let's don't look at him. He might come over here," Serrucho advised.

"Army sent a sergeant to tell Herminio an' Ruthie that Joey died of some stomach problem, dysentery or malaria...somethin' like that," said Maimonides slowly, his eyes on the fire.

"Poor Joey," said Serrucho, buttoning the wrinkled fatigue jacket.

Maimonides coughed.

"You think something like that would'a made Herminio stop drinking, wouldn't it?" said Govinda.

"Gave him an excuse to drink more. Been coughing up blood last couple of weeks. Can't even hold a damn job. Ruthie been working at a factory, building model airplanes ever since...you know, over at the toy factory."

A patrol car approached, slowed down, flashed a light but didn't stop.

The shaggy-haired man, holding tightly to his shopping cart, stepped back, turned, and continued along the sidewalk, his dogs barking.

"Let's change the subject," said Maimonides, finishing his wine.

Serrucho breathed deeply. *"Oigame*, see them dogs?" he said, passing the bottle to Govinda, remembering a story to lighten the mood.

The bearded man was now a shadow moving into the darkness.

"Yeah, big dogs," said Govinda, pouring some wine into a paper cup.

"Reminds me of the time I almost got killed."

"Honest to God, Sarge?"

"Don't call me that, goddamn it."

Maimonides placed his bad leg, an old war injury, closer to the fire, warming it, trying to keep the pain from rushing to his groin.

Govinda scratched his fuzzy white head. "In the war, D-Day, when you attacked Omaha Beach...that's where ya 'most got killed, ha, Serruch?"

"I said change the subject. Don't talk no more about the goddamn war," said Maimonides, his eyes on Govinda.

"Naw. Was after the war," said Serrucho, looking at Maimonides, who poured more wine into his glass jar.

Serrucho leaned forward and said, "When I was gardening."

"Ha, gardening?" said Govinda.

Maimonides turned and smiled.

"I was working for Alfredo Medrano, Bossman," said Serrucho. "He used to pick me up when he had extra work."

"I heard Bossman lost two kids over in Vietnam, didn't he?" said Govinda.

Maimonides kept his eyes on the fire.

Serrucho continued his story. "And the goddamn owner 'a the house where I was workin' told me, 'Don' get caught alone with my dog.' I tell you, I could'a been kilt."

Maimonides shook his head.

Serrucho's stringy black hair fell into his face. He smoothed it back, using his fingers like the teeth of a comb.

Maimonides draped his arms over the back of his cracked chair. He raised one eyebrow high.

Serrucho said, "What chu lookin' at me like that for, Mo? I'm tellin' it jus' like it happen'."

"I didn't say a thing," said Maimonides, taking the bottle and pouring. He shifted his leg. He remembered, 1944, near Verreville, France, two weeks after the invasion, her soft body, warm like the fire at his feet. She was the captain's mistress and had seduced Maimonides, kept him AWOL for two days. He lost his field commission but didn't care. He wasn't officer material anyway. Maimonides smiled at the memory.

"But I know what your thinkin', Mo, *cabrón*. You don't believe me, huh?"

Maimonides laughed. "Cut the shit, 'n tell yer story."

Serrucho narrowed his eyes. "Okay, so the owner, see, he's skinny, all dressed in hippie clothes, always wearin' a beanie cap, says to me, 'My dog's dangerous...special trained. He's a killer. Nobody robs my house 'er my dog'll take care him.' Tha's how he said it, like that."

"Yup, like dat. That's how he say'd it, right, Mo?" said Govinda, nodding his head up and down, spaces between his teeth.

"Damn it, Govy. Why'nt you go to the V.A. an' get them teeth fix't 'fore you lose 'em all," said Maimonides.

Govinda laughed, huffing sounds passing through his teeth. "'Cuz when I got allergies I kin breathe better this way."

Serrucho shook his head, threw a wood chip at his friend, and continued talking.

He described how he had finished cleaning the rich guy's backyard, leaving the freshly cut grass shimmering. He said that as the sun lowered, he could see the entire San Fernando Valley spread out below and the Chatsworth Mountains way off against the haze. He told how he dragged the tools out to the front yard, close to the electric gate and stacked everything into a neat pile so when Bossman arrived with the pickup, they could hurry, load up the tools and get home before dark.

Govinda asked questions, like how many houses were up there on the hills and how much traffic was there and how come they called their friend Bossman. "Ain't he just like us? Why we gotta call him Bossman?"

"'Cuz tha's what he is, the boss," said Maimonides.

"How come we jez cain't call him Alfredo... or Al? He was born just like us," said Govy.

Serrucho spat out, "Shit! You guys gonna let me tell the story or what?"

"Hey, how come Bossman went to Mexico, remember, back around the time the war started in Europe? Stayed there for a few years, didn't he?" said Govinda, thinking deeply, wrinkling his brow.

"Can I tell my story now?" said Serrucho, standing and tugging at his crotch, smoothing the dirt-smudged gray slacks.

"Aw'right, go 'head. Tell it," said Maimonides. "But if ya can't keep our interest... it ain't worth tellin'."

"Well if you'd guys stopped innerruptin'..."

Serrucho sat back down and pushed his hair back again. He explained how he started looking for the rich guy's dog.

"Wasn't Bossman Medrano gone fer three or four years?"

"Why you keep innerrup'n me? Damn it, Govy."

Maimonides cut in, "Because you gotta set up the story. How're we s'pposed to get the mood if ya got no scenery, no landscape... ¿tú sabes?"

Serrucho stared at Maimonides. He turned away, sighed, looked at the fire and continued, describing how the guy had a beautiful house, a swimming pool that was half-inside and half-outside. The shallow end started in the den, and the guy used to go swimming…start right next to his fireplace, dive into the pool, swim under the glass wall to the deep end, which was outside. He never had to step into the cold air, was what Serrucho said.

"What kinda' work he do?" asked Govinda.

Maimonides cut in. "Work! Those guys don't work. Ain't done a' honest day's work in their lives, just drive around in Mercedes and Jaguars, spending all day at their office, taking their secretaries to lunch. You think that's work?"

"You're right," said Serrucho. "This guy didn't have no job, used to sit up in his house writin' songs. Grouchy guy. Don't even talk to his kids. Sit at the piano. Can't sing for shit, but Bossman says the guy's band made a million bucks. Skinny guy, you know, always got that beanie cap on. I seen him and his band on TV every once in a while. I think the band's breaking up. The other guys used to come over, but I ain't seen 'em in a long time, a bunch of *marijuanos*."

"I bet he din't even go to Vietnam," said Govinda.

"War? Shit. He was a skinny bastard. Bossman told me the guy starved his'self every time the draft board called him."

"Rich people always got an angle, a way to get them and their kids out of shit that our kids got to do for them," said Maimonides, spitting.

"Rich people ain't happy anyway. Are they?" said Govy, pulling an old blanket over his shoulders. He wiggled his toes and watched as they pushed against the worn material of his tennis shoes.

"What you mean they ain't happy?" said Maimonides, leaning back, his chair balancing on the two back legs.

"Got too many problems…always gotta worry 'bout los'n th'r money. Don't they?"

"Christ! It's my story," Serrucho cried. "It don't matter if the guy is happy or not. That's got noth'n to do wit' the story. You guys are taking me off the track here."

"Aw'right, go 'head, but let's get on with the action. What's a story with no action? Hollywood movies, all got action. Books, all got action. Let's get on with it. So the guy's grouchy..." said Maimonides, watching Serrucho clench his hands.

Serrucho began again. "Then I seen the dog...a wolf; coulda' put a saddle on and rode him. Goddamn it, I see he's loose, got no leash. He's just lay'n there at the top of the drive-way watchin' me. That dog jez lays there starin', and I know if I stand still he'll get me, and if I run, he'll chase me down. Felt like the Nazis was after me again, *cabrón*! So I stand still, like nothin', and not a thought comin'to my head. Shit, at Normandy I kilt guys, shot three, shoulda got the Silver Star...an' here I am, scared of 'a dog."

"I thought it was a Bronze Star? Didn't he almost get the Bronze Star, Mo?" said Govy, scratching the side of his head.

"Shut up, Govinda. You ain't the only one that got medals. Now LISTEN!" Serrucho snapped.

"I got the Silver Star," said Govinda.

"Yeah, yeah. The Death March. We know. You made us hear it enough times."

"An' I wouldn't surrender. Not me. Lotta guys surrendered."

Maimonides smiled.

"Listen! Damn it. So the dog shows me more teeth, eye teeth. Then, *hijo de la chingada*, here he comes, like a race horse, legs pumpin', body movin', eyes on my neck, teeth like nails, like I'm watchin' him come after som'body else. I squeeze the shovel. His mouth's open. I get ready to swing.

His front legs leave the ground. He's raisin'. I start to swing, and from nowheres I hear… 'FRAKKkkk!'"

"Frak?" said Maimonides sarcastically. "That's a dog's name?"

"God is my witness, like a duck shot out the air, the dog drops, nose at my feet, breathin' like a puppy. My knees 'er rattlin' like maracas. I got the shovel in my hands."

Maimonides leaned forward, picked at his beard, slid his bad leg to one side, and said, "I don't know, Serrucho. Sounds kinda like you're stretchin' it here."

"Stretchin' it? Stretchin' what?"

"You say the dog was off the ground, jumpin' at yer neck, and when the guy calls his name, the dog stops flying and falls to the ground?" said Maimonides, closing one eye in a mocking gesture.

"Come on, Mo," said Govy, bouncing up and down on the couch. "It cou' happen like Serrucho says. Don't those rich people raise animals to do all kinda things? You see 'em at the park, teaching 'em to heel and to flip, to walk backwards to.…"

"All right! All right!" cried Serrucho.

"Yeah, well… maybe. But if't a story ain't believable, what good's it. Don't even matter if it's a lie, so long's we believe it. That's all what counts."

"You sayin' I'm lying?" said Serrucho.

"No, I ain't said that. It's just the way it come out."

"I tol' it like it happened."

"Maybe you told it the way you wanted it to happen, or the way you think it should'a happened," said Maimonides. "Can't nobody ever tell a story the way it really happened. Not really."

Serrucho took a stick and turned a clump of wood onto its unburned side. The flames leaped and sparks jumped into the sky. He was about to speak when the man with the dogs returned. He walked through the gate, across the the parking lot, and close to their fire, the dogs growing larger as they neared.

Serrucho reached for a broken two-by-four.

"Uh, okay if I warm myself?" he said, his dogs sitting at his side.

"You a hippie?" said Govinda.

"Just keep them damn dogs away from me," said Serrucho.

"Suit yerself," said Maimonides.

"Thanks," said the man.

"You a hippie?" Govy repeated.

"There ain't no more hippies."

"What are you?" Maimonides asked, looking the man over. Maimonides had heard that a lot of Vietnam vets had burned out, just sizzled away, turned to ashes, walked the streets carrying signs: Vietnam Vet, Looking for Work, God Bless You.

"Just a guy down on his luck," said the man.

"Purdy young guy to look like you do," said Serrucho.

"I get along."

"You a draft dodger?" Govy asked.

"Ha, man, that was years ago. Burnt my card to a crisp. Whoosh. Was during a protest up north."

"We all veterans, WWII," said Govy.

"Yes sireee, the Good War. My generation got stuck with the albatross. Only suckers went to our war. No way I was gonna go. Shit, got me a deferment."

"A deferment?"

"College. I was in college. Stayed there 'til I took every course in the catalogue. I wasn't stupid. No way."

"Who was stupid?"

"Guys that went to Nam."

Serrucho looked at Maimonides, whose eyes burned into the young man.

"How 'bout some of that wine there?"

"Why was they stupid?" Maimonides asked, his lips barely moving.

"Cuz they went, like sheep to the slaughter, corn to chaff."

"Ain't you felt nothing for your country?" asked Serrucho.

"I pay my taxes."

"Bullshit! You ain't even got a job. Come here askin' for a little heat, some wine," said Maimonides, standing.

"Been down on my luck," the man said, looking up.

"People got to fight for their country. Mo's *sobrino* died over there," said Govy, looking at the dogs. "A lotta kids from this neighborhood died defending their country."

"Defend...from a tenth-rate power, 17,000 miles away?"

"It's what makes us a great country," Serrucho said, sitting up straight.

The man looked at each of them, and he looked at their campfire, at their clothes, at the almost empty bottle of wine. "Yeah? This what you call great, huh?"

"Go try to live in some other country. Try to get a job and survive in Mexico, maybe Africa, Yugoslavia or Poland. See how you like living under Somoza, in Nicaragua. Yeah, we got to defend ourselves, our country, even if it means we die," said Maimonides.

"Need to kill women, old people, an' kids, too? People who don't even know why their country is at war, people just trying to farm their land?"

"Sometimes need to teach hippies a lesson, too," said Serrucho, standing over the man.

The dogs got up. One barked. The other growled.

Serrucho reached for his stick.

The man patted his dogs. "Simmer down now, girls," he whispered to them. Turning to Serrucho he said, "Ain't no need for that.... Look here, mister, I don't mean no disrespect, but it's the way I see things. I may not be a success story, but I had a lot of time to think. There's shit going on in this country that nobody's telling us."

"But to call good men suckers, to say they're stupid for doing what's gotta be done?"

"Just a figure 'a speech. Seduced by Washington, by all of it. Really sad." The man rose to his haunches, hugging his dogs.

"Good or bad, this our country," said Maimonides.

"I appreciate that. You got your opinion. I didn't mean to insult you none. I respect what you did. Just that, I come from a different generation...a different time."

Maimonides handed the man a cup of wine. The man looked at him, drank the wine, and handed the cup back.

"Thank you, mister. If you don't mind my askin', what happened to your nephew?"

"Got sick. Was almost ready to come home. Army said he just got sick, stomach problems. Prob'ly malaria."

"Phewwww. I'm sorry, man. That's real sad...a heartbreaker."

Maimonides shrugged. "He was a good kid. A good ballplayer, loved his mom and dad...no hero, just a good kid."

"I believe you, sir. Uh, I guess I best be on my way."

"Just watch who you call a sucker," said Serrucho, his eyes on the dogs.

"Okay. But there'll be more wars, then what?" said the man, turning and walking towards the gate. "You don't see too damn many congressmen and senators sending their kids off to fight wars. Nope, they're off at Harvard, Yale, Columbia."

"We'll keep doing what we always done. Fight 'em."

"Ours is not to reason why, uh?" said the young man.

They watched him go.

"Hey," they heard the man call.

"What?" Maimonides responded.

"Sorry about your nephew. A damn shame."

The man took hold of his cart and pushed it down the street.

"I could 'a slugged the guy," said Govinda.

"Hippies. *Puros pendejos*, huh?" said Serrucho, sitting down.

Maimonides watched the man and his dogs disappear into an alley. He looked around at his friends, at himself. "Hell. Shit."

"What?"

Maimonides looked into the fire for a long time. "The son-of-a-bitch is right."

"About what? He didn't say nothing," said Serrucho.

"*Pendejadas, puras pendejadas.* Look at us."

They turned to one another.

"Look at my leg...stiff as a goddamn tree. And Joey? And this...." He took the empty wine bottle and tossed it towards a concrete wall. They heard the glass shatter.

"Well, I served. Did what I had to," said Serrucho. "I'll never forget them bodies lying on the sand, floating in the ocean, hundreds of 'em. Guys that cared...guys that knew the chances and did it anyway." He looked into the fire. "I'll always remember. It's all I got."

"Tell another story," Govinda said, bouncing on the couch. "A good one."

"My turn," said Maimonides, dropping a piece of wood into the fire. He told them about Hank Seguin, a used car salesman from Calexico who had made a million bucks on phony real estate deals, cheating relatives and friends of thousands of dollars. Maimonides's voice started low but gained volume as he neared the climax.

There were no cars on the dark, narrow street behind them. Across the street was the railroad tracks where they once played as boys. It hadn't been used in years. Weeds grew through the rocks and corroding ties, and in the distance, the lights from new high-rise office buildings and condominiums hung like candles in the night.

SEVENTEEN
GIVING UP THE GHOST
(MANNY CARDOZA)

I.

When Manny Cardoza's forehead hit the steering wheel, he saw a bright flash, a cameo, an imprint: Beto's face, brown, wavy hair, perfectly combed, his dark skin powdered and pale, eyes closed, lips and nose pressed flat, hands folded across his chest, and a dark, neat hole in the center of his forehead. Manny threw open the car door, and in the light of a street lamp, hopped up the curb and ran down the sidewalk. When he reached the Highland Nursery, he scrambled over the chain-link fence and jumped to the ground.

He felt his way in the dark, dodging trees and plants, moving deeper into the nursery. He heard the screeching tires and dove into a dark space between two palm trees. He lay still. Red lights shone against the trees, reflecting into the dark sky. There was cursing. A chain-link fence rattled.

Manny's mouth was dry. He gulped air, heaved and moaned, desperate to keep quiet. The sirens wailed and the tires skidded. Voices called, echoing. His chest pounded. He pressed his cheek to the ground and the smell of fertilizer rushed through his nostrils.

The ground in front of him brightened, brilliant, as a flashlight searched, leaping from earth to trees. He closed his eyes and dropped his head. The voices neared, getting louder, the boots crunching gravel. His legs shook. He raised his head and saw shadows and lights and night. He rose to his elbows and looked around, waiting. He thought of making a run for it, jumping the fence, and disappearing down the sidewalk. Two men moved past. He hesitated. A blunt instrument struck the back of his head. His side exploded in pain as a crunching blow split his ribs, lifting him from the ground. He coughed, spit out, but said nothing. He tried to raise his head, but a weight pressed against his neck, a shoe shoved his face into the gravel, pebbles scratching his face.

"Move!... Move," said the voice, quivering. "You dirty shit, so I can blow you away."

"Put up the gun," said another, a strong, gruff voice.

Manny closed his eyes tightly.

"We could do it," the shaky voice said, overanxious. "Right here, Mick. We could do it."

Manny recognized the rookie's voice.

"Not tonight! Goddamn it. I ain't dealing with all that shit tonight." Cigar smoke filled the air. "Load his sad ass up. Let's get outta here."

They cuffed Manny, hands behind him, and walked him past the squad cars scattered about the street, red lights flashing, officers standing around, shotguns in their hands, voices buzzing over the radios.

Some people came out of their clapboard homes. They stepped to the sidewalk and porches. It was past midnight. They stood in pajamas, pants, and t-shirts.

The police searched Manny's car, ripping out seats and yanking at the hubcaps.

Mick, a veteran detective, butch haircut, dark suit and tie, huge belly, looked into Manny's eyes, flashlight shining, cigar smoke filling the air. "High as a DC 7. Under the influence," he said. "Told you last time I didn't want to see you around here again, Cardoza. Can't keep that shit out of your body, huh?"

They slammed Manny against the police car's side panel. His knee hit a blunt edge, and he slid to the ground.

"You don't have to be so rough," a woman's voice called from the crowd.

"G'won, you all get the hell to bed. Let us do our jobs here," said a helmeted officer, who stood beside his motorcycle.

"*Siesta* time...*siesta* time," said another officer, gripping his nightstick.

The rookie grabbed Manny by the throat. He squeezed and lifted him to his toes, then shoved him into the back seat. He sat there, dazed, looking down at his shoes, at the clumps of mud. He thought about jail and his knees began to tremble, but he kept his eyes hard, defiant.

A tow truck backed out of the shadows, jacked up Manny's sports car and lifted the front tires off the ground. Manny turned away, as if unconcerned. The tow-truck driver gunned his engine. The heavy auto bucked, lunged forward, and moved slowly up the street.

Manny knew Sharon, his wife, would be sitting at home in front of the television, waiting, her eyes on the screen, seeing nothing but the reflections. The baby would be asleep in her crib.

Sharon's father had told her that Manny was lost and that she should forget him.

Three years earlier, after meeting Manny at Cal State Northridge, Sharon had invited him to her parents' home in Granada Hills. They had all sat down to a nice family dinner. The Foster family listened to the handsome, intelligent veteran who had recently returned from Vietnam excitedly talking about college, about his future. But a year later, Manny had changed.

"He's not the same person, Shari," her dad had said. "Manuel's sick. He needs help, and until you realize it, he'll drag you down with him. Leave him, honey."

"But, Daddy, he's trying."

Her father made a sarcastic expression, twisting the corner of his mouth, narrowing his eyes.

"Okay," she said. "So he quit school. He's still got a good job."

"For how long, Sharon? Don't fool yourself. He's a junkie. He doesn't want help. You took him to the Veteran Administration. He quit the program. Bring the baby and come home, Shari."

"He's my husband."

"He'll end up in jail…again. Next time I won't help, and he won't get off so easy."

After a year's marriage, she had tired. She didn't understand Manny's life, and she was afraid of his friends. They came around at all hours, hard-gang-looking guys, hippies, bikers, and students, always anxious, tense, peering over their shoulders. She knew he tried keeping them away from his home, but they came anyway.

In the back seat of the police car, Manny pushed the thoughts away. He twisted his hands, feeling the hard metal around his wrists.

The rookie sat behind the steering wheel. He took off his hat, placed it on the seat, slid his hands over his thigh, and said, "Shit, wetback bastard made me tear my pants." He reeled around and slammed his fist into Manny's face, just below the cheekbone. There was a crack, a sharp pain, as if someone had driven a nail into his skull.

"Hey! There ain't no need for that," said Mick.

"Ah, who gives a shit."

Manny sat up straight.

269

II.

The patrol car pulled slowly from the curb. People peeked into the back window. A little boy about ten, hair in his eyes, held up his thumb.

They cruised Sunset Boulevard, driving past brick store-fronts, the local high school—Hollywood High—and the drive-in restaurant at the corner of La Brea. Neon lights flickered from marquees at the tops of buildings, advertising movies and record albums. Slowly, the cops turned down Cherokee, a smaller, darker street. Manny's arm muscles tightened, his head throbbed. They cruised past his aunt's house, her front yard overgrown with weeds, an old boat on a broken down trailer parked next to a hedge. He looked to see if any of the guys were out front. At a brightly lighted intersection, they made a U-turn and headed towards the police station on Wilcox.

They passed the brick Baptist church, its three-story bell-tower rising higher than the old concrete apartment buildings. They moved past lawns, gardens, flowers, white fences, sidewalks, concrete curbs, hedges, telephone poles, and electric wires. Manny saw a white Victorian home, long wood porch, steep roof, Mr. Martinelli's place, the one with the corn field next to it, the corn tall, spread out over an acre of land, the last field remaining in Hollywood. Manny thought that if he could have reached the corn field instead of the nursery, the cops would have never caught him.

✪ ✪ ✪

Earlier that evening, he'd been parked across from the Catholic elementary school in front of Junior's apartment. Junior had told him not to leave the house, not until he'd come down some, was feeling *tranquilo*. "¿Sabes qué, Manny?" he had said, "*Te lo juro, ese. Espérate hasta que estés bien suave. Porque si te vas*, you know, you split now, an' the 'man' swoops, *te van a chingar*, bust yer ass, *y* you couldn't fool a nun right now, brother. *Te digo, no ajuantaras otra vez en el bote. Casi muriste las otras veces*...you don' wanna be pullin' no hard time, *carnal*. It ain't your style. They been lettin' you off easy 'cuz you was a Vietnam vet an all, but those days are gone with the wind, *ese*. You're just a hype now," he said, sitting at the kitchen table, leaning back in a chair, wearing his dark Ray Charles sunglasses, nodding his head.

"Hey, Junior, I'm cool, man. I got it together, especially now. I feel good, can't nobody touch me, dude."

"You're still a cherry, Manny. Take it easy, that's all, *¿tú sabes*? You ain't a veteran of the streets like the rest of us."

"Yeah, cool."

"Cool, my ass, *ese*," Junior said with a smirk. Then he said, as Manny walked to the door, "Hey, why don't you bring over one of them fine hippie broads next time you come over? There was some fine ones over at the last party you and your old lady had at your *chante*. I'll turn you on to some free *carga*, man."

Manny laughed. "Those white broads don't dig this scene. Chicanos like you scare them."

"Hey-y-y, man. I can grow my hair long, *ese*. I can look dirty and stinky like those hippie *vatos*. I can even talk like them. 'Out of sight, dudes. Dig what's happening.'"

Manny laughed as he walked down the stairs.

Outside Junior's apartment, Manny had sat in his car, a green 1967 MG Midget hardtop. He had bought it with the money he'd saved in Vietnam. His mom and dad wanted him to invest in a house. He had enough for the down payment. He bought a car instead. All he wanted was to drive around and get high.

The first time he stuck a needle into his arm was in Phan Rhang, two months after Beto's death. Back then, Manny hadn't been able to get the fatal image out of his head. He'd drunk whiskey, smoked weed, dropped Darvon…anything to forget, but nothing helped. He'd see Beto face, then Charley's face. He had memorized each scene. In the rear area, he had talked about it to whomever would listen. He was obsessed with it. In a bar, a secret back room, away from the drunks and prostitutes, a place the M.P.s didn't know, a white dude, Mingus, had shown Manny a different world.

"Stuff will cool you out, Manny. Mellow you, keep you low and slow, man."

He had been offered heroin before. Manny had always declined, even telling Mingus once to go to hell. But there came a time when Manny was willing to try anything, anything to keep the dogs away, to keep Beto's face out of his head. On that day, Mingus had happened along. He had taken Manny to the back room. The place was filled with paratroopers. They sat on couches that lined the four walls. Lou Rawls's deep voice rose above the dense silence, "Move on black snake, stay away from my baby's door."

Manny saw beautiful Vietnamese women moving about the room. One woman, not a girl, but a lady, in her thirties, voluptuous, mature, was fixing a guy who looked like he was already nodding off. She stuck the needle into the young, blond soldier's arm. His bangs fell to his forehead. He looked like an Indiana farm boy. She withdrew the syringe, opened her blouse, placed his hand on her breast, and kissed him deeply on the mouth. The soldier didn't respond. He was somewhere else, somewhere far away. Manny couldn't decline. He sat down and waited his turn. He made the woman open her blouse first, kiss him deeply, and when he could barely breathe, his heart pounding, she slid the needle in.

He returned a few more times. The place had scared him: the drugs and the women, the music and the smoke, the decadent environment.

He arrived home two months later. From Cam Rhan Bay to Los Angeles, just like that, no buffer, no debriefing, just a new uniform, a steak dinner, and an airline ticket.

Manny had been anxious to get home to his family, to taste his mom's cooking, hear his dad's voice, be in the security of their house. Yet, he was also hesitant, guilty. His sins ran deep. How could he face them? Would they ever suspect, ever believe, ever imagine the things he had done and seen?

At the airport his first night in L.A., a taxi had pulled up to the crowded terminal. It was night, and the lights were a blur.

"Come on, soldier, hop in," the cabbie had said. He looked and sounded like Woody Allen, thick glasses, thin hair, melancholic eyes.

"Thanks," Manny said.

It was December. Manny had gotten used to the tropical climate. The concrete beneath his feet was ice. The voices around him, although American, sounded foreign, neurotic, frenetic. He had wanted to plug his ears, close his eyes.

He bent down to pick up his duffel bag, but the cabbie grabbed it first. "Let me get that for you."

A man, dressed in an expensive three-piece suit, walked past the two and placed a suitcase in the trunk.

"I've got to be in Century City in twenty minutes. Let's go," he'd said, and moved towards the back seat.

"Hold on, sir. This soldier was here first."

"I don't have time for this...." the man said. He looked at Manny, who stood in his green winter uniform, ribbons and jump wings over his left breast pocket, his trousers bloused,

the bottoms tucked into his jump boots. "You don't mind soldier, huh? There're plenty of other cabs."

Before Manny could respond, the taxi driver said, "No,
sir," his voice rising, an excited New York accent.

Manny was about to tell him to go ahead. He was in no
hurry.

"The soldier was here first. This is his cab," said the driver, who then turned to Manny and said, "Where to?"

"Who the hell do you think you are?" the man in the suit
growled. He moved close to the cabbie.

They argued. Manny watched. A crowd formed.

"You mind if I take this cab?" the man asked Manny.

"Yeah, mister, I do. It's my cab. I was here first."

"There! You hear that? Hear!" said the cabbie.

"I want your driver's number!" the man shouted.

"It's on the dash. Get it yourself," the driver said, and
walked to the trunk with Manny's duffel bag in hand. He took
out the man's luggage and replaced it with Manny's bag.

"Let's go, soldier."

"You won't hear the end of this, you!..."

"What?" said the driver. "Say it...what?"

"Bastard."

The driver laughed out loud as he opened the car door
and got in.

The man in the suit looked into the car and sneered at
Manny, who was sitting uncomfortably in the back seat,
weary and silent.

✪ ✪ ✪

He never thought he'd get addicted. The first times he did
it back home, he told himself, it was to take away the pain,
the memories. Maybe that was true. Then one day, the memories were extinguished, burned from his mind, and Manny

realized the truth. All he cared about was the high. He craved it again and again. Each time the tip of the needle touched his arm, his mind raced back to Phan Rhang, the woman's open blouse, her bare breast, her lips on his, and the needle entering his skin.

Family no longer meant anything to him. Sharon was a body he lived with. He stopped going to school. He began to miss work.

Then the baby was born. He swore to Sharon that he'd work hard, go back to college and get his degree, but each night after work, he'd drive through Hollywood, buy the stuff, and party.

III.

The rookie chewed a toothpick and hummed an Okie song, *Jumbalaya.* He drove past the streets where Manny had played as a kid.

"Turn here," Mick said.

The rookie turned.

"Stop."

The car halted abruptly. They were in front of Manny's parents' home, a long stucco house on a tree-lined street. At first, Manny turned away.

"Take me to jail, man!" he yelled. The rookie smiled, but he wouldn't move the car.

Manny looked out the window towards his house.

He saw his dad's new Buick parked in the driveway, and beside it, his mom's car, a Nova station wagon. Along the curb was his dad's old truck, the front fender dented where Manny had driven it into the tree when he was fourteen. His father kept the truck as a reminder of the years he had worked delivering plants while he put himself through college, finally earning a doctorate in education. He'd gone from a classroom teacher to a principal, and was now a deputy superintendent for the Los Angeles Unified School District. He urged his children to do the same. The others had all graduated college and were settled in their careers.

There was a light shining in the living room. Manny knew his parents were asleep. They always left one light on.

Above the roof, like a shadowy giant, was the avocado tree, the branches stretching out over the house and sidewalk. Manny saw himself and his older brothers as kids, sliding and swinging from the branches, laughing and calling out, "Be careful, Manuel. Don't fall, ya might break something and Mom'll shit."

He smiled and remembered his first girlfriend, Connie Fujimoto. It was in the fifth grade. He never should have told his brothers that Connie was coming over to visit him. Manny had taken a bath, put on clean Levi's, a blue and green checkered shirt, and combed his hair, parted to one side. A half-hour later when Connie came to the back gate and called out for Manny, his oldest brother had yelled for her to come into the backyard. His three other brothers were in the garage, watching and giggling from behind the door, as the gate creaked open, Connie peeked through. She didn't hear Manny yelling, the tape was too tight on his mouth. She pushed the gate open and stepped inside. She wore red shorts, a white top, and white tennis shoes. When she finally saw Manny, she screamed, stood for a second, turned and ran home, her feet slapping the sidewalk. Except for a pair of oversized work boots, Manny was in his underwear, hanging upside-down, hands bound with a cord, one end of a rope tied to his ankles, the other tied to a branch. He swung back and forth, shaking and struggling to get loose. He never trusted his brothers after that.

Manny slumped back against the seat.

The rookie, fidgety, ran his hands over the steering wheel. He put his head down, then raised it and looked out the window. "Come on, Mick. We've been here ten minutes."

"Wait."

"It's getting late."

"I said wait, damn it!"

Mick was also looking at the house. He'd been on the force a long time, and he knew Manny's father, who was active on boards and committees.

The burly officer looked into his side mirror, studying Manny's face.

Manny dropped his head.

"Let's go," said Mick.

It was after one in the morning when they pulled into the police station. They made Manny wait two hours before he could call anybody. Sharon cried. She said that she couldn't post bail. They didn't have the money and she wasn't about to ask her parents.

He panicked. She'd gotten him out before, somehow. He slumped against the wall. The heat rose to his head. He sweated, and at the same time his hands were cold, frigid. He begged. Still crying, she hung up.

He made another call.

"No more," his mom said, choking. Both of his parents were on the line. He pleaded, like a boy, "Please, Ma...Dad, please come and get me. I'll pay you back every cent. Just post the bail this one last time. I can't stay here. It'll kill me."

"Manny, we can't talk to you anymore," his father said in a soft voice. "This is it, son. We've tried everything. You're destroying us and Sharon, and your son. If you want to keep playing in the sandbox, you start cleaning your own socks and shoes. Goodbye," he said, just like a high school principal, and the phone clicked.

Manny held the phone in his hand, at waist level. "Clean my own socks and shoes," he blurted, laughing, tears clouding his eyes. He stared at the ceiling and saw a fly buzzing around a light. He thought about Lincoln, a biker from Venice who had some good stuff.

The rookie came to take him back to his cell. Manny hollered and tried to pull away. The rookie shoved him, forcing him against the wall. "Fucker!" Manny cried as he threw a wild punch and missed. More cops came. They struggled. Manny hit the floor, and they dragged him back to his cell.

"He couldn't fight his way through cotton candy," one officer chuckled.

"Look here, these bell-bottoms are good for something," said the rookie, taking hold of the baggy pants and pulling as the others laughed.

They dragged him along the smooth floor. Manny could smell the polish. He knew the procedure: the isolation, the sickness, the trial. This time there would be a jail sentence. He was sure of it.

When he reached the cell, he got to his knees, then to his feet and stood up straight. "You shit," Manny said, to no one in particular.

The rookie hit him, the fist catching Manny under the jaw. He bit down, his teeth slicing through his tongue. As he reeled backwards, he saw the Vietnamese woman, her white *ao dai* open above the waist, her breasts exposed. He saw Beto and Charley. They stood beside a tree.

Manny dropped to the ground, his head hitting the corner of a metal bunk bed. He lay still on the floor, sat up, and touched the back of his head. There was a deep gash. He looked at his blood-stained fingers and fell back, his head hitting the floor where a pool of blood formed. He closed his eyes. The officers moved in closer. Blood dripped from the corner of Manny's mouth. A cop stooped down and reached to feel his pulse. The officer squinted. "Somebody get a doctor, fast."

Vaguely, like a lost echo, Manny heard a sound, decreasing in volume with each utter, "Cardoza, ardoza, doza," until it stopped.

"He faking it?" asked one of the cops, looking around nervously.

"No," responded the one who held Manny's wrist.

"Screw him! Bastard! No big loss," said the rookie, half-smiling.

"You don't know shit about nothing, asshole," said Mick as he approached. He pushed the rookie aside and knelt on one knee beside Manny.

"It was an accident?" one of them said.

"Did anyone get a doctor?" another said, angrily.

"Why waste the taxpayers' money?" said the rookie.

"Too late?" asked the cop, still trying to feel a pulse.

"Too late," Mick said, taking a blanket from the bunk and covering Manny.

EIGHTEEN
MEJICO LINDO Y QUERIDO
(DANNY RÍOS)

Poplar and palm trees surrounded the plaza, shading the walkways and gardens from the semi-tropical sun. Blackbirds and sparrows darted from branch to branch. A gardener struck the earth with an old, battered hoe, crushing dirt clods and chopping them into fragmented shards until they settled into a fine silt. He pushed the soil beneath the bushes, forming a dirt moat around each plant. His face was dark, like a chunk of chocolate, and he moved slowly, rhythmically, his straw hat tilted high on his head. He wore faded khakis and weathered *huaraches*.

A white gazebo stood in the center of the plaza. It was made of cement and tile. A staircase wound its way to the main floor up to the flat roof. During the January *fiesta*, fifteen to twenty couples could dance upon the gazebo's floor. Across the narrow street, surrounding the plaza on three sides, were arched porticos, shaded stores, the police department, and one restaurant. The town's main church, constructed in the 1600's, stood at one end of the square. Sixty years earlier, during the first days of the Revolution, San Diego de Alejandria, located in Los Altos de Jalisco, had sent the first men to join the rebel forces in battle against the federal army, giving the region the patriotic slogan, "*Cuna de la Revolucíon'*."

Danny Ríos sat on a stone bench, one of the many benches placed along the perimeter of the plaza. He breathed deeply, closed his eyes and smelled the burning wood, fresh bread, corn tortillas, and dry earth.

The gardener stepped from the lawn area onto the stone walkway. He removed his hat, wiped his brow, and walked towards Danny.

"This is too much work for an old man," he said, and sat down.

"That's what you said last year. I thought you were going to retire."

"Words, my boy. Just words. Besides, all of the young men are working in the North, so someone must take care of things until they return."

"Well, you aren't a young man anymore. And you don't need money, so...."

"I must do something to keep me strong."

"Then, you shouldn't complain."

"Why not?" said the gardener, pushing the hat onto his head. "Everyone needs to complain."

"You should listen to your wife's advice to quit this job, let someone else have it."

"But I like to complain. Why can't people hear a complaint without offering a solution? All the time, do this, do that. I complain just to get the aggravation out. Once it's out, then I'm fine. *Ay, Díos,* Daniel, each year, you sound more and more like a lawyer."

"Once a lawyer always a lawyer."

The old man chuckled. "So, leave your work at home."

The man removed his hat again and fanned himself.

A boy rode by on a bicycle, a five-foot high stack of bread tied to the back, rocking back and forth. He pressed a horn. A bellow came forth like a duck's call. Both the old man and Danny turned to wave.

"Ey...everybody knows you around here now."

"Yes, I keep coming back. I don't want to spend my vacations any place else. An Army friend, Jesus Peña, would always tell me that I should visit Mexico, learn the language of my grandparents. But back then, I never cared, never thought about it, not until I ended up in that hospital after I stepped on a mine and nearly lost my foot. I really thought I was going to die. So many things went through my mind, and now here I am, back in the same town my grandfather left when he was seventeen-years old. There are ghosts here, good spirits, and I feel them."

"We all feel them, live with them every day... and, you say he never returned, your grandfather?"

"Not here. Once, years later, he visited his sister in San Luis Potosí. They were both in their seventies and hadn't seen each other since they were teenagers."

"Hmmm, over fifty years."

"I loved my grandfather. He was a gentle, spiritual man. But I have never been able to understand his actions. It's always bothered me. I want to understand. How could a man leave and never return to his family? I was told his mother came every day to that church," Danny said, nodding towards the basilica across the street. "Every day she walked from their ranch out near Las Amapolas, came to church, and prayed that one day she'd hear from him. She never did."

A man wearing a western cowboy hat, Levi's and boots, a folded newspaper in his hand, nodded to the gardener, walked past, and turned towards the gazebo, where a boy and a girl were standing on the first tier, leaning against the iron railing.

"Why did your grandfather leave Los Altos?"

Danny remembered the story his eighty-nine-year old aunt had told him.

"My grandfather's father had been killed, and my grandfather became head of the house. I suppose he took his job seriously, because when it was time for his sister to marry, my

grandfather refused to give his blessing. Some say he just did-
n't approve of the man his sister had chosen. When she married anyway, he left their ranch and never returned."

"And you say your grandfather and sister saw each other
one more time?"

"Yes," Danny answered.

"And how did the reunion go?"

Danny paused, then said, "An aunt told me that my
grandfather's sister, her name was Carmen, began shivering
the morning my grandfather's plane was to arrive, and she
didn't stop shaking until she saw him. From what I understand, they were warm towards each other but spoke little.
My grandfather cut his trip short and flew home the next
day."

"Why'd he wait so many years to visit her?"

Danny thought for a moment, then said, "Pride?"

The man shrugged. "You'll never know. Maybe it was simply that he loved his sister very much," he said, wiping his
brow again. "Who says you must have all the answers? No one
can know everything, nor should one want to. That's something you should have learned in the war. Why do the good
men die and the bad ones live? No one knows. Life often
reverses itself when we least expect it."

"The war taught me to trust nothing and no one. You see,
I was always unsure of myself, even as a child, and it's always
bothered me. When I joined the Army of the United States, I
wasn't sure if I was doing the right thing, but I did it anyway.
Maybe that's what my grandfather felt when he left home."

"Ah, forever the riddle."

A trashman came by, picked up a barrel, and emptied the
rubbish into the back of a horse-drawn cart. Danny saw a
cockroach skitter onto the sidewalk. It turned one way, then
another, antennas waving. Danny raised his foot. The garden-

er reached to grab Danny's leg. Too late. His shoe slapped the pavement, crushing the cockroach. Danny stood up, leaning awkwardly to one side. He twisted his foot, slid it along the stone walk and sat back down. The trashman glared at Danny, shook his head, clicked his tongue and led his horse down the street.

"You made a grave error," said the old man.

"What?"

"We don't harm these creatures here."

"But...they're a nuisance, nearly impossible to get rid of."

"You aren't at home now."

"Nefertari, they're disgusting."

"What is disgusting in one world may not be so disgusting in another."

"It's a cockroach!"

"Ay, you *pochos*...half-Mexican, half-gringo.... It isn't your fault, I suppose."

"Why shouldn't cockroaches be exterminated?"

"Have you seen a child bitten by a scorpion? In the ranches, up in the mountains, where there is no medicine, children often die, adults become very sick from the scorpion's sting."

Confused, Danny shook his head.

The man stopped talking. He rose from the bench and walked towards three boys who were playing marbles at the foot of a tree. He bent over and said something to them. They turned towards Danny. One boy nodded his head. They gathered their marbles.

"Go with them," he instructed Danny. "They will teach you."

"What?"

"Everything you always wanted to know...answers, *hijo*. Now, go."

He walked back to the garden, picked up his hoe and continued to cultivate the soil.

The boys walked along the main road through town, past painted brick buildings and concrete walls, broken only by wood doors which led to individual homes. At the outskirts, they passed the motel where Danny was staying. It was the only motel in town.

As Danny limped along, using a cane to support himself, the boys skipped playfully. The sun was overhead. The heat and humidity mingled, making the air thick, wet. With no warning, one boy, who wore a Texas Ranger baseball hat, broke from the group and ran towards a grove of trees where new, two-story houses with upstairs patios and spacious yards were in different stages of construction.

The road inclined slightly, and as he hobbled along, his cane searching for solid ground, Danny looked at the fields of wheat, sugar cane and cactus. He could see the river winding along the base of the green hills. At the river's edge, a man stood next to a skiff. He was holding a long pole in his hands, and he waited for customers who needed to be shuttled back and forth across the rain-swollen river.

Another boy, his front teeth stained by a straight yellow mark, leaped from the road and ran to a path that led toward the sugar cane. Danny watched as the boy disappeared into the tall plants.

The third boy nodded with his head for Danny to follow.

"Your leg, it, ahh...hur-r-ts?" the boy couldn't get the question out.

"No. It's nothing," Danny said.

"Crippled?"

Danny shook his head. "When I was a young man I went to the war."

The boy nodded curiously, noting the white hairs at Danny's temples, the graying mustache.

"I stepped on an explosive, a silly mistake," Danny said.

"It hurt?"

"Truthfully, I don't remember," he said, trying to evade the question.

The boy wrinkled his brow.

"I only remember waking in the hospital. Everything else I've forgotten."

"Oh... We're almost there."

They reached the riverbank. Danny asked how long it had been raining. The boy wasn't good with words. He stumbled over phrases.

"Two weeks. Last week it stopped," he said.

Down river, a man stood waist-deep in a hole, a few yards away from the water. He shoveled sand onto a wood cart attached to a scrawny donkey.

"What does he do with the sand?" Danny asked.

"In town...the workers," the boy stuttered.

Danny smiled, waiting patiently for the answer.

The boy swallowed hard. "They buy the sand to make cement."

"Ah, very good," Danny said, watching the man climb from the hole.

The boy with the baseball hat returned. He held a metal cup in his hands. "Where's Rafa?" he said.

The boy with Danny shrugged.

"Ah, he takes too long to do everything. I had the hardest part," said the boy, taking off his baseball cap, slapping it to his leg and putting it on again.

They walked along the shore, ripples of water lapping against the sand. The river rushed over boulders and fallen logs. It raced through the valley floor. Danny gazed at the lush hills. Along the river, a grove of mango trees grew, hanging over the water. Palm trees rose behind them.

Danny came here only in summer, during the time of the waters, when few tourists passed through. He'd go for walks alone, into the mountains, a *mochila* at his side, a wood staff for support. He'd walk the trails, into rock canyons and dense valleys, and he'd remember Vietnam. He'd remember his friends, and he'd try to figure out why. Twenty years later, and he was no closer to the answer. Half of his foot remained on Vietnamese soil, and he remembered nothing about the incident.

The man with the donkey jumped onto the cart, grabbed the reins, and made a clucking sound. The animal walked, its head bobbing up and down, towards town.

Danny and the two boys walked through tall weeds, and came to a clearing. In the middle was a metal ring, the kind used to hold wood barrels together. Kneeling on the ground next to the ring, was the third boy, the one who had disappeared into the sugar cane field. Smiling mischievously, the stain glowing on his teeth, he pushed his hair from his eyes and motioned for Danny to sit down.

"We told you to meet us by the river, *cabron*," said the boy with the baseball cap to the one kneeling.

"Why do you always have to be in charge? I told you I'd meet you here," said the boy, rising to one knee.

Danny looked around, saw a boulder and sat, placing his cane between his knees.

"Okay, boys, let's see what this is all about," Danny said.

With the palm of his hand, the boy whose words often failed him knelt down and smoothed the sand in the center of the ring that looked like an arena. The boy with the stained teeth held a paper cup, his hand over the top. He turned the cup over. A round, fat cockroach, covered in bronze armor, fell to the center of the smooth clearing. It hit the ground, and as if blinded by the light, rushed to one side and stood close to the metal ring. The boy who held the aluminum can moved forward. He removed the plastic lid and turned the can over and a cloth dropped to the sand. Attached to the cloth was a string. The boy grabbed the string, lifted it and shook. The cloth unfurled, and a scorpion, its body long and flat, its tail pointed, landed on the sand, and spun around quickly.

"Scorpion! Scorpion!" the boys uttered, excitedly, their eyes wide, glued to the ring.

The scorpion saw the cockroach.

Danny moved closer, dropping down to one knee. He held his cane tightly, as if grasping a weapon.

The scorpion looked like a crab, armed on all sides, two pincers and a lethal tail. The cockroach stood motionless, fat, unprotected, no weapons, its antennas slightly moving, like radar, calculating, waiting.

Danny spoke, but the boys hushed him.

The scorpion dashed across the sand. It stopped, inches from the cockroach, the poisonous tail raised high, stiff, waiting to strike. The cockroach moved, pathetically slow, like an old tank, out of striking range.

The scorpion neared, slowly, not even ruffling a grain of sand. It stood rigid, for seconds, then moved closer, mechanically, as if controlled by batteries.

The cockroach retreated, its back to the rusted metal ring. Both insects stood lifeless, static. As Danny was about to turn his head away, he saw the scorpion's tail come down upon itself, fast, like a spear. The scorpion reeled back, away from the cockroach to the opposite end of the arena, where it sat motionless, moving its tail weakly, the venom from its own stinger rushing through its body. The cockroach stepped away. It stood firm, unharmed, waiting for the scorpion to die.

One of the boys picked up the cockroach and placed it back into the cup.

"What happened?" Danny asked.

"You didn't see?" said the boy with the cap.

"What?"

"It was too fast for him," said the boy, using the can to scoop the dead scorpion from the sand.

"The cockroach's antenna...it tapped the scorpion on the back, quickly, confusing the scorpion."

"And?" Danny asked.

"The scorpion didn't understand," said the boy with the stained teeth. "It felt something on its back and struck, stinging itself, killing itself."

"How can that be?"

The boy holding the cockroach shrugged matter of factly. "Cockroaches kill scorpions. That's why we don't hurt cockroaches. I almost died when a scorpion stung me. In the summer, when the weather was hot and humid, they come into the houses."

"Once, we found one on our couch," said the boy with the baseball hat.

"Cockroaches protect us," said the boy with the stained teeth.

They left the metal ring in the sand and walked farther along the riverbank, where the boatman waited to ferry people across the wide river. Danny and the boys turned towards the wheat field. They walked along a dirt road and a few moments later came to the highway. They crossed and took the main road into town. Danny thanked the boys. They ran off towards the school yard.

Danny sat in the town's only restaurant and ordered a beer, Superior. Outside, many people crowded the cobblestone streets, some vendors and some buyers. Smoke rose from the barrels where men and women cooked pots of chiles, mixed with pork, beef, and chicken. A man, a rancher whom Danny recognized, took off his white cowboy hat and walked to Danny's table. "Hello, counselor," the man said, "mind if I join you for a beer?"

"Be my guest. Another Superior!" Danny called.

"Now that you are licensed, do you mind if I look you up when I come to San Francisco? I've got some investments I'm thinking of making, a little land in a place called Rocklin, outside of Sacramento, good horse country. I need some advice."

"Sure, come by," Danny said, looking into the man's eyes, astonished that he looked so much like a friend from the Army. "Is it true that cockroaches trick scorpions?" Danny asked, popping open another beer and squeezing a lemon over the lip of the can.

"Have you seen it done?" The man asked, sipping at his beer.

Danny raised his eyes, signalling that he had.

"It's hard to understand, isn't it?"

"I understand less each day," Danny said.

"Yes, yes...that's the beauty of it all," said the man, who called for the waiter to bring two tequilas.

There was a long silence.

On the juke box, a *mariachi* played the song, *Mejico Lindo y Querido.* As Danny listened, he thought about his grandfather, and the words of the song came to him soothingly, sweetly: *Mejico Lindo y querido / si muero lejos de ti / que digan que estoy dormido / y que me traigan aquí....*

The man with the cowboy hat asked Danny more questions. Danny answered, but his mind was on his grandfather, who'd fled to the U.S. Danny wondered about those family members who'd walked the streets of this town, and who'd been buried in lost graves throughout the hillsides. He drank his beer, talked, and listened to the men around him, to their Spanish, so lyrical and suave. Everyone treated him almost like family, yet Danny knew he was a foreigner, a *gringo*.

After three beers, a number of jokes and anecdotes, Danny bade everyone a good afternoon. Someone asked if he wanted a ride to his motel. He thanked them and insisted on walking. Another asked if he was coming back in the evening, that a *mariachi* was coming up from Leon, Guanajuato. Danny smiled and said that, yes, he would be back.

He limped up the cobblestone street, but quickly realized how exhausted he'd become. At a corner where two taxis were parked, he decided to ride back to the motel. As he slid into the back of the taxi, his legs felt very tired, and his foot began to hurt. He knew that a long nap would be nice before listening to the *mariachis* later in the evening.

NINETEEN
CLAIRTON, PENNSYLVANIA
(DAVID ALMAS)

The kids were with their mother. She and David shared joint custody, one week with her, one week with him.

He had come in from a night of heavy drinking. He picked up the receiver and called the Pittsburgh directory assistance.

When the operator asked for the name and city, David said, Clairton and spelled the name P-o-d-l-e-s-k-i. The line was silent. He figured there'd be many Podleskis in Clairton.

"I find only one. Irene?"

His mind went blank.

"Uh...yes, that must be it."

Before he dialed, he went to the kitchen, poured a shot of whiskey, and gulped it down.

The cross-country telephone buzz sounded vague and far away. He wanted to hang up but couldn't.

A tired, older female voice answered. David explained his call. She listened. They talked. There were long silences. She asked why it had taken him so long to call.

"I was afraid, I guess."

"Of what?"

"I never saw Wayne's body, so each year I went on hoping someone had made a mistake. I knew that once I called you, there'd be no more mistakes. Besides, I didn't want to bring you any more pain...you know, by reminding you."

"Son, a day doesn't go by that I'm not reminded. Each time I pass the school, go to church, the market, pass Wayne's photo on the mantel. Forgettin's just not possible." He heard her sigh. "Matter a fact, we miss him more every year. He would'a been thirty-eight."

They spoke for ten minutes. She told him she wasn't feeling well, but that she appreciated the call and if he was ever in Clairton to stop by, she'd really like to meet him. He promised her he would.

The next day he wrote her and her husband a letter, six single-spaced pages, telling them about their son's last months alive. When he described what he'd been told about the night of Wayne's death, he tried to sound casual, and he didn't linger too long on any one point.

David called again, two years later, from the Dulles Airport in Washington D.C., where he had attended an education conference. It was his second trip to Washington. Again, Irene answered. She sounded weak and said that she and her husband, Albert, weren't getting on too well. She'd been in the hospital. "Your letter was beautiful," she said, "'specially the way you told about Wayne's laugh. He was a comedian all right, a real funny boy. And you know, he always liked hanging around with different types of kids, a lot of colored boys, maybe that's why he took to you Chicano boys in Vietnam. Can you come visit?"

"I'd like to, but the conference lasted a day longer than I expected. I've got to get home to my kids. Another time, maybe?"

"That'd be fine. When you get the chance...."

"I hope you and Albert feel better."

"Thank you, son."

The day before his phone call from the airport, he had walked through the Vietnam Memorial and read the names: Wayne Podleski, Jesus Peña, Joseph Serrano, Albert Alvarez, Rudy and Hector Medrano. There had been other names, friends and acquaintances. He remembered their eyes, their voices, and their laughs.

293

Numbed by the frosty air and lucid memories, David had gone back to his hotel on Du Pont Circle. He hadn't eaten dinner that night or attended the evening conference sessions. From his fifth-floor window, he had stood staring at the college students—colorful down jackets, shouldered book bags, mussed hair, and flushed faces—rushing to catch buses to Georgetown and other D.C. universities. He stood there until the violet winter rays were extinguished in the west.

He loved Washington, its ironic, paradoxical power, a potent force that controlled destinies, carved empires, proclaimed liberty, manipulated politics, history and truth. It was a power that permeated everything, seeped into the Potomac, into the stone cold monuments, buildings, sidewalks, cafes, streets and gutters.

As he'd looked out over the city, tears filled his eyes. That was the real reason he hadn't gone to Pennsylvania. It was just too damn painful.

❂ ❂ ❂

Two more years passed. David remarried.

Luz adored Elvis, had even kissed him at a show in Las Vegas years ago, when she was a $1.75-an-hour secretary, and she'd saved every extra cent to pay for the trip. She always wanted to visit Graceland, as well as Hershey, Pennsylvania, not for the amusement park or the hotels, but for the chocolate. She loved chocolate, was addicted to it, and once, when she and David were dating, she had begged him to leave a dance at 1:00 A.M. and get her a Hershey with almonds.

When her company sent her to New York on business, she thought they could make a vacation of it, fly to Memphis, Tennessee to visit Graceland, then to Harrisburg, Pennsylvania to visit Hershey and the Amish country. They could rent a car and drive to Clairton, which was somewhere outside Pittsburgh.

David hadn't talked to Wayne's mom in a long time.

"I don't know," he'd told Luz.

"If you don't go now, you might never make it. 'Strike while the iron's hot,'" she had said.

She made arrangements, and a week later they were walking through Elvis's living room, backyard, private bus, and jetliner. They rented a car and drove the Tennessee back roads, entering Memphis and listening to blues on Beal Street, feasting on grilled Dixie chicken in a neighborhood saloon.

They flew to Harrisburg, Pennsylvania, toured the Hershey factory, gorged themselves on chocolate, and made a quick trek through the amusement park, which in David's view, fell far short of Disneyland, Magic Mountain and Knotts Berry Farm.

The town of Hershey, where the company workers lived, was more entertaining than the amusement park. The streetlights were shaped like candy kisses, the factory and smokestacks were painted the color of Hershey chocolate, and clowns leaped on and off the tourist trams that made their way through the pristine streets. David observed how the only excitement revolved directly around the tram and the tourists. All else seemed quiet, lonely.

The desolation of the eastern "company-town" weighed heavily on the meticulously shaped lawns, trees, and hedges. There was something eerie in the artificial, symmetrical construction. The verdant Pennsylvania landscape was just a little too green, too perfect and implacable; isolated, soulless, heartless, like the inside of a statueless church, just pews and a podium. There was something missing, all symbol and no substance, a host without the spirit.

Arriving in Lancaster County late the next evening, they decided to spend the night in Intercourse, the center of Amish business. As David drove into town, horse-drawn buggies raced up the main street, hanging sharp turns, the whinnying animals clopping wildly along the rutted asphalt.

Luz was tired and went to the motel to read her magazines. David walked across the street to a mini-mart and watched as four-wheel-drive pickups pulled in and out, tires burning, and engines whining. Young ladies wearing proper Amish attire: long gray dresses, white aprons and bonnets, smirked unashamedly from their raised truck seats. The drivers, mostly blond boys, their hair cropped on the sides and long in back, wore tight black pants and white dress shirts. Jumping from their trucks, they swaggered into the mini-mart, walked to the freezer, and exited quickly, their fingers gripping plastic bags of ice.

A sheriff's car turned sharply off the main street, banged its bumper on the driveway, and sped into a parking space in front of the store. The officer, Goliath-size, put on his Smokey the Bear hat and walked into the mini-mart. David followed, pretending he was looking for some chips.

"Ain't no little Amish bitch gonna get away with threatenin' me. Next time I'll put er lights out," said a skinny, scraggly-haired blonde girl behind the counter.

The officer listened, nodded, and left the store.

"Officer," David called, as the man walked towards his car.

The deputy looked over, eyeing the obvious outsider who looked Indian, maybe Italian or Puerto Rican, in his forties, dressed in Levi's, plaid shirt and suede jacket.

"I'm from California. Just visiting," David said. "These kids...they're Amish?"

The officer laughed. "Yeah, y'all don't get to see the real thing. Those Amish kids get a 'nut' on the weekends. Come in here'n raise hell, get all hooched up, park their parents' buggies out there in the fields and whoop it up."

"But the four-wheel-drives. I thought the Amish didn't own cars or use electricity."

"Some of these kids work two, maybe three jobs to buy those trucks. They hide a lot from their parents, and some parents turn their eyes, just like most parents. Know what I mean? Most the kids ain't gonna stay in the religion. They got 'tween the ages of nineteen and twenty to decide, so during that year they raise more shit than a pack 'a fat mules, raise more hell than the reg'lar local kids...don't believe everything ya see in those television documentarries."

The next morning as they drove past Harrisburg, David saw a sign, Williamsport. He pulled to the side of the road.

"What is it?"

"Williamsport, Pennsylvania."

"What's there?"

"The Little League World Series. My Dad always talked of visiting it...said one day he'd take me there to see the place where dreams come true."

"Let's go see it. We've got time."

He paused. "No, it wouldn't be right."

"Why?"

"Going without my Dad."

"You can tell him about it."

"No. This is one thing I'd rather keep alive as imagination. I have a feeling it won't look so great without the fans and the teams, the television cameras. You know?"

She shook her head. "No."

The eight-hour drive from Lancaster County to Pittsburgh took them past some of the greenest land he'd ever seen, hills stretching across the horizon. Solitary figures, in blue overalls and straw hats, hacked away at long, green plants. They piled their produce onto wooden carts pulled by single horses. Silver clouds floated across the deep blue sky. Women in long dresses hung wet clothes over lines that ran from the houses to the garages. There were flowers, trees, grass, and hedges separated only by narrow, black asphalt streets and driveways.

"It's like Disneyland, not a damn piece of trash on the street. Can't hardly believe how peaceful all this is," David said.

As they drove into Pennsylvania's heartland, they saw heavily wooded mountains—the higher ranges cascading into hills and valleys. Forests, like wooded curtains, lined the highway's shoulder and separated Pennsylvania from West Virginia, and long, five-minute tunnels cut through the mountains, circular arteries penetrating the earth.

They stopped for lunch and visited an antique shop in a no-name town, one of many whose sidewalks and streets cast the sun's reflections onto the old two-story colonial buildings that rested along the main street. Like many rural towns, the residents were a mixture of natives and young entrepreneurs, fresh from New York City, looking for a slower-paced life, yuppies who'd traded in three-piece suits for Levi's and flannels.

David drove steadily, silently, no radio, no noise. Luz dozed, waking from time to time to look out the window, smile, lean back and doze again.

Outside the Pittsburgh city limit, the air turned hazy. Through the light smog, they saw a valley, a suspended freeway, a narrow highway, and a wide, slow moving river. Buildings, factories, and numberless smokestacks lined the riverbanks, nestled in a basin surrounded by heavily wooded mountains.

Luz saw the sign, Clairton. She pointed, and David cut across two lanes. He pulled onto a highway that curved along a mountainside, a short stretch above the river. Another sign, a bold black arrow, Clairton, directed them towards an old, steel-buttressed bridge, and below, along the riverbank, they saw the steel mills, aluminum buildings, smokestacks, and asphalt parking lots, half-empty, vacant, ghost-like.

It was Friday, late afternoon. On the town's outskirts, David saw unkempt three-story Victorian homes, precariously straddling the mountainside. Scattered about were smaller wood homes, paint peeling and porches slanted, humble structures in various states of disrepair. There were cars set on cement blocks, weeds growing through axles and picket fences along the sides of homes and across gravel driveways. Broken tree branches lay on rooftops, and rubbish was strewn everywhere.

As he entered town, he slowed to ten miles per hour. Neither he nor Luz spoke as they stared at the cracked, brick buildings and boarded-up windows. Black men, looking exhausted and hopeless, sat on wood boxes as children played on the sidewalk, shards of glass along the curb.

David remembered how Wayne had described the steel town, the images of life, trucks rumbling up and down the highway, shoppers crowding the stores, workers racing for parking spaces, factory whistles shrieking, smoke-stacks billowing, and children running through the streets and parks, and playing along the river.

Two minutes later, David had driven the length of the main street. At the opposite end he pulled into a Stop 'n Go. He dialed Irene's number. "This number is no longer in service," the recording said. He hung up the receiver and walked into the store.

299

Behind the counter, a man about forty, unshaven, hardened blue eyes, watched him enter. "What kin I do fer youse?"

"A friend of mine died in Vietnam. He was from Clairton. I'm looking for his family...Podleski."

"Nope. Ain't heard of them. Lot a Clairton boys died in the war, though."

"There a cemetery around here?"

"Go back toward town, first street, take a right, go up the mountain an you'll see a sign."

"Thanks."

David started for the door and turned. "Say, I heard they made the movie *The Deer Hunter* here...that true?"

"I seen that movie a lotta times. I sure as hell don't know where they filmed it."

"They used the name Clairton in it," David said.

"Yeah, I know. That's why I seen it so much. Still, I didn't recognize a thing in it."

"Okay, thanks again," he said, confused.

He found the cemetery, in the middle of a clean, well-maintained, middle class area. It reminded him of El Sereno, a suburb on the east side of L.A., where the homes were comfortable, wood and stucco, nicely painted, green lawns and gardens, people out front washing their cars.

He pulled into the center of the cemetery, parked on a hot asphalt road, stepped from the car, and leaned on the open door. Luz slid out the opposite door. She adjusted her sunglasses and looked across the length of the grounds. It wasn't a big cemetery, maybe the size of a city block. The grass was thick, dry, yellow, like straw. The sun bore down. Dragonflies and bees skittered over the grave sites, no shade except for a line of trees at the rear, which blocked the view of the river and mill below. There were hundreds of gravestones, flat, peaked, curved, round, elegant, and simple. It was an old

cemetery, forlorn, out of place, as if the homes had unexpect-
edly crowded in on it.

He looked. There wasn't an office or reception center, just
a cinder-block gardener's shed at one corner, a wheelbarrow
and shovel out front.

"I don't know. I feel confused," he said.

"What's wrong?"

"I want to find his grave, touch it, you know, but not here.
I don't want it to be here. This place seems too old and he was
young, you know, a *loco*, like a colt. This place is old, desolate,
just too damn old and lonely."

"There's got to be a directory or something around here,"
Luz said, shading her forehead and looking around.

"Nothing," he said.

"What do you want to do?"

"I'm going to look around. The place isn't that big. I'll just
check out some of the names. It's hot. Why don't you wait in
the car." Before he finished talking, she had already begun to
walk between a row of graves, reading the inscriptions.

They searched for over an hour, brushing away bees and
swiping at flies. They read the names, mostly Poles, Russians,
Portuguese, and Italians, names going back a hundred years,
working-class men and women who carried the smoke and
dust of the steel mills to their graves. He found a lot of
P's...Pachuski, Padua, Petrucceli, Pakowski, Powers, Petrelli,
Paranoski, Postrokov...but no Podleski.

Perspiring and tired from peering at hundreds of tomb-
stones, Luz called out across the cemetery, "Spell it again."

He did.

She shook her head and walked on.

He waved her over.

"It's not here," he said.

"Let's drive through town. Maybe we can find out something there," she suggested, rubbing her neck.

Clairton was bigger than he'd first thought. It stretched up and over a mountain and spread into different neighborhoods, some rundown, others well maintained. As he drove, David looked for the Russian Orthodox basilica he'd seen in *The Deer Hunter*, the neighborhood market where Robert De Niro's girlfriend, Meryl Streep, worked. Nothing, just streets and box-shaped homes.

The sun had slipped behind the mountains. He drove through a newer, modern commercial district, on a hilltop. People were on the sidewalks, entering and exiting stores.

"This is a lot nicer than where we first entered," he said.

"The library," Luz said, pointing. "Maybe they know something."

"It's probably closed."

"Park the car. Let's go and ask."

"It's pretty late."

"C'mon. We're here. We came all this way."

The librarian let them in. "We close at six," she said.

They had fifteen minutes.

"When was he killed?" she asked, after David told her why he was in Clairton.

"1967."

"Oh. I don't know if our materials go back that far. Let's go see."

They walked downstairs. It was a modern library, ash-colored chairs and tables, teak shelves. There were children's paintings and colorful posters on the walls, everything clean and orderly. She led them to a windowless room filled with tables and chairs, a study area.

"Martha," the librarian called, "*The Progress* go back to '67?"

302

"Why?" came a voice from a back room.

"Gentleman and lady here from California looking for news about a friend he lost in the war... a Clairton boy."

"I don't guess so, but I'll look."

"I'll go help her," said the librarian, smiling.

The two women were gone about ten minutes. Silently, he and Luz thumbed through the children's books.

A young woman, matronly, nice smile, long straight dress, walked through an open doorway from the back room. She carried a stack wrapped in brown paper, 1967 written on the top in large numbers. "What month?" she asked, as she set it on a table and tore the wrapping.

"October, towards the end is when he died."

She pulled at the paper and string. "That means it probably didn't come out here until about November. Don't you think?"

"That's right."

She fingered through the stack of newspapers. He wrung his hands, lightly.

"Wayne? That his name?"

"Yes, ma'am," David said, looking at Luz. She raised her eyebrows.

"Came out November 29," the lady said, handing him the paper.

There was Wayne's photo, page one, inside a square at the top right corner. He looked nerdy in his Army glasses, like Buddy Holly, a good, clean-cut all-American boy, not the crazy, adventure-driven kid he had known, slept beside, argued and laughed with, spent months sharing ideas, stories, secrets, fears and hopes.

David stood silently, unable to move.

"Are you closing soon?" Luz asked. The librarian turned to face her.

"You take your time, honey. We'll wait."

David read to himself, his lips quivering, holding the paper so Luz could read, too:

Pfc. Wayne A Podleski, 19, son of Albert and Irene Podleski of 200 Wadnell Ave., Clairton, has been awarded the Purple Heart posthumously. Pfc. Podleski was killed in action on Oct. 15, as a result of a grenade fragment. He was with Co. A, 320th Artillery, First Brigade, 101st, Airborne Division—the Screaming Eagles. Born in McKeesport, on Jan. 14, 1948, Pfc. Podleski attended Clairton High School and was a member of St. Clare's church. In 1966, he left school in the 11th grade to join the Army. He entered military service in June and arrived in Vietnam in January, 1967. Mr. and Mrs. Podleski received the Purple Heart award for their son in a ceremony on Monday, Nov. 20, at 1 p.m. It was presented by Col. M.R. McCartney in his office at Headquarters, 18th Artillery Group, Oakdale.

David turned away so they couldn't see his eyes. Helplessly, he turned to Luz. She took the paper from his hands, handed it to the librarian, and placed her arm through his.

"Could you please make us a copy?" she asked.

"Sure thing, honey."

They followed her up the stairs, where she made five copies.

"Thank you very much," Luz said, as they walked outside.

"Sorry about your friend," the librarian said, and locked the glass doors.

They drove two blocks. "Look, Wadnell," Luz said, excitedly.

He saw the sign. "You sure?"

"One D, two L's."

He turned right.

"181, 183, 185." She read off the house numbers.

"Look on the other side of the street, even numbers." He drove to the next block. Luz said, "There! 200."

He pulled in front of a two-story house that looked like a Crackerjack box set on its side, narrow, steep stairs rising to the porch, looking more like a tenement than a house, no paint, just red roofing shingles as siding and a few small square windows along the sides. There was dirt and a patch of grass in front and little space at the sides or back. It was old and vacant, different than the white wood bungalows surrounding it.

"Was Wayne poor?" Luz asked.

"He never said. I mean, none of us had money."

A vision of his parents' home came to him, a house in the Los Angeles suburbs, near Santa Monica and the ocean, a house surrounded by pine trees and jacarandas, large grass yards, flowers, driveways, and hedges.

Across the street, an older woman stood on her porch.

"Go ask her," Luz said.

"Naw, she probably doesn't know anything. Besides, why bother her?"

"David," she insisted, "go on."

He made a U-turn and parked down the street.

Luz waited in the car.

"You were a friend of Wayne's," the woman said, after he introduced himself. "Well, my gawd. Wouldn't Irene 'a loved to met you. She died last year ya know."

They both turned to look at the house.

"When Irene an' Albert lived there, the house didn't look so sad. It was clean, painted, kept up, flowers out front, kids running around. A fine family. Poor Irene, her losin' Wayne and all. Took it hard, real hard. Albert...he's pretty sick, too. Lives with his daughter out near Pittsburgh. Everything went real bad fer all of us when the mills cut back. Laid off near everyone. Guess you kin see that for yerself."

"Looked pretty bad driving in," he said.

"Didn't used to be like that. Business was going good, an' all the stores down by the river were busy, all painted up, cafes had good food, too. Folks been having a hard time of it."

She told him that they'd been neighbors since Wayne was a child, spent birthdays and holidays together, saw him grow up, run the streets with the other kids, got in some trouble, nothing serious, was always talking about joining the Army. She'd never forget the day they came and told Irene that he'd been killed, putting a damper on the whole street. Poor Irene went downhill from there, loved her boy like there weren't no tomorrow.

She gave him Albert's phone number and said to be sure to call, even if Albert wasn't feeling all too well. He thanked her.

The streets looked different as they drove out of town. The last glimmers of sunlight shone off the heavily wooded mountains. Beneath the bridge, the river moved slowly, taking a barge along with it. Cars raced through the mill parking lot, and laughing, robust steel workers entered a cafe/bar right outside the mill's gates. Smoke billowed from the thick metal stacks, and a loud whistle shrieked across the valley. He thought about *The Deer Hunter*, and the scene where a drunken De Niro ran naked through the streets with Christopher Walken right behind. It was the night of their friend's wedding, and they all knew they'd soon be going to Vietnam. Exhausted, they came to a basketball court and sat down, panting. "I love this fucking place," Walken had said of Clairton. "Promise me, Mike. If anything happens, you won't leave mo there... promise."

✪ ✪ ✪

That night on the telephone, David spoke to Albert for the first time. He hadn't wanted to call, hadn't wanted to be a bother, but Luz convinced him to make the effort. She had seen the anxiety on David's face, but she knew he had to make the call. His eyes welled. She'd never seen him cry. He was always controlled, impregnable, but this time he sobbed, his shoulders shaking, voice choking. She put her arms around him.

When he finished crying, she brought him a wet wash cloth. He wiped his face, and dialed.

Albert's voice sounded weak, far away, as if all hope had vanished. He talked briefly of the mills and Irene's death. He asked a few questions about David and how he'd been. There were uncomfortable moments of silence. The old man was reluctant, maybe from fear of dredging up too much of what he'd tried so hard to put aside.

"I looked for Wayne's grave, but couldn't find it," David said.

"Where'd ya look?" Albert replied.

"At the cemetery, in Clairton."

"Oh, he's not there. Wayne's out near Pittsburgh," he said, giving him the name and directions. "It's a bit hard to find the grave site. Just look for the six columns...big pillars. He's behind the second from yer left as yer drivin' towards it."

"Okay...good, good. I'll go out tomorrow."

Finally, after a long pause, Albert said, "You like to come over?" His tone was friendly but reserved, circumspect.

"Thanks, but our flight leaves early."

"Okay. You take care of yourself and have a safe trip back to California," came the reply.

"Good luck to you, sir."

And the line went dead.

That night on a main boulevard just outside Pittsburgh, they had a bad meal in a flamboyant steak house billed, "The Best in Town." Sixteen wheelers roared past their hotel window all night. He wondered if Wayne had stayed in any of the hotels along this row—a place a high school Romeo might take a girlfriend. How many times had Wayne raced up this thoroughfare, speeding into Pittsburgh, maybe to see the Pirates, or party with friends.

After breakfast the next morning, they packed and headed into the city, following Albert's directions. They took a few wrong turns, corrected their course, and headed into a lush valley. To his left, David saw the cemetery. He turned, cut across traffic, and drove through the arched entrance, grass, trees, and flowers shimmering over soft, peaceful rolling hills. He took connecting streets and turns, made U-turns, rose to crests, drove back down and was about to ask directions at the busy reception office when he came to a hilltop and saw six Roman columns rising gracefully in a semi-circle, close to the curb.

"Look, second from the left," Luz said.

He drove slowly and parked beside the thirty-foot column.

They walked, keeping their eyes to the grass, searching the names engraved in stone.

"Over here," Luz said.

He walked over and read the name, Pfc. Wayne Podleski, Battery A, 320th Artillery, 1st Brigade, 101st Airborne Division, 1948-1967, In Loving Memory.

David reached down and rubbed the letters, carefully feeling the indentations and grooves beneath his fingertips.

Luz stood back to give him room.

"No, come here with me," he told her.

She moved next to him and stooped down.

David was quiet.

"Don't you have anything to say to him? It's only been twenty-five years," she said.

He looked uncomfortable, then began to speak slowly. "Hey, buddy. What's happening?" He looked around, rubbed his jaw. "So. Here I am," he said, looking at the grave. "Just outside of Clairton. What a joke, huh? We were always somewhere outside some place or other, Duc Pho, Phu Bai, Chu Lai, Phan Rang.... I wasn't sure if I'd ever make it, but here I am. Clairton. I guess it's changed some. Hey, man, I'm really sorry about your mom," he said, choked, coughed and stopped talking.

There were flowers in the open container at the head of the stone. He had no flowers to leave so reached into his wallet, took a business card, and placed it in the can.

"Wow!" she said, as she gazed behind her. "Wayne's got a great view."

David looked up and stared across the valley. The Pennsylvania countryside fell at Wayne's feet, long rolling mountains, some covered with grass, others with trees—a bevy of greens, shining emeralds, limes, avocados, and jades—stretching into the distance, not a house or building visible, just the earth and the sky, much like the mountains in Vietnam.

They sat there for a long time. Then it was time to leave. David stood and stared at the grave until he carved the image into his mind. He remembered Wayne's blue eyes, his infectious laugh, his craziest challenge: "Almas, man. Let's smoke so much fuckin' weed that we can't hold no more. You know, just to see what happens, just keep the shit going, one joint after another, until the world fuckin' explodes. Whaddya say?"

309

David reached down and placed his hand on the grave one more time, a goodbye to Wayne and all the dead and missing. Then he rose slowly and walked back to the rental car.

In silence, but for a few sporadic phrases, they drove to the airport. Luz flew on to New York for business. At 1:30 P.M., David boarded Flight 57, American Airlines, Gate 18, Pittsburgh to Los Angeles.

As his plane lifted off the runway, rose higher and banked hard, heading west, David watched the green hills turn into mountains, great mounds of earth rising into the sky, until he could see nothing but blue. His face close to the oval window, he struggled to make sense of it all, Jesse's disappearance, Wayne and Joey's deaths, the deaths of all the others, the spiritually, emotionally and physically maimed who still moved along city streets trying to piece the whole thing together.

The plane flew through the clouds and rose higher, and David wished the plane would never land because peace was in the flight and bad things happened when wheels touched the ground. As an adult David had flown across the country numerous times, but those flights were lost in a mirage of voices, stewardesses, crab-salad lunches, in-flight magazines, movies, and chitchat.

The flights that stayed in his mind were the many military flights he'd taken as a teenager, the one from Travis Air Force Base to Vietnam, the ones cutting back and forth across Southeast Asia, the one from Cam Rhan Bay to Bangkok, and the one from Chu Lai to Phn Rhang and back to the States. After that last flight and the wheels touched United States' soil, a military band, its paltry membership shivering in the Seattle cold, had piped up some kind of pathetic patriotic song. There had been a captain's salute, a rushed steak dinner and a hurried trip to the quartermaster's where a new duffel bag and uniforms were issued, then a quick jaunt to the Seattle airport. A crowd of young veterans mobbed ticket counters and telephones, making connections for flights home. But there was no significance in any of it, and true to fact, as Danny Ríos had once said after Jesse Peña's disappearance, it made no sense at all.

Only his father's words, which had returned to David many times throughout the years, carried a disturbing amount of weight. "Don't ask," his dad had said when David was a boy and couldn't see the logic in patriarchal decisions. "One day you'll see. That's all." And David did see, although he didn't like it and knew it was a line that many people accepted too easily. What he now understood that sometimes the enemy was really the ally, the thief was the hero, the patriot was the scoundrel. David's trust in the world had shifted, a little each day, but no one suspected, and he held the truth inside, placed in a vault slightly below the surface.